THE MISSING RED CARPET MYSTERY

An absolutely addictive cozy murder mystery

RACHEL WARD

The Supermarket Mysteries Book 4

Joffe Books, London
www.joffebooks.com

First published in Great Britain in 2023

© Rachel Ward 2023

This book is a work of fiction. Names, characters, businesses, organizations, places and events are either the product of the author's imagination or are used fictitiously. Any resemblance to actual persons, living or dead, events or locales is entirely coincidental. The spelling used is British English except where fidelity to the author's rendering of accent or dialect supersedes this. The right of Rachel Ward to be identified as author of this work has been asserted in accordance with the Copyright, Designs and Patents Act 1988.

Cover art by Nick Castle

ISBN: 978-1-83526-297-9

*To people worth rolling out the red carpet for:
Ozzy, Ali, Pete and Shirley xxx*

CHAPTER ONE

There was something different about George as she walked into the staff room that Tuesday morning. As general manager, she always carried herself with confidence, but Bea could see that there was an extra spring in her step today, even a twinkle in her eye as she stood at the front and looked round the assembled staff. Beside her, Neville, her number two, was clutching his clipboard lovingly. In fact, Bea noticed, it was a pristine new clipboard, shiny red vinyl catching the light. Bea nudged Ant, who was leaning against the wall next to her, picking at the corner of one of his fingernails.

'Something's up, Ant. Look.'

He raised his bleary eyes to the front. Another bad night's sleep in Neville's spare room. He'd retreated upstairs by eight o'clock, unable to face an evening watching Neville and Carol gleefully trying to beat the teams on the various BBC2 quizzes, while the clues and connections sailed over Ant's head. He'd done some reading practice. With the help of a volunteer coach at the library, he was working his way through the books of a reading scheme. Being able to work out the text for himself was still a novelty and a delight, but it was tiring. After half an hour, he hadn't been able to concentrate any longer, so played games on his phone, then watched a film. By ten o'clock, he turned out the light and tried to sleep, as the signature tune for the evening news played in the room below. He was still awake when Neville and Carol padded up the stairs to bed and, later, when he heard St. Swithin's clock strike midnight. He shouldn't complain — he'd had a good evening meal, he was warm and safe — but was he really *living*? Was this it?

'Ant, look!' Bea nudged him again.

'Wha—?'

George was calling for quiet. They were about to find out what was putting some pep in her step today.

'So,' George clasped her hands in front of her. 'A good day yesterday, volume is a little down on this time last year, which is only to be expected with the current cost of living situation, but revenue is holding up nicely. In fact, we got a pat on the head from Regional Office yesterday, so it's a big well done to all of you. I know things aren't easy for anyone at the moment, but your hard work and dedication are not going unnoticed.

'As you all know, like the rest of Kingsleigh High Street, we've seen a marked rise in theft this year, but following Evan's appointment two weeks ago, and the use of the new Radiolink service so that we can share information instantly with other retailers, we're seeing results already.' Evan was a mountain of a man, and a rising star of Kingsleigh's Sunday league rugby team, whose well-defined shoulder and arm muscles were barely contained by his uniform of white shirt and black jumper with an embroidered 'Security' label on the front. 'There's been a distinct drop in unaccounted-for losses, so well done, Evan.'

There were murmurings of agreement. George tried to start a round of applause but it was only taken up by Neville and a couple of other people, which added to Evan's embarrassment. Standing near the door, he looked to Bea like he wished the floor would open up and swallow him.

All the staff were aware of an increase in shoplifting. There had been talk of carloads of outsiders coming into the town to swipe clothes off rails, empty shelves of perfume and pick up electrical goods. In Costsave, thieves had targeted high value food, like joints of meat, and bottles of spirits, so much so that George had even raised the possibility of storing these items out of sight and supplying them on request to customers.

For the past few months, the security alarm at the main door had gone off so frequently that staff had started to ignore it. Besides, not everyone wanted the hassle or even potential risk a confrontation could bring. Now, Evan had taken that responsibility off their shoulders, but not everyone was a fan.

'Woohoo,' Ant said ironically under his breath. He had a lot of sympathy for people pocketing the odd tin of beans for their kids' tea, or nappies or baby milk because they were desperate, and an ingrained distrust of people in uniform.

Bea shushed him. She was pretty sure George hadn't finished.

'That's not the only good news,' George said, looking round the room. Neville ran a finger round the inside of his collar. What on earth was coming now? Bea wondered. 'I had confirmation late yesterday that Costsave is going to be receiving a very special visitor at the end of the month. A *very* special visitor. We haven't got long to get ready, but I know that we can all pull together and rise to the occasion.' A little ripple of excitement passed through the room.

'Who is it?' Dean called out.

George held a hand up.

'I can't tell you that, I'm afraid, and I'm also going to ask you not to talk to anyone from the *Kingsleigh Bugle* or local radio until there is an official announcement.' There were some audible moans and groans. 'What I *can* say is that I will be forming a small task force to make sure that everything runs smoothly in the run-up to this and on the day itself, and I'm looking for volunteers.' A hush fell over the room as everyone suddenly became interested in examining the coffee stains on the carpet by their feet.

Ant leaned his head close to Bea's. 'This is all a bit over the top, isn't it?' he muttered.

'I don't know,' said Bea. 'I reckon it must be someone important for this amount of fuss. Chief Exec, do you think? Or maybe they're filming an advert here with that soap actor, the face of Costsave.'

'I'm not getting involved,' Ant said, and Bea got the distinct impression he would have taken a step backwards if there wasn't a wall behind him.

'I reckon it might be a laugh. Change is as good as a rest, isn't it?'

She looked round the room and tentatively raised her hand.

'Girly swot,' Ant muttered, shaking his head.

'Bea! That's wonderful,' said George. 'Write her name down, Neville.' Neville got busy with his clipboard. 'Who else? Come on, don't be shy.'

Across the top of the crowd, Bea caught Dot's eye. Despite Dot being Bea's mum's age, she was her best friend at Costsave. She was looking immaculate this morning, as usual — hair bouffant and lacquered, make-up on point. Bea tipped her head towards the front of the room, inviting Dot to join in. Dot gave her a wink and put her hand up.

'Ah, Dot! Fantastic!'

Bea watched as Dot dug her elbow into Bob-on-Meat, who was standing next to her. They had been an official item since last summer. Bob was usually a reliably 'can do' person, so Bea was a little surprised to see him shrug off Dot's attentions and keep his hands resolutely by his sides. She sighed inwardly, however, as she saw someone else volunteer. It was Eileen, the shop floor supervisor. She and Bea had an uneasy relationship at the best of times.

'I will,' said Eileen. 'And my Dean will too.'

Some of the others sniggered, while Dean himself rolled his eyes and groaned, 'Mu-um.' Dean was not known for his positive contributions to teamwork, although he had partly redeemed himself last year by singing a belting solo in the Costsave choir's debut performance at the music festival in the park.

'That's brilliant,' said George. 'I think that'll do for now. Can those of you who volunteered stay behind for a couple of minutes? The rest of you, let's get ready to open up! It's going to be another great day at Costsave!'

Bea watched as most of the staff shuffled out of the room and off to the shop floor, office or stores. Ant lingered to put on a Costsave fluorescent jacket — he was on trolley duty outside for the first couple of hours.

George beckoned those who remained forwards. She was beaming at them, although Neville looked less than thrilled with the self-selecting team.

'Thank you for volunteering. I don't think you'll regret it. I will be in overall charge, but Neville will be running the task force meetings and project managing things, so, over to you, Neville.'

Neville swallowed hard, his Adam's apple bobbing up and down. 'Thank you, George. I'd like to say what an honour it is to be involved in this. I won't let you down.' George smiled indulgently and waited for Neville to get on with it. Out of the corner of her eye, Bea saw Ant shake his head and slope out of the room. Neville cleared his throat again. 'As you said, we haven't got very long to prepare, so I'll be drawing up an action plan looking at the programme, timing, environment, crowd control, security and publicity over the next twenty-four hours. I'll be appointing a sub-team leader who can take the logistics side forward, so please be thinking about that. You will be allowed time away from your normal roles for this work—' Bea thought she heard Dean whisper a long, low, 'Yesss,' to this news — 'so we will have our first formal meeting at this time tomorrow.'

'Since we're in the task force now, and it's just us here, can you tell us who it is, Neville?' Dot asked.

He glanced nervously at George, then shook his head.

'I'm sorry. I can't share any further details yet. George and I do have a pre-meeting today, and I hope to update you tomorrow. So, please think about how we can give the best

Costsave welcome ever to somebody very special, and I'll see you tomorrow.'

Clearly dismissed, Bea and the others started making their way down to the shop floor.

Dean had a big grin on his face. 'Time off from the stores. I knew this task force thing would be a good idea,' he crowed.

His mother rolled her eyes in an affectionate way, 'What are you like, Dean?' and smiled at Bea in a don't-you-just-love-him way. Bea resisted the urge to point out exactly what Dean was like. At the bottom of the stairs, Dot linked her arm though Bea's and they walked towards their checkouts.

'I think someone's been watching too many episodes of *The Apprentice*,' Dot said. 'Action plans? Logistics? Sub-team leaders? You've got to laugh, haven't you? Bea?'

Bea was uncharacteristically quiet. She'd spotted something during the meeting but wanted to make sure everyone else was out of earshot before she shared it with Dot.

'I don't think it's the Costsave Chief Exec, Dot.'

'What?'

'It's not a Costsave bigwig, or that bloke off the adverts. I saw what Neville had written at the top of his paper. This is big, Dot. This is really big.'

They'd reached their stations now. The first customers were through the door, some purposeful, others drifting gently, enjoying the empty aisles. Neville was approaching the Customer Service desk nearby, his face flushed from his moment in the spotlight.

'What was it? What did you see?' said Dot.

'Hang on. Is your pen working?'

Dot reached a biro from by her cash register while Bea broke off a little section of till roll. Dot's eyes grew wider as she watched Bea write two words.

'Oh my god,' she murmured. 'Flipping Nora.'

'I know,' said Bea.

They both stared at the paper for a moment or two, until a customer approached, looking for an open till. Bea snatched up the paper, put it in the pocket of her tabard, then started about her morning routine of setting up her station and logging on. As she prepared to move the 'till closed' sign from her conveyor belt, she glanced across at Dot, who was just applying some hand sanitiser. Dot looked over her shoulder and their eyes met. Dot's eyes were sparkling. She fanned her face.

'I can't hardly believe it,' she said to Bea.

'I know. At Costsave!'

For the rest of the morning, they were both mulling over the words Bea had written down, the words that had put a spring in George's step and got Neville hot under the collar: 'Operation Windsor.'

CHAPTER TWO

Bea found it difficult settling into the rhythm of a normal Tuesday. Her mind was working ten to the dozen, wondering just how special their special visitor would be. The big one? The man himself? If it was, they'd have to tweak Costsave's rather limited organic section. They had organic cabbages and bags of carrots most weeks, but they didn't sell as well as the bog-standard ones. Costsave wasn't the place anyone would naturally choose for premium products although their 'Luxury' range was actually rather good. Somehow, she couldn't picture the King himself browsing the family packs of sausage rolls, economy baked beans and value sliced loaves that were among their biggest sellers. If not him, then who? One of the other three from the top four? Or two of them together?

'Excuse me, is this till open?'

Back in the real world, a woman in her early forties, wearing a leather jacket over a black jumper and jeans was looking at her, one hand on the shopping in her trolley, ready to start loading it up. Her bottle-blonde hair was swept into a tortoiseshell claw and large gold hoops dangled from her ears. Her face was familiar — she was a regular shopper here. Bea felt like she knew some of her background, too, but with her brain full of royal daydreams she couldn't quite remember what it was.

'Oh yes! Sorry, I was miles away.'

The woman started piling her shopping onto the conveyor belt; a chicken in a roasting bag, carrots, cabbage and potatoes, a big bottle of orange juice, two loaves of bread, some biscuits, a multipack of chocolate Crunchie bars, a couple of T-shirts and a pack of pants from the clothing aisle. Nothing out of the ordinary for someone shopping for a family. Bea always noticed what her customers bought. You could tell a lot from people's choices. It was one way of making her job more interesting. Her favourite thing, though, was chatting to them, passing the time of day or having a bit of banter. It was what made her popular. A fair number of people would always make straight for her checkout over any of the others. She was well aware that, for some people, she was the only person they'd talk to all day.

Of course, you had to read the signs. Plenty of people wanted a minimum of interaction while their shopping was processed as quickly as possible. Bea judged this woman was somewhere in between.

'Ooh, these look good,' she said, beeping a large packet of chocolate chip cookies through.

The woman smiled. 'They're for the boys. These are for me.' She held up a box of plain oat cakes. 'Keep getting texts from the GP telling me to eat more oats.' She pulled a face.

'Ha! They taste like cardboard, so they must be good for you,' Bea laughed, then shot a quick look towards Neville. 'Shouldn't say that, should I?'

The woman laughed too. 'You're not wrong, though.'

She finished loading her shopping into bags and then paid in cash. As she reached forward to hand over the notes, a couple of inches of wrist and arm extended from the sleeve of her jacket and Bea noticed the bottom of a rather detailed monochrome tattoo — two wheels and part of the frame of a motorbike, artfully framing the word 'Connor' in beautiful script. Ah yes, now she remembered! This was Patsy

Creech, owner of a long-established Kingsleigh business, Patsy's Diner. She had been widowed a couple of years ago when her husband was in a motorbike accident on one of the country roads to the south of the town. His funeral had caused quite a stir, with his friends in the biking community forming a huge parade behind his coffin which was mounted on a trailer and pulled by a black Honda Goldwing, on its way down the High Street to St. Swithin's.

As the woman passed through the double doors, the alarm went off. The woman looked mortified and stopped. Evan stepped forward and guided her to a quiet spot back inside between the doors and the Customer Service desk, from where Neville was watching keenly. Evan asked her a few questions and examined her receipt. Then Bea saw them approach her till.

'Is there a problem?' she asked.

'Can you remove the security tag from these T-shirts, Bea? I've checked and this lady's paid for them.'

'Oh my god, I'm so sorry,' Bea said. It wasn't like her to make such a silly mistake and she hated having done so in front of Evan. It wasn't that she fancied him exactly, but she didn't not fancy him. She wouldn't mind getting to know him, find out if there was more to him than muscles and quiet charm. Who was she kidding? Muscles and quiet charm would go a long, long way. She hadn't been out with anyone since she'd binned Tom, Kingsleigh's fledgling detective constable, and gently shrugged off Ant's drunken declaration of love at the music festival. She loved Ant, too, in a way, but he was such a good mate she didn't want to risk messing everything up between them by venturing out of the friend zone.

She quickly pressed the plastic tag fixed to one of the shirts into her special machine, removed both halves and handed the clothes back. 'I'm really sorry,' she said again.

'It's okay,' the woman said, although Bea could see that her face was flushed. 'I'm just glad I didn't get all the way home with the tag still on.'

Evan escorted her out again and gave her a little wave as she left. No real harm done, but Bea felt dreadful.

'Incoming,' Dot chirruped, and Bea saw Neville stalking over towards them. Bea cringed inwardly. She knew she'd messed up and didn't need telling.

'Not a good start to the day, Bea,' he said, with a disapproving sniff.

'I know, I know. I'm sorry. It's all sorted now, though.'

'Yes, well, it shouldn't have happened in the first place.'

Bea held one hand out in front of her and slapped it with the other one. She heard Dot give a little snort, but Neville didn't find it funny. She tried another tactic. 'To be honest, Neville, my mind was elsewhere. I was thinking about our you-know-what and how we can make it a really special day.' His expression changed instantly. He narrowed his eyes and looked left and right, then came closer, almost uncomfortably close.

'I share your excitement, Bea, but we must never talk about it on the shop floor. Walls have ears. Need to know basis and all that.' He tapped the side of his rather long and pointy nose.

'Understood,' Bea said. Neville straightened up and walked back to the Customer Service desk.

'Well played, doll,' said Dot. 'This visit is like a golden ticket, isn't it? I reckon any time Neville's on our case between now and the end of the month, we can play the VIP card and he'll be instantly distracted.'

'Like a dog spotting a squirrel,' Bea said, and they both started laughing.

Just before lunchtime, Ant sauntered inside to warm up. He was holding a cardboard box — he'd found that carrying something while you walked around kept Eileen and Neville off your back, for the most part. He'd just stopped by Bea's checkout for a gossip, when a police squad car drew up outside and three people got out; one officer in uniform with a peaked cap and an air of authority, a man in a very nice, dark grey suit and a woman in a pink jacket, tailored dress and sky-high heels.

'Looks like trouble,' he said, watching them walk into the store and report to the Customer Service desk.

Bea looked round. 'Wow,' she said, catching sight of the pink outfit. 'They must be here for the briefing.'

'Briefing? To do with this visit?'

Bea pulled her fingers across her mouth, like she was zipping it up. 'My lips are sealed,' she said.

'Who the hell is it? The King or something . . .' Then he caught sight of Bea's face. 'You're kidding.' He let out a long, low whistle.

Neville was ushering the visitors towards the back of the store. As he swished them past the checkouts, Bea could see that the skin on his neck was pink and mottled and there was the shine of sweat on his temples.

'Nev's already in such a stew over this,' she said. 'I'm worried he's peaking too soon. He'll be an empty, gibbering husk by the end of the month.'

Ant snorted. 'Ha! He does look like he's ready to blow a gasket, doesn't he? But it *is* Charlie-boy himself, isn't it?'

'Shh,' Dot said. 'We're not allowed to say.'

Ant shook his head and smiled. 'Honestly, Ant,' said Bea, 'we'll be in so much trouble if this gets out. You must keep it to yourself.'

'Sure,' he said. 'You can rely on me.'

By the time the security posse had left the management suite and returned to their car, everyone in the store, both staff and customers, were buzzing about Costsave's soon-to-be status: 'By Royal Appointment'.

CHAPTER THREE

'What's all this about King Charles visiting Costsave, Bea?' Queenie didn't even let her daughter take off her coat before she started firing questions at her. 'When is it? Will you get to meet him? Can I come?'

'I'm not allowed to say anything, Mum! Besides, we don't officially know anything yet. We've only been told we're having a VIP visit.'

She shrugged her arms out of her coat and hung it on the back of the kitchen door. Then rubbed her hands together and blew on them — it had been a mistake forgetting her gloves that morning.

'But is it him, isn't it?'

'I honestly don't know! Budge out of the way. Let's get the kettle on. I'm chuffing freezing.'

Queenie had made a start on their tea. She had never been much of a cook. In the past, they had stuck to a strict routine when it came to meals. The same seven items on the menu each week, fifty-two weeks of the year, apart from Christmas Day. Bea understood now that it had been linked to Queenie's long-standing anxiety. It had been one way she could control her life, make it feel safe. Over the past couple of years, she had made great strides in tackling her mental health. She'd overcome her agoraphobia and had started working in the launderette in the row of shops near to their home. She'd branched out when it came to catering, too, responding with glee when Bea brought home something new to try, and even asking her to get the ingredients for a Jamie or Nigella recipe they'd seen on the telly. There had been a few disasters. They agreed to never again mention the time they attempted Jamie's cauliflower stew with olives, but that had been a minor hiccup in their culinary blossoming.

'I've got some spuds in the oven,' Queenie said, 'and I'm going to heat up Saturday's chilli to go with it. That all right?'

Bea couldn't think of anything better to warm her up. 'Perfect. How long 'til it's ready?'

'Twenty minutes?'

'I'll have a quick shower and put my onesie on.'

Later, when they were installed in the lounge, watching the soaps, Bea told Queenie about being on the task force.

'Ooh, what have you got to do?'

'I don't know yet. We've got our first proper meeting tomorrow. Nev's in charge, though. Dot and I only volunteered for the lols, really. Change is as good as a rest, isn't it?'

This week's *Kingsleigh Bugle* was on the coffee table. Bea picked it up and glanced at the front page. Nestling under a colourful banner advert adorned with hearts and flowers, *Valentine's Offers Inside, see page 5*, was the headline, NOT WELCOME HERE — *Police Crack Down on Shoplifting Gangs*. She scanned the article which focused on reports of carloads of criminals driving into Kingsleigh to target local shops before they made a quick getaway. She wondered if she'd ever seen them in Costsave without realising. Probably. They might be put off by the visible deterrence of Evan now, but even so, she would keep her eyes peeled. She started leafing through the rest of the paper.

'I expect Bob's on your task force, too, is he? You need someone practical,' said Queenie.

Bea bridled slightly at the implication that she wasn't, but decided to let it go. 'No, actually. He wouldn't join in.

Bit strange, really, 'cos it would normally be his sort of thing. Come to think of it, he's been a bit subdued recently. I'd better ask Dot if everything's all right.'

The end credits for *Coronation Street* were rolling up. Bea wondered if she could be bothered to go and make a cup of tea during the adverts before the next programme and decided she couldn't. Maybe during the next break.

'It won't be the first time there's been a VIP at Costsave,' said Queenie. 'I don't suppose you remember, but when they opened the new deli counter years ago, they had a comedian in to cut a ribbon. God, what was his name? Dad and I took you down there. He had to put you on his shoulders so you could see over the crowd. They had a red carpet down and everything. Who the heck was it? It'll come to me eventually.'

By the time they went to bed, Queenie still hadn't remembered. Bea made a mental note that it was another thing to ask Dot about. She'd been working at Costsave forever. Like Bea, it suited her, and she positively enjoyed keeping up with the customers. Bea hadn't told Queenie about the mistake with the security tag, but she still went hot and cold thinking about it. Other people might look down on her job, but she knew how valuable it was and she was as much a perfectionist about it as any brain surgeon or rocket scientist. Whatever else was going on, she must keep her standards up.

CHAPTER FOUR

'Okay, so this is where it gets real,' said George. She had invited the other members of the Operation Windsor task force to join her on the rather tired and stained sofas in the staff room after the morning briefing for the first official planning meeting. 'As you may know we met with the Deputy Chief Constable yesterday and two other people to talk about the impending visit. The other two were Sean, a member of the Royal Protection squad, and Amy, one of the palace staff.'

She paused for effect. Before George and Neville had come in, Bea, Dot, Eileen and Dean had made a pact to pretend they didn't know who the VIP was. Now they rather overdid the feigned surprise. Bea gripped Dot's arm. Dot put her hands up to her mouth and squealed. Eileen's jaw gaped, while Dean said, 'Shut up!' so loudly everyone started laughing.

George sighed. 'You all knew, didn't you? How on earth . . . ?'

Bea raised her hand like a guilty schoolgirl. 'I saw Neville's clipboard yesterday — the heading.' Neville immediately clutched it to him, hiding the front. Only twenty-four hours too late, thought Bea.

'I'm so sorry,' he murmured, dropping his gaze. 'It's an unforgiveable breach.' If he had had a sword to hand, Bea thought, he'd have fallen on it there and then.

George put her hand on Neville's elbow. 'It's fine, honestly. It was going to come out anyway — the team need to know.'

'And we only know it's someone royal,' said Dot. 'We don't know which one.'

George shifted forward to the edge of her seat and they all mirrored her, leaning in to catch her announcement, which was delivered in hushed tones. 'I will only say this once. After this, we'll only ever refer to their code names.' She paused again, deliberately building up the tension like Maya Jama about to announce who was leaving *Love Island*. When she was sure they were all hanging on her every word, she whispered, 'It is the top two. It's Charles and Camilla.'

Even Bea, who had been treating this as not much more than an amusing diversion felt a shiver of excitement.

'Shut up!' This time Dean's words were heartfelt. 'The actual King? Here?' He started laughing so hard that Bea thought he'd do himself some damage. He flung himself back on the rumpled cushions, his whole body shaking uncontrollably.

When Eileen snapped, 'Stop it, Dean! Control yourself,' Bea could feel an urge to laugh bubbling up inside her. She tried to swallow it down and clutched onto Dot's arm a bit tighter. Dot glanced at her, saw the muscles either side of her mouth twitching, and corpsed. That was enough. The dam burst and Bea doubled over, laughing until tears streamed down her face.

Soon the whole room was filled with the sound of collective hysteria. When Bea sat up and started dabbing at her face with a tissue, she could see that even George and Eileen had joined in. The only person not carried along on the wave of hilarity was Neville.

'I'm glad you all find it funny,' he sniffed, like an elderly aunt in the middle of a rave. 'But I happen to think it's serious. We have been *chosen* . . . are going to be *graced* by the most important person in this country. The sovereign himself. And we've only got sixteen days to prepare.'

The noise died down and, duly chastened, everyone sat up straight and put their serious faces on.

'Sorry, Neville,' Bea said. 'It's just so extraordinary.'

'It's an extraordinary opportunity for Costsave,' said George, 'and one that I know we won't waste. Everyone's going to get behind this.'

Bea wasn't sure about that, but, like the others, she focused on Neville as he explained the timescale and the tasks involved.

'The theme of their visit to the southwest is thanking key workers, so we understand that in Costsave they want to meet ordinary staff on the shop floor and maybe go into the stores.' Dot nudged Bea and winked at her. Dean looked left and right shiftily, and Bea wondered what secrets lurked in the stores, which were his domain. 'They've got a strict schedule and we've been allocated twenty-six minutes. We pressed for half an hour but that's all they can fit in. So, we need to make sure we make the best of that time and that our facilities are tip-top. I've had George's agreement to order extra cleaning shifts so we can implement a deep clean in the next week, and then it will be up to every member of staff to keep it spotless and tidy.'

'Will the store be closed while they're here?' Bea asked.

George shook her head. 'They've said to carry on as usual. We'll stop people going in and out while they are actually arriving and departing, and we'll have barriers at the entrance so people can wait and see them there, if they want to. But they were happy for there to be customers in store. Obviously, there will be a bubble of security around our VIPs.'

It sounded like a recipe for chaos to Bea, but she didn't say so. If the experts thought it would work, who was she to disagree?

'When you say "facilities", does that include the Ladies' and Gents'?' Dot asked.

'For goodness' sake, Dot!' Eileen snapped. 'Talk about lowering the tone!'

'What? Don't you think Charles and Camilla go to the loo? I've got news for you, Eileen. They're just people, and just like us they—'

'Okay, that's enough!' George leapt in. 'Please don't mention their names again, Dot. From now on, our special guests will be known as Fred and Ginger. Okay? But Dot's actually raised a very important point. We do need to make sure they can take a comfort break if they need to. Not the public loos, obviously. Add the staff rest rooms to the cleaning schedule, please, Neville.'

'They could be a lot nicer with a few homely touches,' said Dot.

Dean sniggered. 'I don't want anyone touching me in the staff bogs.'

'No danger of that, mate,' Bea said, while Dot ignored the interruption.

'A box of tissues. Some flowers in a little vase. They'd make a big difference. I'm happy to take that on,' she said.

'Brilliant! Thank you, Dot,' said George. 'Now, I think the first thing we need to do is to take a tour of inspection of the whole store. If we identify areas that need more than a clean, then I think we can run to a few tins of paint. Let's have this place looking its absolute best. Neville, you and I will do that today.' He made a quick note on his board. 'We'll report back tomorrow.'

Bea raised her hand.

'Honestly, Bea, you don't need to do that. Just jump in. All ideas welcome,' said George. 'Go ahead.'

'My mum reminded me yesterday that we had a VIP guest here twelve years ago. A comedian off the telly. He really drew the crowds, apparently. Do you remember who it was, Dot? Or Neville? You were here then, weren't you?'

Neville straightened his tie. 'I don't think we can make comparisons, Dot. This is in a completely different league.'

'Ha! Of course,' said Dot. 'It was Bobby Ball, from *Cannon and Ball*. Lovely bloke! What a laugh. He had time for absolutely everyone. Such a nice guy. We literally rolled out the red carpet for him. The store bought one and we had it at the main entrance. Surely, we should dig that out and use it again?'

George nodded. 'Great idea! Presumably it's stored somewhere. Dean, can I put you in charge of finding it and making sure it's serviceable?'

Dean started, like someone had stuck him with a sharp pin. 'Yeah, right. Sure.' Bea had a feeling his mind was elsewhere — perhaps on George and Neville's upcoming tour of inspection and guilty secrets lurking in the stores. Maybe she was doing Dean a disservice. He'd changed quite a bit over the last year or two and certainly wasn't the villain he'd been during his first stint at Costsave.

George asked Bea to take a special look at the entrance area and see how she thought it could be spruced up, and the meeting was soon called to a close. Dean shot off down the stairs, like a cork out of a bottle, while the others wandered back to their stations at a more leisurely pace. Bea and Dot opened up their tills, but after half an hour or so, Bea logged off again and headed for the entrance to take an initial reccy of her designated area.

'All right, Bea?' Evan said from his post just inside the doors.

'Hi, Evan. I'm fine. How are you?' Bea said, then felt unaccountably foolish about the rush of words. He hadn't *really* wanted to know how she was. She hurried past, feeling herself blush. Ant was outside pretending to do something with the trolleys in a corner of the car park. Bea smiled as she glanced across and saw him grinding a cigarette end into the tarmac with his foot. He looked up, waved and started to walk over to her.

'What's up, Bea?' he said, nodding approval at her little pink notebook and biro with a fluffy bird on the end. 'Need a bit of a break? Can't blame you.'

'This isn't like your cardboard box ruse, Ant. I've actually come out here to do a job. I've got to make sure the entrance area looks good for our VIPs. I'm just jotting down some ideas.'

He pulled a face. 'What have you got so far?'

'Nothing. I haven't got started yet.'

He surveyed the forecourt and doors. Underneath the overhang of the first floor with its supporting metal pillars, there was a trolley park to one side and a couple of benches the other side, where people waited with their shopping for a taxi or the town bus.

'To be honest, I think there's chuff all you can do to make this look nice. It's a supermarket, isn't it? End of.'

'That's a bit defeatist. There must be something . . .'

For the life of her, she couldn't think what it was, though. They were standing quite near the double doors. A steady stream of customers trickled in and out. A lad in a baseball cap and black zip up top with white stripes down the sleeves, walked past. He stopped close to them to let an older woman out of the doors. Her trolley was rather full and a bit wayward, veering to the left as it trundled down the dropped kerb to the car park. The lad darted forward and grabbed the front of it, righting its course. As the woman thanked him, he flashed a nervous grin, then headed into the store. It's the little things that make a difference to a day, thought Bea.

Still uninspired by the potential of Costsave's facade, she decided to leave it and go back to her till.

'You up for chips at lunchtime?' she asked Ant.

'Try and stop me,' he said, giving her two big thumbs up. 'Saggy was round earlier. He's playing with his drone again. We might see him in the park later if we take our chips there.'

Saggy was Ant's rather dodgy friend. Bea had a soft spot for him, though, since he'd been part of the squad of mates who had come to her aid last summer. She wouldn't mind if they bumped into him later — he was good entertainment value.

Evan was on his radio as she walked past. He looked serious. She pretended to examine some bunches of tulips in a series of buckets on a stand inside the entrance and tried to listen in without much success. She could only hear his side of the conversation.

'Yeah, okay . . . three, yeah? . . . Haven't got an eyeball on them here. Will report when I do.'

'Everything all right?' Bea said, as she switched one bouquet for another for no reason.

'Radio's on fire today. Looks like there's a gang in town. Three of them. They've split up. Jimmy in the off-licence said it looked like one of them was coming our way.'

Normally a pretty relaxed kind of guy, Bea could see a change in Evan now. He'd drawn himself up taller, was tense across his shoulders and was clenching his jaw. His face lost some of its boyishness as he stepped forward and scanned the car park.

'They won't come in here when they see you,' Bea said.

'Maybe not. I'm ready for them if they do, though.'

She didn't doubt it. She preferred him in chilled-out mode and had quite a strong urge to put her hands on the muscles between his shoulders and give them a squeeze, get rid of some of the tautness. She heard someone clear their throat and looked round to see Neville and George standing there. They'd started their tour of inspection.

'Is there a problem, Bea?' Neville said.

'No, no, Neville. Just making a few notes, you know, for the visit . . .' She waved her empty notebook in the air. 'Back to the tills now.'

Neville nodded and George smiled as Bea scurried back to checkout six.

She hadn't been there long before she heard Eileen's voice drifting across the store from one of the middle aisles. 'Hey you, stop right there! Hey! Come back!'

CHAPTER FIVE

Bea and Dot both turned to look where the noise was coming from. They both saw the lad with the baseball cap come haring out of the Hair Care, Bath and Home Remedy aisle. Eileen wasn't far behind. Bea didn't think she'd ever seen Eileen running before, but she was really going for it with a surprising turn of speed. The lad grabbed hold of the end of the shelf unit as he took the corner. It came away from its fixing and toppled over spilling the full panoply of individual chocolate bars across the floor. As he sprinted away, Eileen skidded on a mint KitKat and went flying. She emitted an ear-splitting scream as she went down, and there was an audible thump as her coccyx met the ground.

'Oh my god, Eileen!' Bea and Dot both abandoned their tills to go to her aid.

The lad didn't look back. He was running towards the door and the substantial obstacle of Evan in full defence mode. He was standing square, arms and legs wide, making himself look as big as possible, which, in his case, was pretty massive. Bea heard him shout, 'Stop! Stop there!'

She watched as the lad dodged to the left. Evan lunged at him and the boy darted to the right, managed to get round him and out through the entrance.

'Oh no, you don't!' Evan shouted and set off after him.

Ant was halfway across the car park with a small train of trolleys he'd been collecting in a leisurely fashion. He looked up when he heard people shouting in the store. Someone in a dark top and baseball cap was sprinting towards him. Evan was running out of the doorway now, too, big legs going like pistons.

'Ant, mate! Stop him!' he called out. If Ant gave the trolleys a good shove, he might be able to take the runner out or at least block his path and give Evan a chance to catch up with him.

For a split second the lad locked eyes with Ant. He was only young, Ant thought, probably not even sixteen yet. Whatever he'd done, it couldn't have been that bad, could it? Ant's natural antipathy to authority kicked in. He held onto the trolleys for a moment — long enough for the boy to shoot past — then shoved them into Evan's path. The front edge of the first trolley hit Evan's hip, knocking him off balance. He staggered for a few steps, flailing his arms.

'Sorry, mate,' Ant called out. 'Left it too late. You all right?'

Evan swore at him and, having regained his equilibrium, set off in pursuit of the boy. There was a screech of brakes on the far side of the car park. Ant turned his head to see the lad vaulting over the bonnet of a white van, the driver of which was gesticulating rather graphically.

He's lost him, thought Ant, but Evan wasn't about to give up. If anything, he was running faster than ever and Ant saw them both disappear from view around the corner that led to the High Street.

Inside Costsave, staff were clustered round Eileen.

'Who's our first-aider?' someone asked.

'Anthony,' said Neville and walked to the front to summon him inside. By the time Ant got there, Eileen was being helped to her feet, howling about how much her knee hurt. He tried to examine her but she screamed before his hand got anywhere near her. Tyler, the newest recruit on shelf stacking, was sent off to get one of the wheelchairs they kept for customers. Someone had fetched Dean from the stores. He was almost as white-faced as his mum.

'What's happened to her?' he said, looking at her as if she was a particularly fragile specimen in a museum.

'She had a fall,' George said, which Bea thought was an interesting take on it. George's management training had clearly kicked in — no talk of slipping or tackling a shoplifter. Nothing that could imply Costsave's liability at this stage.

'I think she needs an ambulance,' Ant said. 'She needs to be checked out.'

'Of course.' George took out her mobile phone.

In too much pain to speak now, Eileen was flapping her arm in the air. Bea caught hold of her hand and Eileen's fingers gripped tightly round hers.

'I think it's you she needs, not me,' Bea said to Dean, aware of his panic-stricken expression. She gently transferred Eileen's hand to his and said quietly, 'She's scared, Dean. You just need to be there for her.'

Dean bit his bottom lip, then crouched down so his head was level with Eileen's. 'It's all right, Mum,' he said. 'I'll stay with you. It'll be okay.'

Bea could see Eileen visibly relax. Tyler helped to push the wheelchair nearer to the front entrance, to wait for the ambulance, with Dean on one side and Ant on the other.

'There are some little blankets in Home and Garden, Bea,' said George. 'Can you fetch one to put over her knees?'

Bea immediately set off on her mission. She had to go past the Hair Care, Bath and Home Remedy aisle on her way. As she glanced along there, something on the floor caught her eye, halfway along. Keen to clear up another slip hazard, she diverted down the aisle and picked up the offending item. It was a home pregnancy kit.

She put it back on the shelf and proceeded into Home and Garden, where she quickly selected a red and green tartan fleece blanket and took it back to the front of the store. She handed it to George, who took off the packaging and tucked it in around Eileen's knees herself.

Ant stood back a little, next to Dot and Bob. Bea joined them.

'Poor Eileen,' she said. 'She was within a whisker of catching our little thief just before she slipped.'

'If I'd got hold of him, he'd know about it,' said Bob. 'They're a bloody menace at the moment. It's not a victimless crime — they're stealing from all of us.'

'Well, you didn't get hold of him, and I'm glad you didn't,' said Dot. 'He looked like quite a young lad to me.'

'Old enough to know better,' said Bob, and Bea noticed the distance between them, felt a chill in the air that wasn't anything to do with them standing near to the door.

'Evan was chasing him, too. Did you see him, Ant?' She had been too busy tending to Eileen to take in what had happened in the car park.

'Yeah, I saw him,' said Ant. He looked at Bea, then looked away.

'What?' said Bea.

'Nothing.' He put his hand up to his face, half-hiding his mouth. 'Evan followed him right out of the car park. For a big bloke, he can really shift, can't he?'

'Yeah, he'll probably come back with him tucked under his arm in a minute.'

They all looked out of the doors, but there was no sign of Evan. They could, however, hear the wail of a siren and soon an ambulance, with its blue light flashing, came round the corner and threaded its way past the rows of parked cars to the store.

By now there was quite a crowd of customers and staff gathered near the entrance. They all watched as the paramedics assessed Eileen and then loaded her into the back of the van, with Dean installed beside her. To be honest, he looked so shaken up, Bea felt he could probably benefit from a bit of medical attention himself.

'Okay, everyone,' she said. 'I'm sure Eileen will get the very best care now. Let's get back to doing what we do — providing the best shopping experience in Kingsleigh.'

Everyone started to disperse. Ant retrieved the Costsave wheelchair and started to fold it up. There was still no sign of Evan. Bea wondered how far he'd had to run and where he had got to. She was kicking herself that she hadn't watched the chase across the car park, but, of course, Eileen had come first. Someone hadn't missed the drama, though. George was suddenly standing in front of them.

'Ant,' she said, 'I need a word with you.'

'Okay,' Ant said, waiting to hear what she had to say.

George shook her head, grim-faced. 'Not here,' she said. 'In my office.'

CHAPTER SIX

'See you later,' Bea said, giving Ant's elbow a little squeeze as he set off after George. He pulled a face and she watched as they picked their way past Tyler who was gathering all the chocolate bars. Neville was examining the display rack, then he went back to his Customer Service desk and Bea heard the announcement over the tannoy, 'Ms Smith to aisle ten.' Ms Smith was one of Costsave's facilities managers. In the old days they would have been called a handyman, but although Stacey Smith wasn't a man, she was very handy. Soon, the display was fixed back into place and each chocolate bar was back where it should be. Costsave was back to normal. Not quite normal, though, thought Bea, as she processed the next customer's shopping. There was still an empty space where Evan should be standing, and the familiar figure of Ant having a crafty ciggy outside was missing. She had a feeling today's drama wasn't over yet.

After a few minutes, Dot leaned back and said softly, 'He's back, Bea.'

Bea looked across the shop floor but couldn't see Ant. She swivelled round and there, plodding through the car park was Evan, on his own. He was carrying his jumper and even from this distance she could see that his shirt, soaked with sweat, was sticking to his ample pecs.

Neville had spotted him too. He shot over to the front door and out into the car park, meeting up with him several metres from the store. They stopped and had an animated conversation, then they both walked through the shop towards the staff door at the back.

'Going for a debrief, I reckon,' said Dot. She paused, waiting for Bea to fire back a saucy response.

'Yeah,' said Bea. 'I wonder what happened . . .'

Dot gaped. 'You all right, babe? I left you an open goal there. Debrief. Evan.' She raised her eyebrows.

'What?' said Bea, vaguely. 'Oh, yeah. Sorry, Dot. I think today's been a bit much. I like it when it's quiet and boring in here. I feel a bit, I dunno, off.'

'Understandable. Here, have a mint.' Dot ferreted in the pocket of her tabard and then stretched towards Bea, bearing a packet of strong mints.

'Thanks, Dot. You're a doll,' Bea said, taking one and popping it in her mouth. 'Are you all right? You and Bob seem a bit frosty. Everything okay?'

Dot pressed her lips together briefly. 'I'll tell you later.'

They both swivelled back to their tills. Customer traffic was building up now and they were kept busy until lunchtime. Bea didn't get a chance to talk to Ant when he slunk back through the store and out into the car park. He had the look of a rueful schoolboy after an uncomfortable time in the headteacher's office, though. What on earth had he done?

One person who didn't reappear was Evan. When it was time for her break, Bea went up to the staff area to collect her bag and coat from the Ladies' locker room. On her way there she popped her head into the staff room, and he was sitting on one of the sofas on his own.

'You okay, Evan?' Bea said.

'Yeah. I wanted to get back to work, but George said to take a bit of time out.'

She went into the room and perched on the opposite arm of the sofa, instantly regretting her decision, which felt self-consciously casual and awkward at the same time. Why on earth hadn't she just sat next to him, or on the other sofa, like an ordinary human being? She'd just have to style it out. She shifted position, which just accentuated the expanse of be-legginged thigh and knee sticking out from under her tabard.

'What happened?' she said.

'I chased the lad down the High Street and then he ducked down the alley to the park.'

'So, you lost him?'

'Nah, I followed him in there. Caught up with him. Brought him down with a tackle on the grass just past the play area.' That explained the grass and mud stains on his trouser legs. They were damp where, presumably, he'd tried to sponge them off without success.

'Blimey. So . . . ?'

'I recognised him. He was a kid from school, couple of years below me. Weedy little thing. Grazed both his hands and his chin as he came down. He didn't put up a fight or nothing. Just lay there, then we both sat up. He told me he hadn't nicked anything. He turned his pockets out there and then. He said he was going to pinch something, but changed his mind. Eileen saw him when he was putting something back.'

'Why did he run, then?'

'I don't know. I think he thought he'd be in trouble anyway. And then I set after him and I guess put the fear of god into him. I said we should go back to the shop, explain everything, but he didn't want to. I guess he didn't trust me. There was something about him, something in his eyes. I felt sorry for him, so I just let him go. I got up, helped him to his feet and sent him on his way. Now I'm in more shit than he would have been if he'd come back.'

'You are? Why?'

Evan shook his head. 'I shouldn't have left the Costsave car park, according to George. I'm not employed to "police the town" and I'm not insured either. When I told her about the rugby tackle, she had a face like thunder. I thought she'd be pleased with my commitment. Going above and beyond.

All that. Apparently not—' He stopped and looked beyond Bea. Bea turned round and saw George herself standing in the doorway.

'Bea, do you mind—?'

Bea took the hint and stood up. She shot a quick sympathetic smile at Evan and left the room, heading for her locker. She'd have to be quick, she thought. All this was eating into her chip break with Ant. However, the lure of the potential for gossip was too strong and she paused a couple of paces along the corridor so she could listen in.

'I'm sorry, Evan,' George was saying. 'I've been in touch with Regional about this. In view of the seriousness of your breach of rules, I'm going to have to suspend you. I need to talk to Eileen and others and compile a report. While that's going on, I'm afraid you can't come into work. You will still be paid, for the time being.'

Bea clapped her hand to her mouth to make sure that her horror didn't escape in the form of a gasp, squeak or any other noise which would give her away. Suspended? For doing his job? That seemed very harsh. She tiptoed along the corridor, took off her tabard and retrieved her coat and bag and clattered down the stairs.

Evan was on his way out too. She walked with him into the car park.

'I'm out,' he said. 'Now what am I going to do?'

'I'm so sorry. I'm sure it'll only be for a day or two. George is just following rules.'

'Rules,' Evan snorted. 'What a nightmare.'

Bea's hand hovered behind his broad back. She was within a gnat's whisker of making contact and giving him a little reassuring stroke, when Ant joined them.

'All right?' he said.

'No, got sent home,' said Evan. 'Suspended.'

'Suspended? Bloody hell. I just got a warning.'

Evan looked at him. 'What for, mate?'

Ant suddenly took an interest in inspecting his own his feet, scuffing at some gravel in front of him.

'For not helping you. For shoving the trolleys in your way.' He glanced at Evan, checking his reaction, then held his hands up. 'It's true. I did it. I was going to come and find you later and apologise, but I can do it now. I'm sorry, Evan. I just . . . something kicked in.'

Evan smiled ruefully. 'Listen, man, I wish you'd rammed me a little bit harder and stopped me in my tracks. I wasn't meant to go out of the car park, apparently.'

'So you were wrong for chasing him, and I was wrong for trying to stop you. Yeah, that makes sense. Not.' Ant twirled his finger next to his temple to indicate his opinion of George's decisions.

'Rules is rules,' Evan said.

'Rules is bullshit, if you ask me. I hope you're back here soon, mate.'

'Thanks, Ant. I appreciate that.'

They fist-bumped each other and smiled.

'Do you want to get some chips with us? We're going to take them in the park,' Ant said.

Evan shook his head. 'No, I'm going to head home. Get out of these clothes, have a shower and get my head down. I'm knackered, actually.'

They parted ways. Bea added in a 'Take care,' after her goodbye and then mentally kicked herself for sounding so lame. She and Ant both got a big portion of chips and walked down the alleyway between the phone shop and the nail bar into the park. They picked a bench with a good view across the site which sloped down to the bandstand and the river.

'You like him, don't you?' said Ant. Bea knew who he meant without asking.

'No.' She couldn't quite meet his eye.

'Come on, Bea. I saw you. You were going to put your arm round him. It's okay. Good looking bloke. Bit of a unit. I almost fancy him myself.'

'Was that why you rammed those trolleys into him? You thought I fancied him? I thought we were past all that.'

'Don't be daft. You can fancy who you like. We're mates, aren't we? I just want you to be happy. I shoved those trolleys because I guess I can't help rooting for the underdog. Cos most of the time, all through my childhood, even now I suppose, I know what that feels like.'

'Oh, Ant.' Bea didn't know what else to say, so she dipped her biggest, fattest chip into the pool of ketchup and then held it out to him. He grinned, took it and stuffed it all into his mouth.

'I don't want you to feel sorry for me, Bea. I mean, I'm doing all right these days. I got my job, I'm learning to read. Things are on the up.' The way he said it, though, the tone of his voice suggested otherwise and Bea resolved to spend more time with him, do more together. Not because she felt sorry for him, but because it was like he said — they were mates, and mates should be there for each other.

They carried on eating in companionable silence for a while.

'Ay-ay, something's up,' said Ant, through a mouthful of hot potato and zingy tomato sauce. A marked police car was driving into the park, making its way slowly along the widest path. 'You don't see that every day, do you?'

'No,' said Bea. 'They must have opened the main gates up. Look, there's an ambulance, too. What the hell's going on?'

They watched as both vehicles drove down the hill and parked on the concrete area in front of the bandstand. Various officers got out and set off down the narrower path alongside the river towards the part where the bridge carrying the bypass spanned the valley in the closest Kingsleigh got to a flyover. They soon disappeared from view behind a clump of small trees. Bea finished her chips and walked over to the nearest bin. As she did so, another police car trundled across the park, this time with its siren wailing.

'That's not good, is it? Shall we go and have a look?'

Ant nodded, got up and put his rubbish in the bin, too, and they set off down the hill. Near the bandstand, Bea spotted Tom, her friendly — some might say, over-friendly — contact in the local police. He was a junior detective these days, no longer in uniform, which was rather a shame in Bea's eyes as it had really suited him.

'I might have known you two would turn up,' he said. 'What do you guys do, hack into the police radios or something?' He didn't always appreciate Ant and Bea's efforts as amateur detectives. They'd been involved in three cases, the last of which nearly ended very badly indeed for Bea.

''Course not. We were just here, having lunch,' said Bea. 'What's going on?'

Tom rolled his eyes. 'You know better than that, Bea. I can't tell you.'

Two uniformed officers were rolling out yellow tape now, across the start of the riverside path.

'Listen, I should go.'

'Good luck with . . . whatever it is,' said Bea.

Tom pulled a warning face and wagged his finger at her. He'd been very indiscreet in the past, particularly when he and Bea had been involved, but he wasn't going to go down that road again. Not right now, anyway.

His radio spluttered into life. He turned away, but Ant and Bea both heard his side of the conversation, 'Yeah, it's a body . . . no ID yet. Looks like a young lad. Yeah. No . . . no chance he's alive.'

CHAPTER SEVEN

'Do you think it's the same one?' asked Bea.

'Dunno. I hope not. What did Evan say? He helped him up and sent him on his way? Do you reckon that's what happened?'

Bea was shocked. 'What do you mean? Evan's an honest kind of guy. I can't see him lying about something like that.'

Ant smiled. 'You believe the best of everyone. I love that about you, but people aren't always what they seem. Plus we can all panic under pressure. If he, you know, did something he regretted, he might just be saying what he needs to in order to buy some time. He might be working out what to do now.'

Bea felt a chill run down her spine. 'Do you really think that, Ant?'

'I don't know, Bea. We don't even know it's the same boy, do we? Maybe it's best just not to talk about it until we do actually know.'

But news of the body in the park was spreading quickly. When Bea went into the locker room to retrieve her uniform, Dot was in there, touching up her make-up.

'Someone said there's police in the park. Did you see anything?' Bea told her what she knew. 'Blimey, that sounds bad. It could be anyone, though, couldn't it?'

'Yeah.' She tried to change the subject. 'Is there any news on Eileen?'

'No, not yet. She really came clattering down, didn't she? I felt it when she landed on her bee-tee-em. Made my eyes water.'

'It was her knee that worried me. Her leg ended up in really funny angle, didn't it? I don't think we'll be seeing her for a while. Dean neither, if he has to look after her.'

Dot shuddered. 'I wouldn't want Dean nursing me. Can you imagine?'

'Bit harsh, Dot. You can say what you like about Dean, but he does love his mum.'

'Yeah, you're right. You're so much nicer than me, Bea. Thinking the best of people, instead of the worst. We should all "Be More Bea". Perhaps I'll have some T-shirts made.'

Coming from anyone else, Bea would have suspected snarkiness, but Dot was perfectly sincere.

'Be More Bea,' Dot repeated. 'It's quite snappy, isn't it? Perhaps I'll get an extra-large one printed up for Mister Grumpy.'

'What's up with him? You were going to tell me.'

Dot checked her watch. 'I'm meeting him for a toastie in the café, actually. I'm going to be late. And you're cutting it fine to get back on shift. In about thirty seconds, you'll turn back into a pumpkin and your fairy god-Neville will be after you.'

Bea snorted. Dot might have mashed up the imagery a bit, but she knew exactly what she meant. She didn't need Neville on her back today. She shut her locker, threw her tabard over her head and smoothed down the static in her hair as best she could.

'Look, do you want to go to the pub or something after work? Or the wine bar? It's ages since we had a proper catch-up.'

'Yeah, that would be lovely, babe.' Dot flashed Bea a smile and they left the locker room together.

Bea was two minutes late getting to her till, but although Neville saw her scuttling along, slipping into her chair and logging in as quickly as possible, he didn't move from the Customer Service desk. As Bea glanced over to see whether she needed to brace for incoming trouble, he seemed lost in thought. He woke up when he saw Ant walking past on his way out to enjoy a quiet afternoon's trolley wrangling and intercepted him. Ant was soon turning round and heading to the back of the shop. He called by Bea's checkout on his way.

'Got to cover for Dean in the stores,' he said. 'There's some deliveries coming in this afternoon.'

'Change is as good as a rest,' said Bea. 'Might be a bit warmer in there.'

'Yeah.' He looked a bit troubled. Bea knew about his struggle with reading, had encouraged him to start learning to read in a little group at the library, and celebrated his progress with him.

'Are you worried about it? Reading the labels or anything?'

He flashed her a tight little smile. 'Yeah. Everything happens really fast when a delivery comes in. I've helped Dean with it before, but I just provided the muscle. He told me where to put everything.'

'Is anyone else in there?'

'Don't think so.'

'Ask Nev if Tyler can help you, get some experience in a different department. Then you can have him running about checking labels and barcodes and whatnot, like it's a game.'

Ant's smile broadened. 'You're a freaking genius, Bea. Thanks, mate.'

He trudged back to the Customer Service desk and soon Bea saw Neville accompanying him to the Tea and Coffee aisle where Tyler was stocking up the display of coffee pods.

News of the body in the park was spreading quickly. Customers were talking about it in hushed tones. Sirens were heard drifting in through the double doors. When Dot came back from her break, she had an update.

'I've got a name,' she said to Bea, as she paused on her way to her till. 'Someone came in the caff and said they knew who it was. Said the family were all down there, in the park.

The police stopped them from going through the tape and seeing him.'

Bea could only imagine the distress.

'How awful,' she said. 'Who is it?'

'Everyone's saying the lad's Harley Creech.'

'Oh no.' Bea felt her stomach clench, like a knot forming inside her.

Dot nodded. 'The youngest lad of Connor Creech. That poor family.'

'His mum was in here yesterday,' Bea said. 'I can't even . . .'

'Can you keep the nattering for break time, please, ladies?'

They both jumped. Neither of them had spotted Neville stalking up to them.

'Sorry, Neville,' said Bea. 'Have you heard what's going on in the park, though?'

Neville frowned, then held his hand up. 'I'm not interested in gossip.'

'This isn't gossip, Neville. It's news. They've found a body of a young lad there. We think . . . it might be the boy Evan was chasing.'

Neville's face went slack as he processed Bea's words.

'A body . . .' he repeated. 'Dear god . . .'

He put his clipboard down in Bea's packing area and closed his eyes for a moment, clasping his hands. Bea and Dot looked at each other with raised eyebrows but didn't say anything. After a moment or two, Neville opened his eyes again.

'This is bad,' he said. 'This is very bad.'

Without another word, he picked up his clipboard and headed for the back of the store, breaking into a loping jog which put Bea in mind of an Afghan hound in the Crufts show ring.

'You don't think Evan did something to him, do you?' said Dot.

'No, I don't,' said Bea, but at the back of her mind, there were seeds of doubt. Both Ant and Dot had said that she always saw the best in people. Did that make her naive? Gullible, even? Did the fact that she fancied Evan — she couldn't really pretend she didn't anymore — completely cloud her judgement? 'I don't think he would do anything to hurt anyone,' she said. But before the end of their shift, there was more news on the grapevine. Uniformed police had been seen outside Evan's mum's house and Evan had been taken in for questioning.

CHAPTER EIGHT

Shortly after five, Bea and Dot left Costsave with a little gaggle of colleagues. Bob had offered the two friends a lift home, but they'd explained they had other plans. Did Bea imagine that he looked slightly miffed at the news? She wasn't sure. The weather had taken a turn for the worse. A stiff breeze was blowing an old plastic bag across the car park.

'Catch that, will you, Ty?' Ant said to his new sidekick. 'Can't have the place looking untidy.'

To everyone's surprise, Tyler immediately scampered after the wayward rubbish, chasing it round the ranks of cars until finally grabbing it as it wrapped itself round the bottom of a lamppost. He held it aloft in triumph, while his audience gave a ragged cheer, then stuffed it in the nearest bin.

'Bloody hell, Ant,' Bea said. 'He's keen.'

'I didn't expect him to actually do it,' Ant said. Then, as Tyler rejoined the group, 'Well done, mate. Didn't think you were going to get that. Fair play to you.'

Tyler grinned. 'Cheers,' he said.

'Where shall we go, Bea?' Dot asked as they neared the corner of the High Street.

'Ooh,' said Ant, livening up a little. 'Are we getting something to eat or is it drinks?' He mimed downing a pint.

Bea and Dot exchanged glances. They'd both been looking forward to having a really good chat, just the two of them. It had been quite a day, though, and Bea hadn't forgotten her mental pledge to spend more time with Ant. She raised her eyebrows at Dot, who understood and nodded.

'We're going for a drink. You're welcome to join us. Both of you,' Bea said, including Tyler. 'To be honest, I wouldn't take much persuading to get absolutely bladdered.'

Tyler appeared a little uncomfortable, looking down and shuffling his feet. 'I can't,' he said. 'I'm not old enough.'

Dot pulled a sympathetic face. 'We can still buy you a Coke or whatever.'

'No, s'alright. My mum's expecting me back for tea. She'll worry if I'm late, especially today . . . with, you know . . .'

They all fell silent. Then a horrible thought popped into Bea's head.

'If it is Harley Creech, do you, *did you*, know him?'

Tyler nodded. 'We were in the same year at school.'

'Oh, mate,' said Ant. 'I'm so sorry.'

'We weren't friends or anything. He was in a different tutor group, but it's still . . .' His words trailed off. Bea remembered that one of Harley's older brothers, Norton, had been in her year group.

'It's a shock,' said Dot. 'It's a terrible thing. You'd better get off home, like you said. Give your mum a hug.'

Tyler started to peel away from the group.

'I'll see you tomorrow, okay?' Ant called after him. 'Good job today.'

Tyler's face brightened briefly. 'See you tomorrow.'

'I think someone's got a fan,' said Dot to Ant, as they started walking along the High Street. 'How does it feel to be idolised?'

Ant rolled his eyes. 'Don't be daft. We got on really well, though. He's ever so keen and he did a great job sorting things out.'

'Did you tell him about your, you know, reading . . . ?'

'No. Need to know basis. I'm not ashamed about it, like I used to be, but it's not something you broadcast, is it? I'll tell him if I have to. The thing is, I'm doing really well now. Before too long it won't even be a thing — I'll be able to read, just like everyone else, well, maybe a bit slower.'

'That's brilliant, Ant. I'm so flippin' proud of you,' said Bea.

'Me too,' said Dot. She and Ant had had an unlikely dalliance soon after he started at Costsave. Although that was all in the past, they'd parted on good terms and both retained a soft spot for the other.

'Well, I probably wouldn't have done anything about it without you guys, so I guess the first drinks are on me. Where are we going?' He rubbed his hands together, like he was revving himself up for a good night out. 'If you want to get hammered, Bea, the Old School has got an offer on cider this month.'

Dot pulled a face. 'That dive? I fancy going a bit posh. What about that new place, the wine bar?'

'We're not dressed for that, are we?' said Bea.

'Speak for yourself. I'm ready for anything!' It was true. Dot always looked immaculate and her outfit today — paisley tunic top over some skinny jeans which clung to her curves — would fit right in at Uncorked, Kingsleigh's latest bistro-wine bar.

'Let's do that another day. I'd like to get really togged up to go there. Make a thing of it,' said Bea, knowing that Ant wouldn't feel comfortable in anywhere that frowned on customers whose idea of smart casual was a clean hoodie. 'I'm not really going to get wasted, not on a school night. Let's just go to the Ship.'

There were no objections on settling for their usual hostelry of choice. It was funny how they'd always run through the options and nine times out of ten end up there anyway. Somehow it was a ritual that had to be gone through.

Dot and Bea linked arms, while Ant loped along beside them. As they passed the entrance to the alleyway that led to the park, Bea shivered. Had it only been that morning that Evan had set off in pursuit of that young lad? It seemed much longer.

In the pub, nestled in their favourite spot, the corner table in the back room, there was only one topic of conversation. Bea checked for the latest gossip on her phone.

'Oh shit,' she said. 'Look at this.'

She put the phone on the table and turned it round so Ant and Dot could see. It was a Facebook page: 'In Memory of Harley Creech.'

'Blimey,' said Ant. He scrolled down a little. 'It's been set up by his brothers. Looks like it's official, then.'

'You just read that, didn't you?'

'Yeah. See what I mean?' said Ant, beaming. 'I'm nearly normal.'

Neither Dot nor Bea could suppress guffaws of laughter.

'What?' said Ant.

Dot put a hand over his. 'You'll never be normal, babe. You're a one-off.'

'But we love you,' said Bea.

Ant decided not to be offended and held his glass up. 'Cheers to that,' he said. 'Actually, let's say cheers to Harley, shall we?'

The smiles faded from their faces and they all held their glasses together above the middle of the table.

'To Harley,' they said in unison. 'Rest in peace.'

CHAPTER NINE

'So, are you and Bob all right then?' Bea said, when Ant had disappeared off to the Gents. She hadn't forgotten that was the real reason she wanted to have a night out with Dot.

Dot sighed and took a big slurp of her gin and tonic.

'He's got the hump,' she said. 'And not in good way.'

'What's up with him?'

Dot looked left and right and then over her shoulder. She leaned a bit closer to Bea.

'A few days ago, he asked me to move in with him.'

'Oh, Dot! That's . . . um, good, isn't it?' She checked Dot's expression. 'Or maybe not?'

'Well, it is good, because we get on really well, and I'm happy to leave the dating game behind and settle down again, but . . . I don't know. It was the way he did it. Just so casual, like it wasn't a big deal.'

'No romantic gestures, then?'

Dot emitted a bitter laugh. 'Hardly! We were in my kitchen and I was swilling out the bin juice from my little food waste caddy into the sink, and he was rearranging the stuff I'd just loaded into the dishwasher and he just kind of mentioned it in passing. Do you know what he said? He said,

"Silly to keep paying two sets of bills, we might as well just move in. What do you think?" And that was it.'

Bea pulled a face. 'Oh, Bob! What is he like?!'

'Well, he's lovely and he's kind, and he's pretty much everything my Darren wasn't, but he's not Mister Romance.'

'So, what did you say?'

'I said I'd think about it and I haven't mentioned it since. And he's gone into a massive sulk.'

That explained the big black cloud hovering over Bob's head recently and the frostiness between him and Dot, thought Bea. It didn't sound terminal, though.

'Oh, mate,' she said. 'You know what you need to do, don't you?'

'What's that?' said Dot. 'Leave an Interflora business card lying around? Write him a note? Buy a cattle prod?'

'Sit down and talk to him about it, you daft cow.'

Dot closed her eyes for a moment.

'I know. I should. It's just . . . should it really be this much hard work?'

'You've just got your wires crossed. It won't take much to detangle them. Come on, Dot. He's a lovely guy. He's totally into you, but with someone like Bob, you just need to spell things out a bit.'

'Spell things out? Does someone else having trouble with words?' Neither of them had noticed Ant coming back. Surprisingly, he'd brought another round of drinks with him and he leaned over and placed all three down on the table.

'In a manner of speaking,' said Dot. 'Emotional illiteracy, that's what we're talking about.'

Ant blew his cheeks out. 'Oh god,' he said, with a flicker of panic in his eyes and quickly grabbed his glass. 'I've just seen Saggy at the bar. I might go and hang out with him for a bit, if that's all right with you.'

'Bless him,' said Dot, as Ant beat a hasty retreat. 'They're all the same, aren't they?'

'Well, no, actually,' said Bea. 'There are some real low-lifes out there.' Dot knew she was speaking from experience and reached out her hand to find Bea's and give it a squeeze. 'The thing is, Bob and Ant are two of the good guys.'

'I know. I'll figure things out with Bob, eventually. So what about you and Ant? He *is* a good guy . . .'

'We're so much better as mates, Dot. We're rock solid and I don't want anything to change that.'

'Understood. You've got your eye on someone else, anyway, haven't you?'

Bea was confused. 'No. What do you mean?'

'Oh, come on, Bea. Do you think I haven't noticed you getting a bit flustered round a certain security guy?'

'Bloody hell, Dot. You don't miss a thing, do you?'

Dot grabbed the salt cellar from the next table and, using it as a microphone, launched into an Aerosmith ballad, closing her eyes and swaying in her seat. Bea joined in and soon half the people in the room were watching them. When Bea realised, she shushed Dot and their chorus ground to a halt. There were giggles in their audience, but also mutterings, and Bea realised it wasn't a good look to be singing on such a dark day for Kingsleigh.

'Sorry,' she said out loud to the room. 'Got carried away.' Most people there knew Bea and Dot, at least by sight. It was a friendly crowd, but Bea still felt both judged and a little ashamed.

'You do like him, though, don't you?' said Dot. 'I mean, fifteen feet tall, broad shoulders, polite — what's not to like?'

'Yeah, a bit, maybe. I dunno.' She twiddled with a cardboard beer mat. 'I think I'd go off him if it turns out he killed a kid in the park.'

'You don't think he did that, though, do you?'

'No. I don't and I don't *want* to think that . . . nobody really knows anything at this stage, do they?'

'Except the people who were there.'

'Mm.'

Dot's phone beeped. 'Text from Bob. He's offering us a lift home. What do you reckon?'

'Yeah, I don't really want this drink. I'm ready to call it a day. Wouldn't mind a lift. It's pretty rank out there.'

'Go on, then. I'll summon Prince Charming.'

While Dot texted Bob back, Bea took a few mouthfuls of the cider Ant had brought her, but she was starting to feel unpleasantly full and her head was achy, rather than warm and fuzzy. She pushed her glass away and started to put her coat on. On their way out, Bea stopped to say goodbye to Ant. She was carrying her leftover drink, thinking she would offer it to him or, failing that, put it back on the bar to get poured away.

'I'm going to stay on for a bit,' he said. 'Can't face another long evening at *chez* Neville. Don't know if it's worse stuck in my room or sitting in their lounge. There are only so many improving documentaries I can watch. Bloody depressing, most of them. I have nightmares about global warming . . .'

Saggy had his eye on Bea's glass. 'You're not leaving that, are you? Terrible waste.'

Bea held it out to him. 'It's yours if you want it. Only one careful owner.'

Saggy had no qualms about finishing someone else's drink. He took it and started necking it there and then.

'Don't know why you stay there, mate,' he said, wiping his spare hand across his mouth. 'There's always the couch at my place.'

Ant had experienced Saggy's couch several times. He was sure his back gave a little spasm, just at the mention of it.

'Thanks, bro. I don't want to be rude to Nev. He and Carol have been amazing, taking me in. I do feel like I'm a bit of a project for them, though. An experiment to see how far their Christian kindness can reform me.'

Saggy puffed out his cheeks. 'God loves a trier. Take more than that, won't it? Drink up. I'll get you another one. Then we'll go back to mine and have a can or two and look through that stuff.'

Ant held his hand over the top of his pint glass. 'I can't have too many, mate. They disapprove of drink, well, of people getting drunk. It's awkward.'

'Blimey, you're halfway reformed already! This is serious.'

'Neville works in mysterious ways . . .' said Bea. Dot was waiting in the doorway. 'I'd better go. I'll see you tomorrow, yeah?'

As she turned to leave, Ant said, 'Thanks for asking me. I know you and Dot just wanted a natter. I really couldn't face Nev's tonight, though.'

She looked at him, surprised. 'Don't be daft. You can always come and have your tea with me and Queenie, anyway. Do you want to do that tomorrow?'

'Yeah, that'd be great. I might have some information by then, anyway.'

'What do you mean?'

'Do you remember me saying that Saggy was taking his drone out today? We're going to have a look on his laptop when we go back to his in a bit. He was out all morning. He's got a ton of footage from the park.'

CHAPTER TEN

Despite the alcohol, or maybe because of it, Bea woke up shortly after four the next morning. Before she even opened her eyes, she remembered the park the day before, the police cars, the tape . . . and the name, Harley Creech. Did that really all happen yesterday? She reached for her phone but couldn't find it. She opened her eyes and switched on her little lamp, then leaned up on one elbow and squinted at her bedside cabinet. Her book was there — the latest in her current favourite crime series, which imagined the late Queen as an amateur detective — but her phone was not. She groaned and peered over the side of her bed. The phone was on the floor. She grabbed it and settled back on her pillow, then trawled all her favourite sites and forums for the latest news.

The Facebook memorial page had hundreds of comments now, a chorus of grief at the loss of such a young man.

'One of Kingsleigh's finest. Rest in peace.'

'Gone too soon. With the angels now.'

'Only the good die young. Sleep well, Harley.'

People criticised social media, but twenty years ago this would never have happened. Here was a space where anybody could come and pay tribute. Bea thought it was moving and really rather brilliant. She wondered if Harley's family would get comfort from it. She hoped they would.

Less comforting were the local forums. These were a mixed bag at the best of times — people asking for recommendations, posting up photos from their walks, making political comments or having pointless arguments. Tonight there was poison spreading through their threads, almost like a mediaeval crowd bearing flaming torches and pitchforks. The object of their ire was Evan.

'. . . seen chasing him down the High Street.'

'Man the size of a brick shithouse chasing a young lad like that. For what? Completely out of order.'

'They should lock him up and throw away the key.'

'Give me five minutes with him. I'd teach him about rough justice.'

Oh no, thought Bea. How quick people are to judge. She shut off her phone for a moment and closed her eyes, replaying her conversation with Evan in the staff room. Yes, he'd chased the boy, and yes, he'd tackled him, but he categorically said that he'd helped him up and 'sent him on his way'. At the time, she hadn't doubted what he was saying at all. She and Ant had been involved with three investigations of their own now. She'd made some catastrophic misjudgments but she liked to think that she was learning to be observant and could read people's body language pretty well. Evan hadn't displayed any 'tells' that he wasn't being truthful. No ear scratches, no hiding of his mouth, no avoidance of eye contact. He'd told his story and the only feeling that Bea had got from him was one of confusion. He thought he'd been doing the right thing.

Now, the 'People's Court' of Kingsleigh had found him guilty before even hearing his side of things. It wasn't the first time they'd formed a virtual lynch mob. They'd done the same with her late dad, both when he was alive and years after his death, had judged him responsible for something terrible without knowing the facts. She and Ant had moved heaven and earth to defend him. Perhaps they should do the same now, get the old team back together. She smiled as she remembered that Ant was ahead of her on this one, and she wondered what Saggy's drone footage might have revealed.

She fired up her phone again and clicked on her messages. Ant always used to prefer voicemail to texts, but recently he'd been delighting in sending and receiving written messages — another sign of his progress. She typed rapidly and pressed send, *Wanna meet b4 work? Bacon roll at Cath's caff, 7 a.m.?*

Ant wasn't known as an early riser (unless he'd been sleeping rough, which he'd had to do in the past, when he would get up early and call in at the leisure centre for a wash and brush up). The chances were he'd still be asleep at seven and she'd have to wait for her gossip fix until later, but you never knew. If he did wake up early, she didn't think he'd be able to resist the offer of bacon and white bread.

She was about to shut down her phone and try to get back to sleep when she had second thoughts. She remembered how she felt when her dad's name was being dragged through the mire. How isolated. How desperate. How angry at the unfairness of it all. She searched her contacts list and composed another text. She paused for a moment, and then pressed send.

Evan. Don't know when you will get this but stay strong. I believe you. I'll help you prove your innocence. Bea xx

She switched off the light, put her phone on the bed next to her and turned over.

Less than a minute later there was a telltale ping of an incoming message.

She checked her phone again. It was Evan.

Thanks, Bea. I'm home now but keeping things on the low down. Dunno what to do. E x

Keep the faith. Your friends will help you. B x

I'm being stitched up. Thrown to the wolves.

CHAPTER ELEVEN

As she suspected, Ant didn't even read her message until long after the suggested rendezvous hour. At 7.35 a.m., she got a quick text from him. *Cya at work*. It was frustrating on one level, but she couldn't help smiling. He wasn't likely to change any time soon. In fact, Ant caught up with her halfway along the High Street on her walk into work.

'Hey,' he puffed, 'sorry about your message.'

'That's okay. It was a long shot.'

'Really sorry about the bacon sarnie, though,' he said. 'The House of Neville has gone sugar-free. No Coco Pops. No Frosties. Breakfast is either porridge and walnuts, or something that looks like toenail clippings and skimmed milk.'

'Sounds grim.' Bea thought fondly of her two slices of thick white toast, slathered with butter and marmalade. She still felt a little peckish, though. She should have gone for a third slice. Perhaps she'd have a bun at breaktime.

'The kids are bloody miserable. I told little Amy I'd try and sneak a packet of Pop Tarts into the house.'

'Don't get caught, mate. Nice as they are, I don't think Nev or Carol will want you undermining their parental authority.'

'I tell you, that household's getting weirder by the minute. It's like I'm living with Kingsleigh's only Amish family.

Before I know it, they'll be getting rid of the telly and making us wear straw hats and shit.'

Bea thought, not for the first time, that Ant really needed to find somewhere else to live. There was a lot of new housing going up in Kingsleigh, but none of it affordable on Ant's wages. Someone's spare room was really the best — the only — option at the moment.

'I can't see you in a straw hat, somehow.' They were turning into the Costsave car park now and running out of chatting time. 'Anyway, did you look at Saggy's drone footage? Did it show anything?'

'I did and it did. It's complicated, though.'

'Why?' Bea had a sinking feeling.

'What Saggy's got — I don't think it will help Evan.'

'Oh.'

'It might not be a disaster, though. You know what Saggy's like. He won't go running to the cops with it.'

'If they get wind of him having had the drone up, I reckon they'll ask for it. Or seize it,' said Bea. 'Is it really bad?'

They had walked round to the side door. Ant held it open for Bea and they bundled inside, out of the cold.

'It's not terrible, but it's not good. Shall I ask Saggy to bring his laptop to yours this evening and you can have a look?'

Bea hesitated. Although Saggy had been on the little team that had rescued her when her last investigation had gone badly wrong, she still wasn't sure whether he was sufficiently house-trained to admit into her and Queenie's home.

'I'll tell him to be on his best behaviour,' Ant said, and Bea cursed his ability to read her mind. 'He's a lot better than he used to be.'

'Okay,' she said. 'Sure. Let's all have tea together. Queenie will love having company.'

Numbers were noticeably depleted at the staff briefing and the atmosphere was muted. Tyler was standing on his own, so Ant and Bea made their way over to him. Bea was pleased to see Bob and Dot came in together, until she realised that their body language was still prickly. When George and Neville walked in, they didn't have to ask for quiet — the room hushed at the sight of them.

George started with an update.

'I understand that yesterday was a very challenging one for everyone. I want to thank you all for dealing with the most difficult circumstances and carrying on for the rest of the day like the true professionals you are.

'I have to report that it has been confirmed that the young man who was found . . .' she paused, unable to say the word they all had in their minds, '. . . who was found in the park yesterday lunchtime, Harley Creech, was the same one who was involved in the incident here. We don't know the details, but I think the least we can do is have a minute's silence for him now. Please join me.'

She clasped her hands in front of her and bowed her head. Everyone else followed suit. After a very long minute, George looked up again.

'Thank you,' she said. 'To update you, Evan has not been arrested nor charged with anything, but my own enquiry into yesterday's incident is ongoing, so he will remain suspended for the time being. Obviously, I need to respect a colleague's medical details, but Eileen will not be back at work for at least a week.'

'Torn cartilage and a bruised coccyx,' Kirsty blurted out. She was Eileen's best friend among the staff. 'Pretty nasty. She's dosed up to the eyeballs with painkillers at the moment.'

'Yes, well, thank you, Kirsty,' George said, sending her a look which was the opposite of thankful. 'Given this news, Dean will also be absent for at least some of the time, on carer's leave. I will be relying on all of you to be flexible in the roles we ask you to do, and there will be extra shifts available. Now,' she said, and bounced on her heels a couple of times, trying to change the energy in the room, 'Neville, can you update us on our VIP visit?'

Neville rummaged with the sheets of paper on his clipboard. 'Certainly. With Eileen and Dean out of action, we have two vacancies on the task force, so I'm looking for more volunteers. We'll have an emergency meeting straight after this briefing. If you are interested in joining in, please stay behind.'

'Will the visit still be going ahead?' Kirsty asked.

Neville blinked rapidly, then squinted at Kirsty like he didn't understand the question.

'Of course. Why wouldn't it?'

'Well,' she said, 'if Evan's charged with murder, they will hardly want the King getting tangled up in that, will they?'

Neville shot a glance at George, who said smoothly but insistently, 'I think we're getting ahead of ourselves here. Firstly, I don't want to hear any more talk about what Evan did or didn't do. That subject is now closed, do you understand? Secondly, this incident and the royal visit are two entirely separate things and I want to keep it that way.'

She carried on with the general notices and it was soon time to open up the store. Most of the staff trooped out. As he turned to join them, Bea tugged on Bob's sleeve.

'Are you going to join us on the task force, Bob?' she said.

'No, I don't think so,' Bob said, although Bea thought she detected a little hesitation. Bob was usually in the thick of things at Costsave.

'Come on. It's fun and we could do with someone—' she remembered what Queenie had said to her — 'practical.'

His face brightened. A little flattery goes a long way, thought Bea.

'Well, maybe, if everyone thought I'd be useful. If I was *wanted*.' He gave a meaningful look at Dot. Bea raised her eyebrows at Dot, then cleared her throat. Finally, Dot took the hint.

'Don't be daft, Bob. 'Course you are,' she said. 'Wouldn't be the same without you.'

Tyler had also stayed behind. As a substitute for Dean, he was a definite improvement, Bea thought. This little team was shaping up nicely.

Neville started by running through the checklist of responsibilities and reallocating the jobs he'd previously given to Eileen and Dean — Bob was charged with finding the red carpet — then asked Dot to report back on her plans for sprucing up the toilets. Dot had not skimped on her plans, which included a lick of paint and a feature wall, new mirrors, fresh flowers in vases, tissue boxes, and liquid handwash and moisturiser at the sinks. Bea approved. She could see that Dot was using this opportunity to create the sort of work toilets most people could only dream about.

'Thank you, Dot,' said Neville. 'That is admirably thorough. A little over the top maybe?'

'I don't think so,' said Dot. 'Can you imagine Camilla using the loos as they are now?' She gave a visible shudder. 'I'd be mortified. We don't want our facilities letting the whole store down.'

Neville nodded. 'Point taken.'

Tyler put his hand up.

'When Princess Anne visited our primary school, we were all given little flags to wave. We got on the local news and everything. Should we get some flags and hand them out?'

'I think people would like that,' said Bea. 'They can keep them as souvenirs of the day.'

Everyone agreed and Tyler was tasked with finding out the cost of various quantities of flags and bunting. As the meeting broke up and they made their way to their stations, they continued discussing their plans. Just for a moment it was as if the previous twenty-four hours had never happened.

There was a stark reminder of the reality, though, about half an hour later, when a dark saloon car drew up near the front entrance and two men got out. Bea immediately clocked that one of them was Tom, her detective friend. He acknowledged Bea on his way past her checkout but didn't smile. His grim expression told her all she needed to know. Yesterday, the police focus had been on the park. Today, their enquiries had shifted to Costsave and Evan.

CHAPTER TWELVE

When Bea, Ant and Saggy walked in through the kitchen door, they were met with some very welcoming smells.

Bea had warned Queenie that she had invited Saggy and Ant for tea. They didn't have many visitors, so Queenie had been rather excited at the prospect. She had done an early shift at the launderette and then pottered about all afternoon, getting ready.

'Wow, Mrs J, what's cooking?' Ant said.

Bea was also curious. She wondered whether her mum had fallen back on an old favourite or was trying something new, although the aroma filling the kitchen seemed comfortingly familiar.

'Mary Berry's lamb tagine,' said Queenie, rather proudly.

'Blimey,' said Bea. This was a new one.

'Except, I didn't have lamb, so it's beef. And she puts in a lot of funny spices, but I didn't have half of them. And you don't like celery, do you Bea, so I left that out, and did carrots instead. And no honey, because putting honey in a stew is just plain weird, isn't it?'

'So,' said Bea, trying to work it out, 'you've made a beef stew?'

'Sort of.'

'Well, whatever it is, it smells bloody lovely,' said Saggy. He was a bit on the scrawny side, but Bea had seen him tucking into a chip supper or two and had warned Queenie that, despite appearances, he was like one of those tiny mammals on the nature programmes they both liked watching — he needed to eat his own weight in food every day in order to survive.

Queenie beamed. 'It'll be ready in about half an hour. Hope you can wait that long.'

'Do you need any help, Mrs J?' asked Ant.

'No, I'm fine pottering in here. Go into the lounge, if you like. I'll bring you all a cuppa.'

They filed into the next room, where the TV was playing to itself.

'Do you need any help, Mrs J?' Saggy repeated in a whiny, sing-song voice, clutching his hands in front of him like Uriah Heap.

'Shut up,' said Ant, grinning. 'Just being polite, innit.'

'He's such a nice boy,' said Saggy, fluttering his eyelashes.

'Let's see who gets extra helpings, mate. Let's just see . . . Anyway, where's your laptop? I want to show Bea the footage.'

Saggy set his laptop up on the coffee table and they all sat in a row on the sofa and watched. The image was really clear, although the path the drone took seemed a bit random to Bea.

'I've edited it. This is just the bit with Evan in it. Here we are — 10.36 a.m. onwards. There! That's the boy running and there's Evan.'

Bea could see two figures entering the frame from the bottom left. The drone flew over them as they raced across the park. The second person, large and powerful, was clearly gaining on the first and then he launched himself, catching the other around his legs and bringing him down so that the two people became one heap on the ground. By now the drone was passing over. The heap was in the middle right of the picture and then it was gone.

'Can you zoom in?'

'Yeah. I did a copy of it and went in as much as I could. It's pretty brutal.'

Saggy played the second video. This time they could see much more detail; Harley's baseball cap, Evan's uniform. And they could almost feel the crunch after Evan sailed through the air, wrapped his arms round Harley's legs and they both hit the tarmac of the path. The last thing visible was Evan moving his legs a bit, while Harley was ominously still.

'Jeez, you can see why he's in the first team. He's a beast,' said Ant. 'He's easily twice the size of Harley, width wise.'

'I mean, it *is* brutal, but it doesn't actually contradict what Evan told us,' said Bea. 'He did say that he rugby-tackled Harley; brought him down.'

'Look at him, though, Bea,' said Ant. 'Harley's flat out. He's not moving at all. What if that was it? What if he flattened him in one hit and then made the rest up?'

Bea sat back on the sofa. 'Is that all you've got?' she said to Saggy.

'I've got loads of footage but that's all I managed to capture of the attack. I haven't got any from when he dumped him under the bridge.'

'Tackle, not attack,' she corrected. 'And, besides the fact that he said he let him go, it must be nearly a hundred and fifty metres, maybe more, from there to the path under the bridge. If he'd carried Harley there, someone would have seen him, surely.'

'Well, there were lots of people in the play park at the top, but the way the hill is flat and then curves down, I don't think they could see.'

Bea made a mental note to go to the park as soon as possible and check out the sight lines. Saggy could well be right that the tackle and what happened afterwards had taken place in a sort of blind spot.

'Why didn't you fly the drone back, Saggy? If I'd seen that on my phone or laptop or however you were following it, I'd have been right on it. Were you even watching where it was going?'

'Yes, all right, Miss Marple.' Saggy couldn't keep a note of tetchiness out of his voice. 'I *was* watching, but I've been having a bit of trouble with the controls, that's why I took it out. See if I'd fixed it or not.'

'You took a dodgy drone out over a busy park? Weren't you worried it might hurt someone?'

'I was pretty sure I'd fixed it. Anyway, the steering's still a bit unpredictable. It went off over the industrial estate and by the time I managed to turn it round there wasn't anything to see. When it passed back over the park Evan and Harley had both gone — I guess Harley was lying under the flyover by then, but it was before his body was found. There's no sign of anything odd, no police there or anything.'

'Have you given a copy to the police?' said Bea.

Saggy reached forward and shut his laptop. 'I don't want to get involved.'

'It's evidence, though.'

Saggy shrugged. 'I've got this thing about the cops. I don't bother them and I hope they don't bother me. I like to keep things under the radar.'

Queenie popped her head through the door. 'It's ready, everyone. It would be a bit of a squeeze round the kitchen table, so come and fetch it and we can eat in here.'

They all filed into the kitchen and collected plates of what looked suspiciously like beef stew and mashed potato.

'No couscous?' said Bea.

'You buy it, I'll cook it, love,' said Queenie, 'but I thought mash would go nicely with this. There's no chickpeas, either, because I know they give you the wind.'

'Mu-um! Do you have to?'

The lads tried to stifle their laughter, but it snuck out anyway. Saggy blew a squeaky raspberry and Ant doubled up and held onto the back of a kitchen chair until he could compose himself.

'Sorry, Bea. It just came out,' said Queenie, which set Saggy and Ant off again. This time Bea and Queenie joined in, with Queenie laughing so much that tears started trickling down her face. She dabbed them away with a tea towel. 'I'm so sorry. What am I like? Come on, everyone. Get stuck in before it all gets cold.'

They took their plates through to the lounge. The local news had just started and the lead story was a report on a press conference held by the police about Harley Creech. No one touched their food as they watched. First a police officer gave the facts as they knew them, which were fairly sparse. Obviously, he mentioned 'an incident' at Costsave and then said that they were waiting for the results of the post-mortem to confirm the cause of death, but were treating it as suspicious. Then Harley's mum, Patsy, appealed for help. Flanked by her two older sons, Norton and Brough, who both towered above her, she was wearing a similar outfit to the one she was wearing when Bea saw her in the store, earlier in the week — leather jacket, black top. Her face was pale and haggard, though. She seemed to have aged years in just a couple of days.

'Harley was my baby boy, the brightest star in our family. We all loved him, especially his dad. Since Connor died, Harley has been my little man — always helpful, always thoughtful. None of us know what we will do without him and we just want to understand what happened. If you know anything at all, please come forward. We don't want revenge or anything like that. We want justice. Justice for Harley.'

CHAPTER THIRTEEN

'That poor woman,' said Queenie. 'Justice for Harley. Amen to that.'

They picked up their knives and forks and started eating with various degrees of enthusiasm, although Bea couldn't touch hers. She was thinking that Saggy shouldn't — couldn't — ignore Patsy Creech's appeal for evidence. He'd have to hand in the drone footage now. It didn't necessarily make things worse for Evan but it certainly didn't make them better. Queenie noticed her lack of appetite and felt a pang of concern.

'What were you all looking at just now?' she said, casually.

'Just footage from Saggy's—' Ant started.

'Nothing!' snapped Bea.

Queenie gave her a hard stare.

'Bea,' she said, 'I don't want you tangled up in anything. You know how close I got to losing you last time. I know that was personal, darlin', and part of me is very grateful for everything you did, but you put yourself in terrible danger. It's only thanks to these lads, and the others, that you're still here.'

Ant and Saggy smiled modestly.

'Look me in the eye,' Queenie continued, 'and tell me you aren't doing another of your investigations. Bea—'

Bea forced her eyes to meet her mum's. She managed to keep them steady for a second or two, but then couldn't help looking away.

'Oh no, no, no. This won't do. Boys,' Queenie said, appealing to the others, 'I'm very happy to see you here at any time, you know that, but please don't encourage this one to get involved in stuff that's best left to the police.'

Ant stared fixedly at his food and carried on shovelling it in as fast as he could, in his trademark style. Saggy suddenly seemed absorbed in the next news item on the TV screen.

'Boys!' Queenie said sharply. Saggy's fork fell out of this hand and clattered onto his plate. He and Ant both stopped eating and looked at her.

'Yes, Mrs Jordan. Sorry, Mrs Jordan,' Saggy said.

'Ant?'

'Yes, Mrs J. We won't encourage her.'

He shot a glance at Bea. She was watching their reaction to her mum with amusement.

'Promise?'

'Promise,' they both said, solemnly.

'All right. Eat up, then. There's seconds, if you want them, and lemon meringue pie for afters.'

The atmosphere lightened instantly as Ant and Saggy indulged in a speed eating contest. After two helpings of 'tagine' and a generous wedge of pie each, they all sat slumped in a very agreeable food stupor.

'I should get back to Neville's,' Ant said, 'but I'm too stuffed to move.'

'Yeah, me too,' said Saggy. 'I can't remember the last time I was this full. It's bloody brilliant. Is there any more pie?'

'There's a sliver, but I'm keeping that for my elevenses tomorrow. I've got an afternoon shift and the morning always seems to drag, so I like to have a little treat with my coffee.'

'I like your thinking, Mrs J.'

They watched the soaps together, but when *Dragons' Den* came on after that, Ant roused himself to go.

'That's me off,' he said, getting to his feet.

'Don't you like this one, love?' said Queenie.

Ant stood in front of the others, blocking their view of the screen. He pretended to adjust an imaginary tie, then cleared his throat. 'I've got a product which will automatically wipe dogs' arses and I'd like half a million quid for two per cent of my company.'

The others tittered.

'Well, as a pet owner myself, I have no end of trouble with my shih tzu and so I'm going to offer you all the money but I want ten per cent,' said Saggy in the poshest accent he could manage. 'Do you need to talk to the wall?'

Ant grinned. 'No, but you can talk to my hand,' and he made a rude gesture at Saggy. 'Come on, mate, time to go.'

Saggy gathered up his laptop and they both took their empty bowls through to the kitchen. Ant offered to wash up, but Queenie told him it would all go in the dishwasher. After they'd gone, Bea made some tea and she and Queenie settled down in their chairs to watch the rest of the programme.

'I really enjoyed this evening,' said Queenie. 'They're good lads, aren't they?'

'Yeah. I like how they are on best behaviour round you. It's hilarious.'

'Was that best behaviour?'

'Trust me. Yes.'

They lapsed into silence. Bea started scrolling through her phone, while Queenie kept nodding off to sleep. Her eyes kept closing, and every now and again she jerked upright in her seat. Finally, she emitted a rather loud snore which woke her up properly. She glanced over at Bea, who pretended she hadn't heard her, although really, Bea thought, she had no obligation to spare Queenie's feelings after that chickpea remark earlier.

Queenie shifted in her chair and discreetly wiped her mouth with her hankie.

'I can't help thinking about poor Patsy Creech. She'll never see her boy grow up.'

'It's terrible, isn't it?' Bea was idly scrolling on her phone. 'Oh, there's a Just Giving page for him now. To help pay for the funeral costs.'

'Shall we give something, Bea? Go on, let's give her a tenner. I'll go halves with you. I feel so bad for her.'

'Okay.' Bea clicked through the stages on the online form and donated. 'Done,' she said.

'It's not much but it's something, isn't it?' said Queenie. 'Show her we care.'

Soon afterwards, they went up to bed. Queenie paused in the doorway to her bedroom.

'Bea, you won't do anything silly, will you? Just let the police deal with this one.'

'It's okay, Mum,' Bea said. 'I won't do anything silly.'

Queenie closed her door and Bea uncrossed her fingers from behind her back.

CHAPTER FOURTEEN

The Just Giving page wasn't the only development online. As Bea lay in bed checking her phone, the Neighbourhood app was on fire with posts about a disturbance on the Church Bank estate. There were reports of police cars clustering round one of the houses there, gangs of people refusing to go home, and, finally, some video footage of someone with their hood up and a black scarf across their face lobbing a brick through a front window.

It was quite clear from the comments that the house under siege was where Evan lived.

Bea immediately texted him.

Are you ok? Are you at home?

It wasn't long until she got a reply back.

I'm ok. I got out earlier. Someone warned me they were coming for me.

Bea wanted to ask him where he was but could see it might be better for him if no one knew.

So glad you are safe.

A little frisson ran through her at his next message.

Can I call you? I need to talk.

She'd hardly had time to reply, *Sure*, when her phone started vibrating. She clicked on the call accept icon.

'Hello? Evan?'

'Hi.' His voice was low and quiet. 'I hope you don't mind this. Everything's falling apart.'

'No, it's fine. I'm glad you rang. Are you somewhere safe? Is your mum all right?'

'Yeah, she's staying with her friend in Saltford. I didn't go with her, because I want to keep her safe. I'm the one with the target on my back.'

'Oh, Evan. Have you talked to the police? They need to protect you.'

She could hear a sigh of frustration.

'I rang them and said I'd been told people were coming to get me. They said they'd send a car round. We didn't see anything after two hours, so we just got out.'

'Do you need anything? Food? Water? Clothes?'

'No, it's okay. I'll just lie low tonight. See what happens tomorrow. My phone will run out of charge eventually and I didn't bring any food with me. I don't see how I can go to the shops right now.'

'Look, I've got one of those little power pack things. I could bring it to you.'

'I dunno. Maybe it will all blow over.'

Bea could hear rain battering against her bedroom window. 'Are you inside somewhere? It's awful out.'

'Yeah. I'm inside.' There was a pause, then, 'I didn't do it, you know, Bea. I don't know how Harley died, but it wasn't me. He had a few bumps and bruises, but he was okay when he left me. Do you believe me?'

'Yes. I do.' She had believed him the first time he told her about it, and now the sincerity of his tone convinced her even more.

'The cops think it was me. They made that very clear when they interviewed me. I don't trust them to find out what really happened. Is there any way you can help?'

'I'm on it already. Ant and me, we're on the case.'

'Thank you.' His voice was thick with emotion. 'I just need someone on my side.'

'You've got us. Text me where to leave the battery charger, and some food. I'll do it before work tomorrow. I won't tell a soul. You can trust me.'

'Thanks, Bea. I'll try and get some kip now.'

'Okay. Goodnight, Evan.'

'Night.'

He rang off. Bea kept hold of her phone for a long time, replaying their conversation in her head. It was almost blowing a gale now. Normally she liked being safely tucked up in bed, listening to wild weather outside, but tonight she couldn't shake the image of her friend, on his own, god knows where. Tonight's storm might blow over quickly, but she had a feeling that things were only going to get worse for Evan.

CHAPTER FIFTEEN

Bea set her alarm for six o'clock. She slept fitfully before that, waking and dozing, constantly checking the time. At five forty-five, a text came in.

Waste bin in far corner of Bristol Road car park, next to toilet block. E x

E x, thought Bea. Did the kiss mean anything? Whether it did or not, it was enough to propel her out of bed and cancel her alarm. She quickly went to bathroom and dressed in her work clothes. Then she unplugged her battery charger, rootled around in a drawer for a spare connecting cable, and headed downstairs. In the kitchen, she tried to think quickly what food she could take. She found some cereal bars and a packet of Hobnobs in one cupboard and there were some sausage rolls in the fridge. She was sorely tempted to put the leftover slice of lemon meringue pie in a Tupperware pot, but then rejected it on the grounds of potential mess during transport and the repercussions when Queenie discovered it was gone, so she grabbed some bananas and an apple and put the whole lot in a Costsave carrier bag. Her coat was on the back of the chair and her handbag was all ready and waiting. She put on her 'good' trainers, the ones that were comfortable to walk in and smart enough for work, and let herself out of the kitchen door.

It was dark and cold outside, but at least it had stopped raining. She walked along the familiar roads and alleys towards the middle of town. The car park Evan had nominated was about a quarter of a mile beyond the other end of the High Street. It was a bit of a hike but she didn't mind. She was on a mission.

There was hardly anyone else about. She passed a milk float making its rounds of the estate, and a very early dog walker on the rec, but mostly she was on her own with her thoughts, which suited her just fine — it was important that nobody spotted her leaving the bag. She wondered whether to bypass the High Street with its CCTV cameras mounted at strategic intervals, then decided that it wasn't the anonymous CCTV operators that she needed to be worried about, it was the sort of people who had formed the mob outside Evan's house, and she guessed that after last night's shenanigans, they wouldn't be up and about this early.

She walked down the empty High Street. Some shops were dark. Others sent warm light spilling onto the pavement. It was a familiar scene, and yet strange in this silent, unpeopled state. She imagined Harley appearing at the far end, tearing along the road towards her, before crossing over and ducking down the alleyway to the park. Within half an hour of taking those steps, he had died. She stopped for a moment, opposite the entrance to the alley. Everyone had been so focused on his death, and on Evan's possible role in it, that perhaps they hadn't thought enough about Harley himself. Evan had said that the boy had emptied his pockets to show he hadn't stolen anything. But she herself had found a pregnancy test on the ground in aisle seven, hadn't she? And Eileen must have thought he was nicking something to make such a fuss. Why did he need a test like that? There was a lot they didn't know, and perhaps she was the person to find out.

Headlights lit up the road, as a car trundled down the street behind her, drew level and passed on. In its wing mirror, the driver's eyes were checking her out. She dipped her head, gathered her handbag closer to her body and set off walking again. The car pulled up about twenty metres in front of her. Oh shit, she thought, a kerb crawler, that's all I need, regretting now that there was no one else about. She kept her head down and increased her pace. As she drew level with the car, she noticed that the front passenger window was open and she heard someone shout, 'Beatrice!'

Beatrice? There was only one person who called her that. She stopped and peered in.

'Neville? What you doing out so early?'

The assistant manager, in his sensible anorak, leaned across the passenger seat.

'I was just about to ask you the same thing.'

Bea cursed herself for not preparing a cover story. 'I couldn't sleep, so I'm getting today's steps in,' she said, tapping her wrist to indicate a fitness app on her smartwatch, and hoping Neville didn't know that she had never owned such a thing in her life. 'Why are you up with the lark?'

'I'm just heading into work to get ahead with Operation Windsor,' he said. 'There's a lot to do.'

Bea frowned. 'Oh, right. I'll press on and get my number up. I'll see you later.'

She watched as the window wound back up and Neville's car proceeded to the end of the High Street and round the corner to the Costsave car park. She and Bea had joked about him blowing a gasket over the royal visit, but it was clearly getting to him. Why on earth was he in such a state about it?

She passed St. Swithin's church and joined the Bristol Road, which sloped gently downhill. When she reached it, the car park was empty. She trudged across the unmade surface to the far side where a toilet block stood near to the entrance to the grounds of Kingsleigh Town Rugby Football Club.

There was only one bin near the toilets. It felt weird putting a bag of nice food into it but she knew, logically, that the plastic would protect everything until Evan could pick it up. She looked around, wondering if he was close enough to be watching her. The RFC clubhouse and changing rooms were to the left of the site entrance. She thought she saw movement in one of the windows. She held up her hand and waved, in case it was him.

The movement stopped. Perhaps she'd imagined it anyway.

She started composing a text. *Package delivered*, and added, *B x*, before pressing send.

She looked back at the window, but there was no further sign of life. She sighed. If he wanted to meet her face to face, he would have said, wouldn't he? She understood that he needed to be cautious, but, even so, she was disappointed. She raised her hand again towards the window and then turned and walked back across the car park. When she reached the road, she looked back, but it was just a dark, empty space.

What now? She checked the time on her phone. 6.42 a.m. Dear god, still a good hour until she could reasonably turn up at Costsave for her shift. Neville would be there, of course, making a very early start. The night staff would be taking the early deliveries in the yard, so she could hang out with them or at least have the reassurance of knowing that someone else was about if she went up to the staff room. Her very first investigation had left her with qualms about being in Costsave out of hours, though. No, she thought, she'd wait until the other day staff started rocking up.

It was too cold to hang around anywhere for long. Perhaps she would do what she'd told Neville and get an hour's exercise. It wasn't a bad idea, she reflected, as the gentle uphill slope of the Bristol Road started to make her puff. She'd hated PE at school and had never developed a gym habit like many of her friends, but maybe she should think about getting a little bit fitter. Power walking round Kingsleigh was as good a way as any.

When she reached the mini roundabout by St. Swithin's, instead of carrying on into the High Street, she turned left. The road would take her across the bypass and river and eventually into the countryside, but before then there was another entrance to the park. It was just starting to get light. The park was a creepy place at night, but there was a different vibe to the early morning. Bea reckoned she'd be all right in there now. She had a little torch in her pocket, but her eyes had adjusted to the low light anyway — she didn't think she'd need it.

CHAPTER SIXTEEN

Bea didn't usually enter the park from this direction. It was the wilder part of Kingsleigh's green space — with the ruins of Kingsleigh Abbey at the top of the site and then a grassy slope with a few trees dotted about, which was designated as a dog-walking area. I'd better watch where I put my feet, thought Bea, as she set off down the hill towards the river. Grossed out by the thought of stepping in something unpleasant, she switched on her torch and directed its beam onto the path in front of her.

As she approached the flyover, she saw that the police tape was still there, barring the way. She sighed. She hadn't even thought about that — she'd have to walk back the way she'd come or take an even longer route, doubling back across a footbridge and then round by the road. Still, while she was here, she might as well have a quick look at the scene of the crime.

She walked along the riverside path towards the cave-like space created by the concrete arches. There were bunches of flowers and tea lights and photographs on the ground, spreading along the side of the structure and up the hill — another sign of the town's outpouring of grief. She shone her torch onto some of the messages.

Harley — absolute legend.
RIP Harley — with your dad now.
Tears from heaven for our Harley.

The photographs were mostly grainy shots of Harley with various friends — groups of blurry faces looming up to the camera. Some were in plastic wallets. Others were unprotected and already disintegrating. In fact, the whole display looked rather soggy and sad. Bea wondered how long it would be until the police or maybe the council cleared it all away.

She was crouching down to read the small handwriting on another card when some movement caught her eye. She tensed. She was perilously close to rat level here and the park was known to have a healthy rodent population close to the river. She directed the torch beam into the archway and the light picked out a dark figure at the other side, crouched down like her. It was dressed all in black, hood pulled up. In its hands was a single flower. It looked up and squinted in the torchlight.

'Sorry,' Bea called out, moving the torch quickly to point down. 'Didn't mean to dazzle you. Sorry!'

The figure jumped up and started running away. Damn, thought Bea, Whoever they were came here for a quiet moment of contemplation, and I spoiled it. She'd thought it was a young lad when she'd seen them crouched down, but in the torchlight she was fairly sure it had been a girl's face framed by the hood, pale eyes showing panic, like a rabbit in the headlights. She was curious to see if the person had left anything. She considered nipping under the tape and tiptoeing across, after all the police must have gathered all the evidence they could from the scene by now, but she couldn't quite bring herself to do it. She checked her phone again. She had plenty of time.

She doubled back along the riverside path. The sky was pale grey now, too cloudy for the sun to show. Bea switched off her torch and went across the little wooden footbridge over the river and then turned right to skirt along the other side next to the road. Another right-hand turn and she was almost at the park's main entrance. She gasped as something low and fast ran out from under the gate. The streetlights were still on and she watched as the fox bounded across the road and disappeared into the shrubbery opposite. The main gates were locked but a side gate had been left open. As she walked across the grass, she kept her eyes peeled for the mystery mourner, but she'd gone, melted away somewhere into the sleeping town, just like the fox.

Within a few minutes Bea was at the more familiar side of the flyover. She found a single flower not yet sullied by the weather — a large white rose, almost luminous in the soft morning light. There was no message attached, no photo or other keepsake, just the flower, but Bea was certain that it had been left by the girl.

The curved concrete of the flyover's arches was covered in graffiti. Puddles dotted the path and the murmur of the river echoed off the surfaces. There was no white tent, no painted line to mark the site of a body, but Bea couldn't help wondering if a darker patch towards the metal railing at the top of the riverbank was the spot where Harley Creech's life had come to an abrupt halt. The official cause of death hadn't been released yet. Had it involved the spilling of blood?

She turned again and walked up the slope towards the alleyway to the High Street. It was still too early to go to Costsave. She paused at the entrance to the play area and was toying with the idea of sitting on the swings for a while, when her stomach gave an alarming rumble. She suddenly realised that she'd been in such a hurry to take Evan his supplies that she hadn't had anything to eat or drink herself this morning. The café at the corner of the High Street, which had distinct greasy spoon tendencies, was the only place that opened this early, but that would do her nicely.

The front window of the café was reassuringly bright. Condensation was frosting the glass on the door, promising warm, sticky air within. As Bea stepped across the threshold, the first thing she saw was Ant, sitting at the table nearest to her, both hands around an enormous bap with bacon spilling out of it on all sides. He paused, mouth open, as he spotted Bea.

'Busted!' said Bea.

Ant grinned. 'I just couldn't take another day of sawdust and toenail clippings. My arteries were begging for a bit of lubrication. Can I get you something?'

She shook her head. 'Nah, I'll go and order. You dig in.'

She walked up to the counter, feeling a sudden surge of warmth. It wasn't just down to the temperature inside the café, which was pleasingly toasty. It was seeing a friendly face after her strange, sad walk. When something bad happened, it made you appreciate the things in life that really mattered. For Bea, that meant family and friends. It was easy to take them for granted. She wondered if the girl by the river had anyone special to go home to and felt a sharp pang of sadness. When she'd ordered — a classic eggs, bacon and sausage with a fried slice and a mug of tea — and paid, she returned to the table near the front.

'Can I have a hug?' she said, as she took off her coat and draped it on the back of a chair.

Ant looked up, a little startled. He'd almost finished his bacon bap. A tiny ribbon of grease ran down from one corner of his mouth.

'Sure,' he said, putting the remains of the sandwich on his plate. He stood up and wrapped his arms round Bea, while she encircled his waist and leaned her head on the top of his chest, perilously close to his shiny chin.

When they drew apart, he looked into her eyes.

'You all right, Bea? What's that all about?'

'Nothing. Just, you know, feeling a bit bleak.'

'Mate . . .' he said, and hugged her again.

CHAPTER SEVENTEEN

The mood was distinctly subdued at Costsave. George was absent from the daily briefing. Neville, standing in for her, seemed to have double the usual volume of paper on his clipboard and to be endlessly riffling through it, unable to find what he needed. He got more flustered and tetchier with every minute.

When Dot asked if the task force should stay behind, he snapped, 'As nobody but me seems to be actually doing anything to prepare for this visit, I can't see the point. Please get to your stations with everyone else.'

Stung, they dispersed along with the others.

'That was a bit harsh, wasn't it?' said Dot. 'I've really put a lot of time and effort into my toilet plans.'

'Don't take it personally, babe. I keep telling you he's getting his knickers in a twist over this visit,' said Bea. 'I saw him coming into work shortly after six this morning.'

'Six? What were you doing—?'

'Long story,' said Bea, looking around for something to change the subject with and spotting Bob on the stairs ahead of them. 'Hey, Bob, you were here for the last VIP visit. Do you remember it being this stressy?'

Bob waited at the bottom for them.

'I can't even remember if it was Cannon or Ball that visited, Bea. Can you remember, Dot?'

'It was Ball, you daft lump! How can you not remember Bobby Ball? He was lovely!'

'All right, all right,' said Bob. 'I knew it was the little one with the curly hair. I just didn't know which was which.'

Dot rolled her eyes. 'Blimey, Bob, what are you like? They were completely different. Not like Ant and Dec. No one can tell them apart.'

Bob nodded sagely. 'No one.'

Bea was about to launch in and explain how clearly different Ant and Dec were, but thought better of it. Life was too short and she was glad to see Dot and Bob agreeing about something for a change. Perhaps Dot had managed to have that talk with him. She'd ask later.

'Anyway,' Bea said, 'it doesn't matter if it was Cannon or Ball, what matters is not reinventing the wheel this time. Any luck tracking down that red carpet?'

They were on the shop floor now. Bob was about to peel off to go to the meat counter.

'I reckon we should just get a quote for buying a new one,' said Bob. 'You know, just in case. Take the initiative.'

'Hmm, you might be right,' said Bea. 'Tyler's costing up flags and bunting. I'll ask him to add red carpet to his list. I could ask Dean where he looked, if you like. I'm going to ring him and check on Eileen later.'

The morning rattled along. Fridays were usually busy with people stocking up for the weekend. Bea saw quite a few of her regulars. They passed the time of day, chatted about the weather, or last night's TV. A few mentioned Harley, and the mini riot on the Church Bank estate.

'Nasty business,' said Charles. He was one of Bea's favourites, a customer who had become a friend. She'd looked after his golden retriever when he had been in hospital and now often popped in to see him in his bungalow on her way home from work. 'People behave like animals when they're in a mob, don't they?'

'Most animals are a bit nicer, though.'

He smiled. 'Agreed. You wouldn't catch Goldie lobbing a brick through anyone's window.'

'I was thinking I might take her out for a walk tomorrow. Would she like that?'

'Like it? She'd love it.'

'I'll come round in the morning. Oh, you've missed an offer here, Charles. There's a bogof on kitchen roll. Do you want your free one? Might as well. It won't go off in the cupboard, will it?'

'I can't be bothered to walk back, Bea.'

'Don't worry. I'll get someone to fetch it.' Tyler was on his way past, pushing a metal cage full of boxes of crisps on his way to restock the depleted snack aisle. 'Tyler, can you go and get another packet of these? Aisle four.'

'Yes, sure.'

He parked the cage and set off jogging. Neville darted out from behind the Customer Service desk and intercepted him at the corner of aisle four. Bea couldn't hear what was said, but it was clearly some sort of telling off, and it was a rather chastened Tyler who returned, walking, to Bea and Charles.

'Here you are,' he said, handing the kitchen roll to Bea who beeped it through.

'Did Neville have a go at you?'

'Told me off for running. Said we didn't need another accident.'

'Well, he's right, I suppose, but don't take it to heart. He's got the hump today.'

'Thank you for these, young man,' said Charles, putting the packet in his shopping bag on wheels. 'That was very helpful.'

Tyler smiled and his shoulders relaxed a little bit. He went back to the metal cage and pushed it into the crisp aisle.

'See you tomorrow, love,' said Charles, shuffling towards the exit.

At breaktime, Bea found the staff room too noisy, so she took her mug of tea and her phone downstairs, and stood outside the staff door at the side of the building. Ant joined her for a crafty cigarette and watched as Bea dialled Dean's number.

'Shall I put him on speaker?' she asked.

'Not bothered,' Ant said, blowing a long plume of smoke out into the air, but Bea did it anyway.

Dean sounded surprised when he answered the call.

'Bea! Everything all right?'

'Hi Dean. I've got you on speaker. Ant's here too. Just wondering how you both were. How's Eileen getting on?' she said.

'She's off her tits on painkillers,' Dean replied.

Ant guffawed, and Bea waved at him to keep quiet. 'Oh god,' she said.

'No, it's really nice. She's much mellower than usual. I'm seeing a different side to her. When she's all better, I might have to have a conversation with her about recreational drugs. I really think she'd like them.'

'Be nice to have something in common, eh?' Ant said, leaning in towards the phone. She heard Dean laugh.

'Yeah. Can you imagine? Me and Mum at a rave, giving it large. It'd be a whole new world, mate.'

'I'd pay good money to see that,' said Ant.

'Yeah, I don't think I'll mention it to her yet. She's in bed with her little telly, and I'm up and down the stairs twenty times an hour. I'll be glad to come back to work for a rest. Don't know when that'll be, though. She's not safe to be left on her own yet.'

'I'd take your time, if I were you. Anyway, that was it really. Just checking up on you. Oh, I was wondering if you'd found that red carpet before everything kicked off. Neville's doing his nut about everything and it would be nice to tick one thing off the list.'

'Nah. I did have a look. It's not in the back of the shop and I had good look round the yard and couldn't find it. It wasn't with all the seasonal decorations and crap in the metal lock-ups. Are there any cupboards upstairs?'

'I don't know. I'll ask. Thanks, Dean. Send our . . .' Bea hesitated. 'Love' was rather too strong a word in relation to Eileen. '. . . best wishes to your mum.'

'Will do. George rang yesterday. Wanted to talk to Mum about how she fell over, but I told her mum's too out of it for that. I also told her we were lawyering up. All those adverts, "Have you had an accident at work?" and now she's finally had one. Reckon we might be quids in.'

Ant's mouth fell open.

'Bloody hell. Are you going to sue?'

'No, 'course not, but it won't hurt to let George think that we are. Could get interesting . . .'

'Ha, premium play, mate. Respect.'

After Bea had rung off, she and Ant finished their tea and trailed back upstairs.

'Do you reckon they'll get compensation?' asked Ant.

'I dunno. Maybe. George won't want anything going to court, will she? We've got enough bad publicity over all the stuff with Evan.'

'Dean might be right. They might get a big payout. Good luck to them.'

CHAPTER EIGHTEEN

The radio was on in the staff room at lunchtime, tuned to a local radio station playing middle-of-the-road hits. Bea didn't really notice when the music was interrupted, but somebody shouted 'Shush,' and soon everyone was listening in silence as the DJ read out a newsflash.

'. . . just received the news that Somerset and Avon Police have confirmed that they are now conducting a murder investigation in Kingsleigh. The body of sixteen-year-old Harley Creech was found in the Memorial Park on Wednesday morning. The results of the post-mortem indicate that he died from a blunt trauma injury to his head. Police have renewed an appeal for witnesses and have also issued an arrest warrant for local man, Evan Edwards. There will be more on this item at our update on the hour.'

Bea was sandwiched between Dot and Tyler on one of the sofas, while Ant was sprawled over a dilapidated armchair. She was still feeling full after her cooked breakfast, so was just having some tea and a few biscuits for lunch. Ant had sprinted down to the kebab shop and brought back a huge pitta bread stuffed with lamb. Now he appeared to be in some sort of meat coma.

'Arrest warrant now. Blimey,' said Dot.

'They're going to stitch him up,' said Bea. 'I know it.'

Ant opened his eyes and shifted to a more upright position. 'It's an easy win for them, innit?'

'Exactly.'

'But what if he did it, Bea?' said Dot. 'I mean, it might have been some sort of accident. He could have been trying to restrain him and somehow he hit his head. It could happen, couldn't it?'

'But he told me he didn't. He told me quite clearly.'

'When did he tell you that, love?' She asked the question casually, but Dot's eyes were drilling into her.

'On Wednesday, Dot. He was sitting right here, before George sent him home.'

'Ah, yes. Have you spoken to him since then?'

Bea didn't want to lie to her friend. 'We texted. I was just checking he was all right.'

Dot put a hand on her arm. 'I know he's one of us, and I know you like him, Bea, but this is a nasty business. Don't get involved.'

'What do you mean? I'm not involved with anything. I just think the guy's innocent and I'm worried about him. His house has been attacked. The cops are after him for something he didn't do . . .'

'All right, all right. But with feelings running so high, it might be better for him, for everyone, if he turns himself in,' she said, pointedly. 'He can set the record straight and be protected from the idiots with bricks.'

'Well perhaps the police should do something about the idiots with bricks, instead of hunting an innocent man!' Bea slammed her mug down on the table, got up and brushed biscuit crumbs off her lap onto the floor. 'I need some fresh air.' She stomped out before she could say anything she would regret, ignoring Dot's cry of, 'Bea!' as she left the room.

She found a quiet spot by the recycling bins, sat on a little wall and started scrolling through her phone. She looked at her messages. The last one from Evan just said, *Thx. E x* It was timed at six thirty. She couldn't believe she'd missed it. He must have found her care package, then. That was something, at least. She was just wondering whether to text him again, and what to say if she did, when Ant appeared.

'Here you are. All right, mate?' he said, warily.

'Yeah. Fine,' she said, her sulky tone indicting the exact opposite.

'Good. It's all good,' he said, lighting up a cigarette.

'It's not, though, is it?'

He smiled. 'No, it's a mess. I don't know if we can sort this one out, though, you and me.'

'I've got some leads, things we can follow up. If you're with me, that is . . .'

Ant turned to face her. ''Course I'm with you. We're Kingsleigh's finest crime-fighting team, aren't we?'

'I don't know about that.'

'Think of the fucking state this town would be in without us!' He flung his arms out, sending ash flying off the end of his cigarette, narrowly missing the end of her nose.

She jerked her head back, then, despite herself, smiled. 'Well, there is that.'

'So what are the leads?'

Bea quickly told him about seeing the girl at the crime scene earlier that morning, and about finding the pregnancy test on the floor of aisle seven.

'There's more to this story than anyone knows,' she said. 'Why was he nicking, or thinking of nicking, a test? Who's that girl? If Evan didn't kill him, which I'm sure that he didn't, he must have either met or bumped into someone else in the park, so who else was there?'

Ant listened intently, taking it all in.

'Yep,' he said. 'There's all sorts of stuff to check out. We need a plan. I'm in stores again this afternoon, should give me plenty of thinking time. Do you wanna meet up after work?'

'I need to get home. Queenie's cooking again. I could have a quick drink, though. Half an hour.'

'Let's do that then,' said Ant.

'Better go back in,' said Bea, as she looked round for the source of a low rumbling noise. 'There's a lorry just coming into the yard — is that meant for you?'

Ant sighed. 'Oh, shit, yeah. I'll nip round the side. See you later. And Bea?'

'Yes?'

'If something bad happened to you, I'd never forgive myself and Queenie would kill me.' Bea wondered where he was going with this. 'Let's stick together on this one. No going rogue.'

CHAPTER NINETEEN

'You can say what you like about Dean, but he's got a nice little set-up in the stores.' Ant and Bea were back at the corner table in the snug of the Ship. 'After Tyson and I had dealt with a couple of deliveries, we had a brew in the man cave Dean's got there. Couple of garden chairs, crate as a table, nipping into the cold room for some milk. It's pretty sweet. And I had time to do this.'

With a flourish, Ant produced a sheet of folded up paper from his pocket. He spread it out on the table and then moved it, so Bea could see. When she realised what it was, Bea felt a lump in her throat. Ant had written a plan — three bullet points in his best handwriting. She was so overwhelmed that at first she didn't take it in. When she read it a second time, though, it was actually really sound.

Find girl Bea sore
Was Harley nicking? Wot did Ileen see?
Who was in the park? Saggy drone

'That, my friend, is bloody brilliant.'
Ant grinned. 'I know right. I thought about what you told me, and then I thought about what we could do about it.'

'I can see that. I'm not going to lie. I'm impressed.' She high fived him and then they held their glasses up and clinked them together. 'Good call about Eileen. Dean might have told the police they can't interview her, but he'd let us in, wouldn't he? Especially if we took some flowers or something.'

'Yeah. Flowers should do the trick — that's genius. We could go now . . . oh, you've got to get home. Tomorrow morning? Are you working?'

'No, I've got the weekend off.'

'Nice, and I reckon after we've been to Eileen's, we should go round to Saggy's and look at the rest of his footage. If Evan didn't do it, someone else did. He might have them on camera and not know it.'

'Okay. Then in the evening, there's a vigil for Harley in the park, down by the bandstand. I was going to go anyway, but we should observe the crowd, see who turns up. They do say, don't they, that the murderer often revisits the scene.'

'Busy day tomorrow, Bea. Just as well. I never know what to do at the weekends at Nev's. I've got to get out of there, Bea. Get my own place somehow.'

They both knew the chances of Ant being able to afford to buy or rent on his own in Kingsleigh were negligible. Some problems seemed too hard to solve.

'Oh. I just remembered . . .'

'What?'

'I said I'd take Goldie out for a long walk. I can't let Charles down.'

'No problem. We can bring her with us. She knows Dean's dog, doesn't she? They can have a play in their garden.'

'Yeah, I s'pose.' Goldie was getting on a bit. In dog years, she was about as old as Charles, which, Bea estimated, must be approaching ninety. 'I could drop her back after that. I don't think I should take her to the vigil.'

'Sounds like a plan. Have you heard anything else from . . . you know.'

Bea knew he meant Evan, but wisely wasn't saying his name out loud here.

'No. Shall we talk outside? I'd better get home anyway.'

They were downing the remains of their drinks when someone asked, 'Are you going?'

Bea looked up to see Tom.

'Oh!' They both said, together, then smiled, awkwardly. Despite their rocky romantic history, Bea still held a bit of a candle for Tom — she couldn't help herself.

'We're just leaving,' said Bea. 'Do you want this table?'

'Yes, that'd be great.' Tom, in a smart shirt and leather jacket, proceeded to shepherd his companion through the crowd, a young woman with perfectly styled long hair and wearing a pale lilac suit, with a white vest top underneath which displayed an impressive cleavage. They were obviously on a date. 'Thank you,' he said, as Bea and Ant edged their way out.

'Blimey,' said Ant as they stepped into the bracing air outside, 'he's punching above his weight!'

'Just a bit,' said Bea, although she thought, with some regret, that the two had actually looked quite good together.

'You don't mind, do you? I mean, you're well rid of him, Bea.'

They started walking along the street. Bea dug her hands into her pockets to protect them against the cold.

'You never liked him,' she said.

'Obviously not — he's a copper. And a snake. You're way too good for him.'

'His heart's in the right place, Ant.'

'If you say so. Anyway,' he looked around, checking the coast was clear, 'do you know where Evan is?'

Bea also looked around before drawing a bit closer to Ant.

'No. Well, yes. I did know. I left some food for him in the car park next to the Rugby Club this morning. I reckon he was sleeping in the clubhouse. Obviously, he'll have to move. It'll be busy down there tomorrow.'

Ant flipped his fingers.

'I knew it! You're no good at keeping secrets, Bea. Not from me, anyway. Do you think he's still there?'

'I honestly don't know. I messaged him earlier to ask if he was all right, but I haven't heard back. He knows that we believe him, though, that we're on his side.'

'It's just as well he's keeping out of the way,' Ant said. 'If people round here get hold of him, they'll rip him to shreds.'

CHAPTER TWENTY

Just before she went to sleep, Bea tried another text to Evan.
Are you okay?
Her phone pinged almost immediately this time.
Yes.
Do you need anything?
No, all good. Thx, Bea. Xx
She wanted to ask where he was, if he was still in Kingsleigh, but he would have said if he'd wanted her to know. Perhaps it was enough to be reassured that he was still alive and keeping safe somewhere.
Ant and I are on the case. Will keep you updated. She paused before pressing send. Reading it through, it sounded a bit lame, and his previous text had an air of 'conversation closed' about it, so she deleted the words and put down her phone. It was easy to feel powerless when things were going wrong, but in this case she and Ant had a clear plan, at least for tomorrow. She turned over and cuddled the nice warm microwavable owl that was her habitual bedfellow through the winter. As she drifted off to sleep, she had visions of something — *someone* — else keeping her warm, imagined the considerable bulk of Evan in bed next to her, and pictured herself snuggling her face into the comfortable place between his neck and shoulder . . .

She woke up after a delicious night's sleep, feeling warm and cosy and snug. It was light behind the curtains at her window and she had a moment's panic that she'd missed her alarm before remembering that it was the weekend and she had two glorious days off. She loved her job and had no real thought of working anywhere else, but the last week had been upsetting and stressful. Two days away from the place, even though she would be busy, seemed like a good idea.

She checked her phone before she got up, but there was nothing particularly new. The focus of the community chats was Evan's whereabouts, which started a flutter of anxiety in her stomach. With so many people looking for him, Evan would have a difficult job staying hidden. Maybe Dot was right — he'd be safer if it was the police who found him, or if he turned himself in. It wasn't Bea's decision, though, and Evan would have more confidence making that choice if there was evidence backing up his story or pointing the finger elsewhere. That was today's job. She sat up and then swung her legs out of bed. Breakfast, pick up Goldie and then meet Ant.

Queenie was pottering about the kitchen in her nightie and dressing gown. There was a packet of flour out on the kitchen bench and she was mixing up something in a glass bowl.

'Thought I might make pancakes for brekkie today. What do you reckon, lemon and sugar or orange and golden syrup?'

'Oh, Mum, I'm just going to grab a bowl of Crunchy Nut and go. I told Charles I'd take Goldie out this morning.'

She felt awful as she saw her mum's face fall.

'I've nearly made the batter now. Why don't you just have a couple? It will only take me a minute to make them.'

'Okay, I'll get ready.'

'Where are you going anyway?'

'Ant and I are going to call in on Eileen, take her some flowers.'

'Oh, that's lovely. I bet she's suffering. Knee and coccyx, wasn't it?'

'How on earth did you know that? I don't remember telling you.'

'Someone at the launderette said. I think it was Sharmila. She lives next door to Kirsty's cousin.'

Bea shook her head in disbelief. The Kingsleigh grapevine was more conductive than a lightning rod. She found her comfiest trainers and started putting them on while her mum melted some butter in the microwave and added it to the eggs, flour and milk.

'Ooh, get you!' said Bea. 'These are going to be fancy.'

'You can't go wrong with Delia,' Queenie said. 'Here goes.' She poured a pool of batter into a hot frying pan. After a minute's sizzling, it refused to flip and she had to chip it off with a palette knife. 'That didn't go very well, did it? Do you want to take this one for Goldie?' she said.

'Um, I don't know, Mum. I do really have to get going.'

'Wait, this one's looking better.'

Queenie tossed the next pancake with a dramatic flourish. It landed with a satisfying plop into the middle of the pan. Soon it was on a plate and ready for Bea to add her topping of choice. She opted for orange juice and syrup and it was quite delicious.

'Blimey, that's amazing. Just one more and then I'll set off.'

Six pancakes later, Bea had crossed the fine line between pleasantly full and uncomfortably overstuffed.

'Oh my god, Mum, that was awesome. I've got to go now, though.'

'All right, love. Hold on a minute, though. I've got something for you to take to Eileen.'

'No, Mum—' Too late. Queenie had bustled out of the kitchen and Bea could hear her rummaging in the understairs cupboard. She reappeared with a plastic bag.

'What's that?' said Bea.

'A rubber ring. It's got the air pump in there, too.'

'What the hell, Mum?'

'Eileen will know. It's the best thing ever if you've problems sitting down. I had mine after my operation for my you-know-whats.' Haemorrhoids was the word, but it was on equal footing with Macbeth and Voldemort in the Jordan household and was never spoken out loud, in case it summoned the painful visitors back.

'I can't take this,' said Bea. 'I mean, really.'

Queenie tried pressing the bag into her hands.

'Eileen will thank you for it. Better than flowers, that's all I'm saying. If she doesn't want it, bring it back, but I guarantee she will.'

Bea sighed and took the bag.

'What time are you back?' said Queenie. 'I was thinking I might go to the vigil in the park later. Show my respects. Shall we go together?'

'Yes. That's a great idea. I might not be back until this afternoon, but we can definitely walk down to the park together. See you later. And thanks for breakfast.' She put her coat on, then swooped on Queenie and planted a kiss on her cheek. They didn't often express their affection like this and Queenie was positively glowing as Bea went out of the kitchen door.

Although she was running late, Bea's stomach was so full she had trouble walking faster than a stately waddle. When she got to Charles' bungalow, he offered her a cup of tea and a Tunnock's Teacake. She knew what he really wanted was a chat, but she couldn't face sitting in his over-warm lounge, and was meant to have met Ant half an hour ago. She'd texted him but hadn't had a reply and was getting anxious about making him hang around waiting.

'Maybe later,' she said to Charles, as Goldie nuzzled her hands gently. 'Right, young lady, ready for a walk?'

Goldie's leisurely pace matched hers this morning. They plodded along to the High Street, and found Ant outside the flower shop, holding a bunch of bright pink and purple blooms, artfully gathered together with some foliage.

'Sorry I'm late,' she said. 'Queenie was cooking pancakes.'

Ant clutched his chest. 'You're killing me. Bloody hell, if only I'd known . . . I got these,' he said, tipping the top of the bouquet towards her. 'Do you think they'll do?'

'They're lovely. Shall I give you half the money?'

'Nah. Buy me a pie or two at lunchtime.'

They walked away from the centre of town and into the estate where Dean and Eileen lived. When they reached the neat, link-detached house, Bea knocked at the door, which set off a volley of gruff barking inside. Goldie, unfazed, just sat down, grateful for the rest. The door was soon answered by Dean, looking more dishevelled than usual. Still in his pyjamas, his hair was lank with grease and there were toothpaste stains on his top. They had texted him and arranged to visit, but, even so, it looked like they'd caught him on the hop.

'Hi guys,' he said. 'Am I glad to see you! Come in. Bring the dog.'

This was more warmth than either of them expected. Ant and Bea exchanged surprised looks and stepped into the hallway.

'Mum's still in bed.'

Bea had already gathered that from the dulcet tones drifting down the stairs.

'Dean! De-an! Who is it? Did you find my reading glasses? Dean!'

Dean rolled his eyes, then shouted, 'It's Bea and Ant from work. They've come to see you.'

'Tell them to fuck off.'

Bea caught Ant's eye and they started laughing. Bea put her hand over her mouth to try and muffle the noise.

'Sorry, guys,' Dean said to them, quietly, then bellowed, 'Mu-um! They're right here! They can hear you.'

'Okay. Hi Bea! Hi Ant! You can fuck off now.'

Ant and Bea both creased up. Bea had to cross her legs to prevent an accident.

'We'd better leave you to it,' said Bea when she could talk.

'No!' Dean yelled. There was desperation in his eyes as he grabbed Bea's arm. 'Don't go. Please don't go. The hospital only gave her enough good painkillers for two days. She's just on paracetamol now and she's . . . oh god, guys, she's a monster.'

CHAPTER TWENTY-ONE

'Just chill for a minute,' said Bea. 'Have you had your breakfast yet?'

'I haven't done anything,' said Dean. 'I overslept and was late with her pills and she needed help going to the bathroom and I haven't taken the dog out and—'

Dean's dog, Tyson, was still barking and had started scrabbling in a very determined manner at one of the doors leading into the hall. It sounded like one of the hounds of hell was kept in there, but Ant and Bea, and Goldie, were familiar with Tyson. He was just an over-friendly ball of energy. There was no harm in him.

'Okay, okay, shut the front door, Ant, and then we can let Tyson out. Then I'll make some tea for everyone and you can have a shower and get dressed, Dean. It's going to be all right, you'll see.'

Dean's look of gratitude was almost too much for Bea. He meekly did as instructed. Tyson, released from the lounge, launched himself at them in a friendly way. Bea told Ant to take the dogs into the back garden, while she put the kettle on and Dean went upstairs. The kitchen was in a truly impressive state. Bea wondered how on earth such mess could accumulate in only three days, but there was no point speculating about Dean's domestic inadequacies. She found an unopened packet of rubber gloves in a drawer, put them on and set about bringing some order to the chaos.

By the time Dean reappeared, looking like a drowned rat, but a clean one, Bea had washed a mountain of dirty dishes, wiped down the surfaces, taken a stinking bin bag outside and mashed a large pot of tea. She also had a big pan of porridge bubbling on one of the gas rings.

'Where's your golden syrup, Dean?'

He found a tin in one of the cupboards and she divided the porridge between three pudding bowls and two dog bowls, and drizzled syrup onto the ones destined for human consumption. Then she put a mug of tea and a bowl of porridge onto a tray.

'Do you want to take this to your mum,' she said, 'or shall I?'

Dean leaned against the kitchen bench, to all intents and purposes an empty husk of a man. 'Could you do it, Bea? I've been up and down those stairs like a fiddler's elbow the past few days.'

'Okay. Can you tell Ant breakfast is ready, then?'

Bea set off up the stairs, carefully carrying the tray. The door to Eileen's bedroom was open, but Bea approached tentatively, unsure of her welcome.

'Knock, knock,' she called out. 'Are you decent?'

'Oh, it's you.' Eileen's voice rang out. 'I want my Dean. Tell Dean to come up.'

Bea ventured as far as the doorway. Eileen was slumped in bed, in an awkward position halfway between sitting up and lying down.

'He's just having some breakfast, Eileen, so you've got me. I've brought you a cuppa and some porridge.'

'I don't think I fancy porridge. Dean will bring me something later.'

There was something about Eileen's sulky tone that tickled Bea. She had babysat for a few of the neighbours' children over the years and Eileen's grumbling was only a hair's breadth away from, 'You're not my mum. I want my mum.'

'What about some tea? Do you need some help sitting up?'

'I can't sit up. It hurts too much. These painkillers are rubbish. They're not touching it.'

Bea put the tray down on Eileen's dressing table and approached the patient.

'When my dad was ill, we made him a sort of nest with pillows. Let's see if I can remember how to do it.'

She managed to help Eileen shift up the bed a little and then lean forward, while she created a supportive cradle of pillows behind her. When Eileen leaned back, she winced and closed her eyes, but after a moment or two opened them again and said, 'Actually, that's really nice.'

Bea smiled. 'Just try and relax. I expect all your muscles are in a knot. Do you want a sip of tea?'

'I could try.'

Bea handed her the mug and waited.

'Maybe I am hungry,' Eileen said, after a while. 'Is there syrup on that porridge?'

'Two parts syrup, one part porridge,' said Bea.

'Go on, then.'

Bea helped Eileen put the mug on her bedside table, then fetched the bowl for her. She was soon tucking in with relish.

'Do you mind if I sit down?'

Eileen waved her porridge spoon at the end of the bed and Bea perched there.

'Has Dean told you what happened after your fall?'

Eileen swallowed another mouthful of porridge and took a breather.

'Some of it. He said that shoplifter was found dead in the park. Pretty shocking. I mean I think we should throw the book at the little shits. Stealing is stealing, isn't it, and someone needs to teach them right from wrong, but he didn't deserve that.'

'Are you sure he was stealing?'

'I saw him with my own eyes, Bea. Are you calling me a liar?' Eileen's ability to take umbrage was never far from the surface.

'No, not at all, Eileen. I'm just interested. After all, you were in the centre of things. You're the key to this.' A little flattery usually worked, and Bea could see Eileen's ruffled feathers smoothing down already. 'What did you actually see?'

'Well, I was walking through the middle of the store, checking that all the end-on displays were up to scratch when I noticed a young lad lingering by the medical section in aisle seven. I mean, there are things there that some people might find embarrassing, so I don't usually hang around there if they look a bit sheepish, but there was something about this boy. He had no basket with him and he was jittery. When you've worked there as long as I have, you get a sixth sense about people. You just know.'

Bea was inclined to agree. Reading people was one of the perks of the job, in her book. She liked observing, listening in sometimes, speculating about her customers' lives. Some people might call it nosy. She preferred words like 'interested' or 'engaged' or even 'caring.' Yes, she thought, it was a way of caring.

'I stayed at the end, on the corner, and adjusted the display of special offer cakes and biscuits. That reminds me, is the multipack of Jaffa Cakes still on at two pounds twenty-five? I was going to pick one up . . .'

'Yeah, it is. I'll bring you one.'

'Oh, that'd be lovely. They're quite light to nibble, if you fancy a little something, aren't they?'

Bea was trying not to grind her teeth in frustration. Eileen showed no sign of coming back from the tangent she'd strayed onto.

'They're the best,' Bea said, calmly, trying to think of a way to steer the conversation seamlessly round to aisle seven again.

'I've always thought they were a cake, but we've got them with the biscuits, haven't we?'

'Yes, this lad wasn't after Jaffa Cakes, though, was he? What did you see him take?'

'Well, Bea, that's the thing. He was taking stuff off the shelf and looking at it, reading the boxes, I reckon. He did it a couple of times and then he just slipped one in his pocket. I saw him, then he started walking away from me, down the aisle.

'I left my display then, and started to follow him. The odd thing was, he stopped, put his hand back in his pocket and doubled back. He had a box in his hand by now. It was obvious I was watching him and when he clocked me I saw a flash of panic on his face, and he started running. I mean, that's the sign of a guilty conscience, isn't it? So, I guessed that that wasn't the only thing he'd nicked. He must have had his pockets full.

'He dropped what he was holding and ran towards the checkouts and the exit. I went after him and the rest is history.'

'Did you see what it was he dropped?'

'No, I was focusing on him, on not letting him get away.'

Bea didn't want to deliberately upset Eileen and, let's face it, it was so easy to do unintentionally. So, she chose her next words with care.

'Do you think when he stopped that he might have been about to put it back?'

'I don't know, Bea. I know he took it, and he knew I knew. That's why he ran. With how things ended up, I wish I hadn't chased him. If I'd just let him go, I wouldn't be up shit creek and he wouldn't be . . .'

'It's not your fault, Eileen. Whatever happened in the park, it wasn't your fault.'

'I can't help thinking about him, though. His little face. You know some of them are hard, aren't they? Even twelve, fourteen years old, they can have hard little faces. Like they don't care.'

Bea knew exactly what she meant. Quite a few of the kids she saw in the store and on the streets were old before their time, had had the corners knocked off them before they'd even left school.

'This boy wasn't like that, Bea. I just keep thinking about him.'

She'd been talking so much that half her porridge was still in her bowl, cold now. Eileen put it down on the bed next to her and reached for a tissue, wincing as she twisted her spine. Bea was alarmed to see her dabbing her face. Eileen was crying.

'Eileen, listen,' she said, leaning forward and putting a hand gently on her arm. 'It wasn't your fault.'

'It's not that, Bea,' she said, sniffing hard. 'It's the pain. My tail end is killing me.'

'I've got something that might help. Mum's sent you a rubber ring to sit on.' She narrowed her eyes, expecting a verbal onslaught, but instead Eileen brightened a little.

'Has she really, Bea?' she said. 'That's just what I need. Your mum's an angel. Can you fetch it and set me up on that chair? I could watch a bit of morning telly.'

Bea took her breakfast away and returned with the rubber ring. She had some fun and games inflating it, but eventually she was able to help Eileen out of bed and get her comfortably seated on an armchair near her bedroom window with a dressing gown round her shoulders.

As Bea prepared to leave, Eileen looked at her. Bea thought she was about to thank her. It seemed like their relationship had taken a new and rather heartwarming turn.

'Bea,' Eileen said, 'do you think I should text Neville about the Jaffa Cakes? Suggest he puts them in with the cakes, not the biscuits?'

CHAPTER TWENTY-TWO

Bea and Ant left Dean in a much better state than they'd found him in. With his mum comfortable upstairs, and himself washed, fed and looked after, he settled down for a good session with his PlayStation.

'Cheers, guys,' he said. 'I owe you one.'

Goldie and Tyson were stretched out on the floor at his feet, front paws touching. It seemed a shame to disturb the older dog, who was so sound asleep that she didn't stir when Bea put her coat on.

'Dean,' said Bea, 'do you mind if we leave Goldie here for an hour or two? We're going to Saggy's and I think the walk there and back might be a bit far for her.'

'No problem,' said Dean. 'I'm not going anywhere.'

'So,' said Ant, as they walked out of the estate, 'did you learn anything from the Dragon?'

'Not a huge amount, except that everything she said backed up what Evan told me. She only saw Harley take one thing and then he turned round and could have been about to put it back. It sounds like he panicked when he saw that Eileen had been watching him.'

'She has that effect on me, too,' said Ant. 'One look can put the fear of god into you.'

Bea laughed. 'She's honestly not that bad. Well, she is, but I saw her human side today.'

'So,' said Ant, and Bea could almost see the cogs whirring inside his head, 'if she backs up what Evan told you, then it's another reason to believe him. Which I did anyway, but you know . . . it's good to have some collaboration.'

'Corroboration.'

'That too. So, we definitely need to find out who else was in the park that morning.' He rubbed his hands together and Bea could tell he was excited. 'It's a buzz, isn't it? Investigating?'

She smiled. 'It is. It feels like we're doing something that really matters. Something important.'

'Yeah. Although you do something important every day. I watch you at work sometimes, not in a creepy way, you understand, and you're so good with all the customers, Bea. They love you. I'm just pushing trolleys or lumping boxes around but you . . . you're making people's days better.'

Bea didn't know how to react. It was such a nice thing to say, on so many levels. After a little pause, she swallowed down a big lump in her throat and just said, 'Thanks, mate,' and they carried on walking in companionable silence.

When they reached the edge of the ex-council estate where Saggy lived, Ant asked, 'Have you been to Saggy's before?'

'I don't think so.'

'Ah.'

'What does that mean?'

'Nothing, just that it's sometimes a bit . . . well, it's sometimes a lot. That's all. If it gets too much for you, just give me a wink or something and we'll leave.'

'I'm not going to wink at you. Let's just think of a word or something. A code.'

'Okay. What, like sausages?'

Bea tutted. 'How could I use that without looking like an idiot? No, something ordinary. How about rain?'

'Rain.'

'Or raining. Both. If I make any rainy references, it means I'm not a celebrity but get me out of there anyway.'

Ant grinned. 'All right, then.'

'But I mean, how bad can it be?'

It wasn't long before she found out. Saggy's house had a small front garden, filled with the sort of furniture you'd normally keep indoors — a sofa, a sideboard, a TV cabinet and assorted dining chairs.

'We can just go round the back,' said Ant. 'Everyone does.'

He led her past the furniture and along a path at the side of the house. There was a ramshackle lean-to, dripping with condensation. He knocked loudly and went in. Bea followed, closing the door behind her. The lean-to ran along the back of the house and was populated with a washing machine, tumble drier, plastic baskets overflowing with washing (it wasn't clear if it was dirty or clean), garden equipment, bicycles, and towers of cardboard boxes. It led into the kitchen where a friendly-looking woman, wearing leggings and a T-shirt and with her hair tied in two plaits was peeling a mountain of potatoes.

'Hello, Ant,' she said. 'There's tea in the pot, if you want it, love. Who's this?'

'Hi, Mrs Reynolds, this is Bea.'

''Course it is. Stanley's mentioned you. Do you want a cuppa, Bea?'

'Um, no thanks,' said Bea. 'We just had one.' Bea had never heard Saggy's real name before and smiled to herself.

There was a loud thumping from somewhere above them as if someone was practising clog dancing or perhaps karate.

'Just ignore that. The kids have had a sleepover. You go through. Stanley's in the front room.'

Bea followed Ant further into the house. They found Saggy on a comfortable sofa with his feet up on a coffee table as he played some sort of shooting game on a large TV screen with the volume turned up to ear-splitting levels.

'All right?' he said as they entered the room. Ant slumped down next to him, while Bea cleared a heap of magazines off a chair before sitting down. Saggy carried on playing. 'I'll just finish this. I'm killing it today.' Bea watched as he literally killed dozens of opponents. She wasn't a fan of violent games and there was too much blood spatter with this one for her tastes. The sound was so loud, she wondered if Saggy had problems with his hearing. It was a blessed relief when he finally exited the game and the room went quiet, even though there was still background thudding and squealing from upstairs.

'Good game,' said Ant, offering Saggy a high five.

'Do you want a go?'

'Nah, we've come to look at that drone footage again, like I said. The unedited version.'

'Oh yeah. My laptop's here, but I can run it through the telly if you like.'

Saggy cued up the video and they started watching. It was a slow process. They watched the whole thing once through, which took twenty-five minutes, then they started again. Bea kept asking Saggy to pause it and rerun sections so frequently that he handed the remote control to her.

'I'm going to fetch some drinks. I've got some cold ones in the fridge. Want one, Ant? Bea?'

Ant opted for a beer and started chatting with Saggy about the merits of various games, but Bea didn't want anything. She was intently focused on what the footage was showing.

'Guys, shush a minute,' she said. Ant and Saggy exchanged looks but did as instructed. 'Apart from the families up at the play park, I've counted half a dozen or so people in the bottom part of the park between 10.20 a.m. and 10.45 a.m., some on the bandstand side and some on the dog-walking side. It would be brilliant to find out who they all are, but I'm really interested in this one.'

She froze the screen and walked up to the telly.

'Look at this. It's 10.26 a.m. There's someone inside the gates. Here.'

Ant looked. 'Okay.'

'And then . . .' Bea fast forwarded the video before stopping it again. 'It's 10.34 a.m., two minutes before Evan and

Harley came into the park and I reckon this is the same person here, sitting on the edge of the bandstand. Saggy can you zoom in on them?'

Saggy fiddled with his laptop and the little figure on the big screen got larger and larger.

'That's the best I can do,' he said, a little apologetically.

'No, that's brilliant,' said Bea. 'It might not look like much, but that hoodie, those trainers. I don't know who it is, but I've seen them before. I'm pretty sure that's the girl I saw leaving a rose under the flyover.'

CHAPTER TWENTY-THREE

Bea went over the recording once again, this time making notes on her phone about everyone the drone captured in the bottom half of the park during that small window of time. Saggy had finished his beer and wandered off somewhere and Ant had stretched out on the sofa and closed his eyes. She'd nearly finished when the noise from upstairs grew louder and there was suddenly a burst of activity as what sounded like a herd of elephants thundered down the stairs. Six small girls charged into the room and started chasing each other round the room, screaming at the top of their lungs. Ant opened his eyes wide, saw what was going on and closed them again, tight.

Mrs Reynolds appeared in the doorway.

'Girls! Girls! Enough! Come and get your food.'

Her words were met with squeals and cheers and the herd moved out of the room and towards the kitchen. Ant opened one eye and squinted out.

'Is it safe?' he said.

'For the time being,' said Bea. 'Two more minutes and then I'm done, and we can get out of here.'

'It's definitely bloody raining now, isn't it?' Ant winked, significantly.

'Yeah.'

Saggy reappeared with two plates of sausages and mash. 'Mum sent these in for you.'

'Oh, it's all right, Saggy, we'll—' Bea stopped and looked at Ant's face. 'Is it still raining, Ant?'

'No,' he said, taking a plate from Saggy. 'I reckon the rain will hold off ten minutes. Cheers, mate.'

Saggy joined them with his own plate, shutting the door to keep the hordes out.

'Your mum's a great cook,' said Ant.

'We can put the sun lounger up in the conservatory for you again, Ant. I always thought you and Neville whatsisname were an odd match.'

'We are, and I've got to find somewhere else, but your mum's got enough on her plate without me here. I'll find somewhere.'

On their way back to Bea's, they diverted via Dean's to pick up Goldie, then dropped her back with Charles. He'd obviously been on his own all day, so this time Bea didn't refuse his offer of tea and a Tunnock's. She and Ant had a nice chat with him, although, even with her coat and jumper off, she was uncomfortably hot in his tiny sitting room.

'There's a vigil for that young lad this evening,' said Charles. 'I'm too old to stand out in the cold, but I'm going to light a candle for him and put it in the window.'

'That's lovely, Charles,' said Bea. 'We're going to go to it, so we'll see the candle when we walk down — Queenie's going to come too.'

They managed to get away after half an hour's small talk. As they crossed the rec, Bea's phone pinged. She fished it out of her pocket.

'It's Evan, isn't it?' said Ant, seeing her frown.

'Yeah. He says can he call.'

Ant shrugged. 'Do you want me to leave you alone?'

'No, it's okay.'

She texted *yes* to Evan and within a minute her phone was vibrating in her hand.

'Evan? You okay?'

'Bea? You on your own?'

'Yes.' A lie this white was hardly a lie at all. She guessed the call would be short and she didn't want to frighten Evan off or waste time explaining that Ant could be trusted. 'Are you all right? Do you need anything?'

'I could do with some stuff from home. I'm going to pop back when it's quiet.'

'There's a vigil tonight, in the park, six thirty. I reckon everyone will be there.'

As soon as she said it, she regretted it.

'Right, I'll go home then.'

'I don't think that's a good idea. There could still be someone watching the house, Evan. The police want you, you know.'

'Yeah. I know. I can nip round the back, though. I'll be careful.'

Even with the eyes of K-town elsewhere, Bea still thought that Evan's house was too hot a location for him.

'Look,' she said, 'why don't I go instead?'

'I can't ask you to do that. You haven't got a back door key or nothing.' If she couldn't get in, she was pretty sure that Ant could. His dad was currently spending time in a local facility at his majesty's pleasure for breaking and entering. Ant had told her that his dad had taken him on some of his night-time jobs when he was little.

'Honestly, I could do it. It's too risky for you to go back there.'

'I don't want you getting mixed up in this, Bea. I'll be fine. Like you said, everyone will be at the park.'

'Have you got somewhere to stay tonight?'

'Yeah. Don't worry about me. Some clean clothes, a bit of food. My big jacket. I'll be good. Look, I'm going to ring off. You never know who's listening, but thanks, Bea. I'll keep in touch.'

Before she could say anything else, he'd gone.

'Did you get any of that?' Bea asked Ant.

'Yeah, he's going to go home and pick up some stuff while the vigil's on.' Ant puffed out his cheeks. 'I wouldn't, if I was him.'

'Me neither. I just hope he can be in and out in a few minutes and then go wherever it is he's got in mind.'

CHAPTER TWENTY-FOUR

That evening, Ant, Bea and Queenie were in a good mood as they set off. It was a cold night, but Queenie had cooked soup and sausage rolls to warm them up and walking in the dark together felt almost like Bonfire Night or the Victorian Evening — there was an air of common purpose and anticipation. That started draining away when they passed Charles's bungalow. A single candle burned in the front window.

'Ah, look, Mum. A candle for Harley. Charles said he'd do that.'

'That's nice, isn't it?'

It wasn't the only sign of remembrance on their route. Other houses had candles on display, some next to photographs of the young man, cut from the *Kingsleigh Bugle*. There were handmade signs, too.

'It's like the whole town is in mourning, isn't it? We've lost one of our own,' said Queenie. 'I think this is going to be emotional.'

As they got nearer to the town centre, they saw more people on the footpath ahead of them. It was soon clear that half the town was converging on the park. As they filed though the main gates there was a bit of chatter around them, but the noise died down as they followed the path between the sparse February flower borders. Bea gasped as she looked down the hill to the bandstand. There were hundreds, maybe thousands of people there, all silent.

A sea of flowers and candles spilled out from the area in front of the stage. Bea had brought a pack of Costsave tea lights with her and a bunch of early daffodils. They joined the quiet and orderly queue to pay their respects. Bea felt a pang when she realised that the couple filing silently along ahead of them were Ginny Meldrum's parents. Ginny had been a friend and colleague at Costsave, cruelly murdered on a cold winter night, not unlike this one. Another young person lost much too young.

When Bea, Queenie and Ant got to the front, Queenie added their flowers to the edge of the tributes and Bea crouched down and lit three tea lights, one from each of them. They all stood briefly and tried to take it in. The scent of flowers filled the air, joined every now and again with the note of melting wax and it took Bea back instantly to the flowers and candles at her dad's funeral in St. Swithin's. She was hit with a wave of raw grief. It was a familiar feeling, but one which had become less and less frequent over the years, as time worked its magic. It never really left you, though. It was always there, could appear when you least expected it, and then it was like the intervening years had never happened. The grief was new. The loss was new. You wondered how you'd ever cope without them.

She glanced at Queenie, who was studying some of the messages, blinking back tears. Was she thinking about Harley or was it mixed up with her own grief, too? She squeezed her mum's elbow. There was no need for words. Queenie looked at her, red-eyed, and then they hugged each other for a little while.

When they broke apart, Bea looked across the memorial and saw Patsy Creech's face, lit up in the glow of the candlelight. Her expression was calm, almost blank. Bea imagined that she had no more tears to cry after the past few days. She was flanked by her surviving sons. Someone was crouched down in front of her, tending to one of the tea lights. When they got up, they stood looking down at the ground, face hidden. Patsy put one arm round their shoulders and whispered something in their ear, which made them look round and Bea could finally see their face. It was the girl with the rose. The girl on the drone footage.

'Oh my god,' murmured Bea.

'I know,' said Queenie, looking in the same direction. 'That poor woman.'

Ant tapped Bea's arm.

'Come on,' he said. 'Let other people have a turn.'

Bea shuffled close to him and stood on tiptoe to lean her head closer to his. 'The girl in front of Patsy Creech,' she hissed. 'It's her. It's *the* girl.'

CHAPTER TWENTY-FIVE

'Did you see her?' Bea asked, after they had moved to the edge of the crowd.

'Yeah,' said Ant. 'Are you sure that was her, though? The girl you're looking for? That's Harley's sister, Scout.'

'Harley's sister? I didn't even know he had one.' Bea's mind was in overdrive now.

'What about Harley's sister?' said Queenie, who, Bea thought, was looking tired and sad.

'Nothing,' said Bea, 'just she's very young, isn't she? Horrible age to lose someone so close. Isn't that Bob and Dot over there? Do you want to go and say hi?'

Bea waved her arm towards her friends and Queenie brightened instantly.

'Oh yes! I haven't seen Dot for ages. Are you coming?'

'In a minute.'

She watched her mum make her way around the back of the crowd. When Dot spotted Queenie, she started walking towards her and they met in the middle, sharing a quick hug. It was that sort of evening. Bea let her eyes wander over the rest of the gathering. As you'd expect there were a lot of young people, huddled in groups, holding onto each other, crying. This will affect them for the rest of their lives, thought

Bea. Everyone in the school will remember where they were when they heard that Harley Creech had died.

She recognised quite a lot of them, either from school or from them coming into Costsave. Groups of teenagers bundling into the store after school were a bit of a blight. She didn't think they swiped the big-ticket items, but there was certainly an uptick in the pilfering of sweets and chocolate bars at that time of day, and Eileen had taken to studiously tending the alcohol aisle at about half-past three to act as a visible deterrent.

There was a group of lads, about Harley's age, standing apart from the main crowd. They were jostling each other, not as cowed and shocked as the other young people. Bea wondered if Harley had got in with the wrong lot. Nicking a pregnancy test could easily have been some sort of dare, a challenge to prove himself to one of the local gangs. She made a mental note to find out who Harley had been friends with at school.

The biking community were out in force, clustered near to the Creeches. They were various shapes and sizes but all in the same basic outfit of black leather jackets and either jeans or leather trousers. Bea found their presence rather reassuring — she hoped that Patsy felt supported by the people who had been Connor's friends. They were certainly putting on a good display of solidarity.

The local community support officers walked through the crowd, stopping to talk to people. It felt like they were there to join with the expression of respect rather than to police the crowd and they were the only people that Bea could see wearing an official uniform. She spotted Tom, though. He was dressed down in jeans and puffer jacket, but he was clearly scanning the crowd, just like her. Their eyes met. Bea knew Tom had seen her, but he didn't acknowledge her at all, just looked and then looked away. He's working, she thought, and wondered how many other plain-clothes police were there.

At seven o'clock the church bell rang the hour, its chimes drifting across the park. A hush descended and about twenty young people walked onto the stage. They lined up in two rows, looking solemn and nervous. One of them looked towards Patsy, who nodded at them, and then they started to sing. Bea was expecting something modern and poppy, but, surprisingly, it was one of the songs the Costsave choir had tackled last year, 'You've Got a Friend.' The singing was a bit wobbly to start with but then the singers grew in strength and confidence. They split into pitch perfect harmonies, and the music took wings and soared into the cold air. The crowd started to join in and Bea found tears running down her face as she, too, sang along.

Other teenagers moved among the crowd handing out black helium-filled balloons. At the end of the third song — Ariana Grande, another of Bea's favourites — balloons were delivered to the choir, who then held them aloft. The lead singer stepped forward, 'For Harley,' she said, her voice ringing out loud and clear. She let go of the balloon and everyone else followed her lead. Hundreds of balloons sailed upwards. It was quite a sight.

'Not very environmentally friendly.' Bea looked round to find Tyler beside her.

'No, 'spose not. Better than those lanterns, though, that set fire to things.'

'Marginally.'

'That why you're not joining in, handing them out and whatnot.'

Tyler shrugged. 'I wasn't friends with him. I mean, I wasn't not friends with him, if you see what I mean, but I didn't know him very well.'

'Who did he hang out with?' asked Bea.

Tyler pulled a face. 'I dunno. I don't think he hung out with anyone much, especially after his dad died. I think he worked at the diner after school. I don't think he went out to the pub or the skatepark or anything. He used to be in one of the football teams but that stopped. He was just helping his family out.'

'Ah,' said Bea. 'Poor kid.' She knew what that felt like. Her dad had died when she was about the same age. For her, it had been the catalyst to Queenie's mental health problems and Bea's years as an unofficial carer.

Ant interrupted. 'I don't like the look of that. Something's going on.'

Bea followed his gaze. A section of the crowd was getting agitated and noisy. The sound and the movement seemed to radiate from one corner. It reminded Bea of a film she'd seen in a Physics lesson — a cartoon of how energy moved through the molecules of a gas or liquid, she forgot which. Something was moving through the people in the park. Soon it reached the people nearest to her. She strained to catch what they were saying.

'He's been spotted . . .'

'Church Bank estate . . .'

'. . . we'll get him.'

He.

She immediately thought of Evan. Oh god, she'd forgotten about him while the choir was singing.

People were streaming away from the bandstand now.

'I think they're going up to Evan's house,' she said to Ant. His eyes widened.

'Oh shit,' he said.

'I wonder if the police know.' Bea looked around but she couldn't see the community support officers or Tom. She got her phone out and sent him a quick text.

Big crowd going to Evan's house. Trouble? Need police?

He texted back. *Tx. On it.*

'Shall we go too?' said Ant.

'Okay. I'd better tell Mum.' But she, too, was lost in the crowd now. Bea hoped that she was still with Dot and Bob, but she couldn't be sure. She didn't want to leave the park without knowing that she was safe. 'I can't see her, Ant. Where is she?'

They walked halfway up the slope and looked back. The atmosphere had definitely turned nasty. About ten young men ran towards them, jostling each other and whooping. As they barged past Bea, she felt an elbow in her ribs. She staggered backwards and Ant caught her.

'Hey!' he called after the lads, but they didn't hear or didn't care. 'Are you all right? I think we should go home, don't you? We'll find Queenie and I'll walk you both back.'

'No, Ant, I need to know that Evan is okay. Hang on.'

She got her phone out again and texted Evan.

Get out now. B x

She waited, staring at her screen. The message had been sent but wasn't marked as delivered or seen.

'They're going to kill him, Ant. I know they are.'

CHAPTER TWENTY-SIX

They found Queenie, still with Dot and Bob.

'Oh, Bea, this crowd's a bit too much for me,' said Queenie. 'Shall we go home now?'

'Ant and I were going to go for a drink,' Bea said, improvising. She knew her mum would be upset if she thought Bea was getting involved in any argy-bargy. She instantly regretted her choice, though, as Bob's eyes lit up at the thought of a pint.

'Where are you going?' he said. 'The Ship?'

'I can't face the pub,' said Dot. 'Why don't we let it thin out a bit and then walk back with Queenie?'

Bea could see that Bob was torn. Which would he choose — duty or pleasure? He plumped for both.

'We could have a little warmer at yours, Queenie,' he said. 'Have you still got that whisky? If not, we could pick something up on the way.'

The plan went down well. Bea gave her mum a hug before leaving.

'Don't stay out late, will you, Bea? There's a funny atmosphere now. I won't sleep 'til you get home.'

'I won't be long, Mum. See you later.'

Ant and Bea joined the people funnelling through the gates. It was easy to see the ones who were heading for Evan's estate — they were walking swiftly, overtaking slower groups, buzzing with energy. Bea wondered if there were any shortcuts to get them there more quickly and warn Evan, but she realised that was pretty futile. The early leavers would be halfway there by now. She just hoped that he was out by now and well clear of the area.

'It's lucky there aren't many pitchforks in Kingsleigh,' said Ant. 'This lot are out for trouble, aren't they?'

'It's lucky there aren't many guns,' said Bea.

'True. There might be other stuff, though. You know what some of the kids round here are like for carrying blades. It could get hairy. If you want to go home with the others, I don't mind going up there on my own. I can report back later.'

Bea was touched by his concern, but unfazed.

'Do you even know me, Ant? Do you think I'm going to be put off by some idiots trying to act the big man?'

She glanced across at him. She expected him to be grinning at her, but his face was dead serious.

'I do know you. That's the trouble. I know what you're like. If things kick off, mate, you and me are getting out of there. It's not our job to protect Evan or his house. We're just there with our eyes and ears, okay? Promise?'

He held his hand out towards her with the little finger extended. She linked hers with his.

'Pinky promise,' she said. 'Come on. We're nearly there.'

There was a substantial crowd in the road outside Evan's by the time they got there and a palpable air of menace, punctuated now and again by shouts of 'Justice for Harley!' and roars of approval. Ant and Bea stood a little way apart from the throng. Bea noticed that the bikers seemed to be absent. The people here were more like the ones she'd see spilling out of the pubs on a Friday or Saturday night or piling into the Kingsleigh Town Football Club on a Saturday afternoon wearing their red and white club scarves. Mostly men, mostly young, but quite a few in their thirties or forties and one or two much older than that, with faces that bore the scars of pugnacious lives.

Now, she could hear the wail of a siren above the shouting and saw a flashing blue light approaching along the suburban street.

'Here comes the cavalry,' said Ant. His reaction was mild compared to some. As the car drew to a standstill at the edge of the crowd and two uniformed officers — one male, one female — got out there were boos and jeers. The officers looked rattled. The older of the two got on his radio straight away, then they both nodded at each other and made their way on foot to stand in front of the gate of number fourteen.

'You need to go home now,' the male officer shouted. 'There's nothing to see here. You're doing no good being here. Let's move along.'

Instead of prompting their dispersal, his words had the opposite effect on the people gathered there and they surged forward. The officers were pushed against the gate. The woman officer drew her truncheon and shouted, 'Get back! Get back!'

'This is getting nasty,' said Ant.

'I know. I don't like it. It's scary.' She strained her ears, hoping to hear more sirens. Help didn't seem to be coming. She knew that Tom was aware but would he come up here as a plain-clothes detective or leave it to the uniforms? There was no way two people could hold back this crowd.

The woman officer was still shouting. Her colleague had drawn his truncheon, too. Were they really going to start hitting people? What would happen to them if they didn't? Bea watched with open-mouthed horror, her eyes focused on the centre of the action, when suddenly everything changed.

A bright light arcing over the crowd caught her attention. The glare burnt a path on her retina, and just for a second she saw a golden rainbow in the night sky and then she heard breaking glass and there was a flash of light in the front window of the house.

'Jesus Christ,' Ant murmured.

There was an orange glow from the room where the missile had landed and soon smoke and flames were licking out of the broken window. A roar of approval went up from the crowd, but, for some, things had gone too far and there were screams of horror, too.

Bea got on her phone and dialled 999.

'Fire service. Quickly!' she said when asked which service she required. She was put through to the control room, and gave the address, all the time watching as the house become engulfed in flames.

'Is there anyone inside?' the operator asked.

'I don't know,' she said. 'I honestly don't know.'

CHAPTER TWENTY-SEVEN

It only took a few minutes for the first fire engine to reach the scene. By then, though, the house was well and truly ablaze. The crowd had retreated away from the front wall, driven back by the heat of the fire, but as the fire crew ran towards the house, Bea saw some dark objects sail across and land nearby. She followed their trajectory backwards and saw the lads she'd seen at the park, with scarves pulled over their mouths and noses now, at the far side lobbing stones. Thankfully, they missed their intended targets, but the officers were forced to withdraw to their vehicle to regroup.

Bea was glad Queenie wasn't there to witness this. What on earth had happened to boring, humdrum Kingsleigh? This was next level.

A minute or two later, with the house burning unchecked, a second fire engine appeared, closely followed by two white vans. Bea watched as the rear doors of the vans swung open and teams of police in full protective gear got out and started assembling in the road.

'It's time to get out of here,' said Ant.

'What if Evan's still in there?'

'That's his problem. Seriously.' He put his arm round her shoulder and started to steer her away.

'Ant, please, I have to know. Can we just go over there and I'll ring him?' Bea pointed thirty metres or so along the street to a couple of ornamental planters.

'Okay.'

They jogged to the planters which were made of little brick walls about half a metre high, each filled with bare soil and with an ornamental tree in the middle. Ant jumped onto one of the walls and held on to a tree trunk.

'Up you come,' he said, leaning down and offering Bea his hand. Her ascent was less graceful than his, but she got there. It was a great vantage point. Bea checked her phone. There was no answer to her text. She tried calling, and held her phone close to her ear as she and Ant watched the riot police forming a solid rank with their shields to create a wall in front of them. The phone rang and rang. Bea shook her head and killed the call. On an agreed signal, the police started moving down the street.

A couple of stones flew right over the crowd and hit the shields. Bang! Bang! The officers didn't flinch. They just kept going. It wasn't a charge. In a way it was more chilling than that — a slow, steady advance. Bea didn't think she would ever forget the sound of their boots on the tarmac, a drumbeat that signalled that they were in charge now. They would not brook any opposition.

The message was received loud and clear. Bea could see bravado and excitement turning to terror on the faces of those people nearest to the oncoming force. They started backing away, then turning and trying to run, their exit blocked by the bodies behind them. Their panic infected those nearest to them. Movement rippled through the crowd — people turning, pushing, running. To Bea it looked like the video of a flock of starlings she had seen on Facebook once, making patterns in the sky. What was the word? Murmur something. Murmuration. That's what it was, people bunching up, spreading out, reacting to what their neighbours were doing as the whole mass moved away from Evan's house and along the road.

'This is fucking mental,' said Ant. He had one arm round Bea's shoulders, and he held her tighter. Bea didn't object. It was one of the most frightening things she'd ever seen.

The police stopped twenty metres or so past Evan's house and formed a roadblock. And now the fire fighters got to work, moving the vehicles closer, unrolling hoses into the front garden, running back and forth. Soon two immense jets of water were being directed at the house. By now the fire had spread to the upstairs rooms. The windows glowed orange. Smoke was leaking out of one of the windows.

'Think they're too late to save it,' said Ant. 'Look at that.'

Bea saw flames starting to lick out between the tiles on the roof. Then there was a splintering sound as part of it collapsed inwards and a shower of sparks danced into the dark air and spiralled upwards.

'Too late,' she echoed. She wanted to go home now, but she couldn't tear herself away.

'There can't be anyone inside, Bea. If Evan had been there, he'd have got out early doors. Gone out the back and cut across the gardens.'

'Do you think so?' She wanted to believe that it was true.

'Yeah. I know so. Shall we go home now? Seen enough?'

'Yes.' Now that the adrenaline was starting to wear off, she felt sick to her stomach and very, very tired.

'Let's go round the other way, bypass the crowd,' he said. He took his arm away from Bea, let go of the tree and jumped down. Then he held his arms out to help her. 'Ready?'

'Yeah.'

The burning house was sitting in a haze of light, smoke, and water spray. Bea gave it one last look, finding it hard to believe that such destruction could happen so quickly. Not just the house, but Evan's whole life. Up in flames in a matter of days. Life really could turn on a sixpence.

The figures of the fire fighters were silhouetted against the bright glow, but as she looked there was something else close to the house. Some movement.

'No. Wait! Oh my god, Ant. Look!'

Ant turned towards the house. He could just make out two figures in the glare, one tall and in uniform, the other bent over as if they were having trouble walking and were being propped up. The taller figure was shouting.

'Over here!'

Others ran to help as the second figure collapsed and the fire fighter lay them down as gently as he could.

'Oh, Ant,' said Bea. 'He was in there all along. He was trapped in there. Those animals did it. They killed him.'

CHAPTER TWENTY-EIGHT

'That's not him, Bea.'

'What do you mean?'

'Evan's massive. I don't think one bloke could've dragged him out like that.'

'Then who . . . ?'

They watched, aghast, as a paramedic team raced to join the group of firefighters gathered round the prone figure on the ground.

'Here, give me a hand and a hitch up, can you?'

Bea looked down from her perch to see who it was. Beneath a rather distressing comb-over was the familiar face of Kevin, the photographer for the *Kingsleigh Bugle*. He gave her the creeps at the best of times, and this wasn't the best of times. There was no way she was going to let him touch her hand or share the planter. It might not be a confined space, but it would be way too close for comfort.

'Sorry. Find your own spot.'

'Oh, it's you! I might have known. You're always in the thick of the trouble round here. Come on, Bea, have a heart. I've got a job to do here.'

'And she said no,' said Ant, 'so push off before I push you.'

'Oh yeah?' said Kevin, puffing out his chest. A strand of hair was flopping over the wrong way, making him look even more like a little bantam cockerel squaring up for a fight. He must have seen something in Ant's eyes, though, because the bravado didn't last long. He was soon backing away. 'All right, all right. Keep your hair on, mate.' He scuttled off down the road, clutching his camera bag.

'You worry about your own hair,' Ant muttered. 'Tosser.'

'Thanks, Ant,' said Bea. 'I can't stand him.'

'Me neither. Can you see who it is yet?'

'No. Oh, hang on. They're moving them, I think.'

One of the paramedics had fetched a blanket from the back of their van. Now Bea stood on tiptoe to try and see over the heads of the people clustered around the victim.

'They're up, Ant! They're walking!'

The fire fighters made way for the two paramedics now. Between them they were supporting someone walking very slowly. As they passed through the garden gate, Bea could see that it was a woman. She had the blanket round her shoulders and was making heavy weather of the short distance to the ambulance, but she was very much alive and not obviously badly injured.

Instinctively, she took a snap on her phone. She had a fleeting thought that taking pictures like this made her as much of a vulture as Kevin, but she tried to bury that thought. She only wanted a photograph to help ID the woman, although from her age and general appearance, there was only one obvious candidate. Evan's mum.

The woman was helped into the ambulance. On impulse, Bea jumped off the planter and started running towards the vehicle.

'Bea, what are you doing?' Ant shouted. 'Hey! You can't—'

The back doors were still open. The woman was propped up on a gurney now and had an oxygen mask over her face. Her eyes were shut.

'Mrs Edwards?' Bea called.

The woman opened her eyes and seemed to be trying to focus on Bea, perhaps wondering if she knew her.

The paramedic who was next to her in the van stared at her.

'Are you family?' she asked, sharply.

'No, I'm—'

'I'm sorry, you'll have to step away. Barry!'

Her colleague was next to Bea now. 'Out of the way, please.' Bea took a couple of paces backwards, her eyes still fixed on Evan's mum. The paramedic closed the first door.

'I'm Evan's friend. Is he still in there?' Bea shouted.

Evan's mum shook her head. Bea felt an inkling of relief, but she needed to be sure.

'He got out?'

The woman nodded.

'Oh, thank god. Take care, okay?'

'Move away now. I need to shut this.' The paramedic closed the second door and checked that it was secure, then went round and got into the driver's seat. Bea walked back to Ant, who was still hovering near the planter.

'It was his mum,' she said. 'And she nodded when I asked if he'd got out. They must have met there secretly. He left before she did and then she got trapped.'

'Bloody hell.'

'I'm going to text him.'

She sat down on the little wall and quickly composed a message.

Yr mum out now and on way to hosp. She ok. B x

She got a text straight back.

Hosp? Wtf?

If Evan had left before the mob got there, he wouldn't know about the fire. How could she break it to him gently?

Smoke, prob. House on fire, but being put out now. Don't worry. Yr mum is okay

OK Thx Bea

Bea got to her feet. 'He didn't know,' she said. 'I reckon he left when he got my text earlier.'

'Well, that's something. Your warning worked.'

'But his mum . . .'

'Bea, that's not your fault. You had no idea, did you? And he should have told her to clear out, too. Come on, let's go home.'

They took the back alleys and little lanes to avoid the remnants of the crowd. By the time they got to Bea's house, the whole incident seemed unreal.

'Do you want to come in for a cuppa?' said Bea.

'No, I'll get back to Neville's. It's been a long day, hasn't it?'

'Meet up tomorrow?'

'Yeah, maybe. I'm gonna try and sleep in.'

Bea walked down the side of the house and let herself into the kitchen, surprised to see Bob and Dot sitting at the table with Queenie. By the looks of things, and the half inch of liquid left in the bottle in the middle of the table, 'one glass' had turned into a bit of a session. They were all chuckling as Dot delivered the punchline to one of her stories.

'. . . and then he said, "I can't put that in my mouth, I'm vegetarian!"'

Queenie screamed with laughter and Bob had trouble holding onto his mouthful of whisky. Bea felt that she'd walked out of one world and into another one. The contrast was so surreal.

'Oh, hello, love,' said Queenie, who was sitting nearest to the door, turned round in her chair. 'Did you have a nice time at the pub?'

The pub? Of course, that had been their cover story.

'Yes, um, I mean, it was okay.'

Queenie narrowed her eyes. 'What's up?'

'Nothing. I think I'll just go to bed, leave you party people to it.'

She really wanted to stay up for a while, decompress, but she couldn't face faking the jollity she'd need to join in with the others. She hung her coat on the back of the door. Queenie wrinkled her nose.

'What's that smell? Have you been smoking?'

'No, 'course not. It's—' Bea sighed. They'd all find out soon enough what had gone on this evening — 'it's smoke from a fire.'

'A bonfire?'

'A house fire. Someone chucked a bottle full of petrol through one of the windows at Evan's house.'

The atmosphere in the room changed in an instant. It was like she'd thrown a bucket of water over the three of them.

'What? Is that where you've been?' Queenie was on her feet now.

'Mum, calm down. I just went up there because I wanted to make sure that Evan was safe.'

'Was he there?' said Bob.

'No. He wasn't —' no harm in a little white lie — 'but his mum was. She had to be rescued from the fire.'

'Oh my god!' Queenie's hands went up to her mouth.

'I know. It sounds worse than it is.' It couldn't, really. Things were as bad as they could possibly get without someone dying. 'She's okay, I think.'

'What were you thinking, Bea? Have you learnt nothing at all?'

'I was with Ant, Mum. We were all right. Safety in numbers.'

Bob and Dot stood up, too. 'We'd better go. I'm glad you're all right, love,' said Dot. 'Bob, pass me my coat.'

'You don't have to leave,' said Bea. 'I don't want to break up the party. I could actually do with a drink.'

'You have a quiet one with your mum,' said Dot. 'I think you need some time together.'

Bob held Dot's coat for her and eased it over her shoulders. She put both their empty glasses on the draining board and then she and Bob bundled out of the kitchen.

'Do you want a cuppa or a drink drink?' said Queenie.

'I could just finish that up,' Bea said, eyeing the whisky bottle. Queenie fetched her a glass and they sat down opposite each other.

'I don't know what to do with you,' Queenie sighed. 'I really don't.'

Bea knew it came from a good place, but she was too tired and shaken up for a telling off.

'You don't have to do anything. I'm all right.'

Queenie reached forward and put one hand over one of Bea's. Her grip was surprisingly strong. Bea wanted to wriggle her hand away, but she couldn't.

'You're bloody brilliant, Bea, you know I think that, but you're also a nightmare. Why on earth do you have to get involved in things?'

'You know why. This is the same as it was when everyone was slagging Dad off. I can't stand injustice. If I can help to put things right, then I will.'

'And it's this Evan lad this time, is it?'

'Yeah. He didn't do it, Mum, and now half of K-town is after him, as well as the police. They nearly got him this evening, too.'

Queenie frowned.

'So, he *was* there, and you knew about it.' She squeezed Bea's hand even harder. 'Bea, he's wanted by the police. If you're keeping information from them, you could be in very hot water indeed.'

'I'm not saying anything, Mum. Not now. Not yet.'

'To me or the police?'

'Both. I can't.'

Now Queenie withdrew her hand.

'It's like that, is it?'

'It is. It has to be. Until I've got evidence that he didn't do it.'

Queenie slammed her hand onto the table, making Bea jump.

'It's not your job!' she shouted, enunciating every word.

Her mum so rarely expressed anger about anything that Bea was truly shocked.

'Mum! Stop it. It's not helping. It's been a horrible day. I'm going to bed.' Perilously close to tears, Bea scraped back her chair and stood up. Queenie mirrored her and then moved so that she was between Bea and the door to the lounge. 'Mum, please. Just let me go upstairs now.'

'Okay, I will, but come here first.'

Queenie opened her arms. Bea reluctantly drew close. Her mum wrapped her arms round her, while Bea's stayed by her side.

'I love you, Bea,' Queenie said into her ear.

'I know. I love you, too. I'm tired. Can I go upstairs now?'

They separated and Queenie let Bea walk past into the lounge, heading for the stairs.

'Bea?' She stopped and turned round. Queenie's eyes were glittering with tears. 'Please, Bea. Please don't get involved. I couldn't bear to lose you.'

CHAPTER TWENTY-NINE

On her days off, Bea normally liked to ditch the routine, sleep in for hours and spend as much of her day as possible in her pyjamas and dressing gown. After her shower last night, she did manage to get to sleep, but she was awake at half-past four and that was all the rest that her mind and body would allow her, even though she did everything she could to nod off again. She didn't turn on her phone. She kept her bedside light off and tried calming breathing. When that didn't work, she started counting backwards in her head from one thousand. She got down to eight hundred and eighty-seven, clear-headed and wide awake, before she gave up.

She sat up in bed, propped a pillow behind her shoulders and fired up her phone.

'Holy crap.'

Kingsleigh hadn't just hit the headlines on the *Bristol Live* website, it had made the national news. Several online sites carried the story of the mob and the fire at Evan's house. Bea clicked on one which was normally her 'go to' site for celebrity gossip. She would never in a million years have expected to find her little town covered, but there it was.

The headline *SOMERSET ON FIRE — Riot in Market Town* was accompanied by half a dozen photos of Evan's house in flames, the crowd gathered there and the line of police in riot gear. Bea got out of bed and fetched her laptop from her dressing table so she could have a proper read. It was not good.

> *Lawlessness came to the streets of a sleepy market town on Saturday, after locals firebombed the house of a murder suspect and then pelted firefighters with stones to stop them tackling the blaze. Riot police were called in, believed to be the first time they have dealt with an incident in Kingsleigh.*
>
> *One person, believed to be the owner of the house and not the suspect, was rescued from the fire, which completely destroyed the house. Earlier in the week police issued an arrest warrant for Evan Edwards, 19, of Croft Road. As we understand it, he is still at large. No arrests were made at the scene in relation to public disorder but a police press conference is expected later today.*
>
> *One local resident, who watched the carnage from their house on Croft Road, and did not want to be identified, said, 'It's absolutely disgusting. I've lived in this street for forty years and we've never seen anything like it. It's like society has completely broken down. The kids round here are feral. You've got to look at the parents, haven't you?'*
>
> *'The incident came after a peaceful vigil was held earlier in the evening in Kingsleigh Memorial Park for local youngster, Harley Creech, 16, who was found murdered there on Wednesday.'*

Bea found articles on several other sites. She had never been particularly fascinated by party politics, but she couldn't help noticing the different spin each site put on the events, according to their political allegiance.

LAWLESSNESS ON THE STREETS.

BRITAIN FIGHTS BACK — VIGILANTES TAKE MATTERS INTO THEIR OWN HANDS.

PAYING THE PRICE — CUTS TO POLICE SEES CRIME SOAR IN ENGLISH BACKWATER.

LOCK 'EM UP — CALLS FOR TOUGHER PENALTIES FOR PUBLIC DISORDER OFFENCES.

However you interpreted it, and wherever you looked, though, it was not a good news day for Kingsleigh. She checked the time. It was still only five-fifteen. She groaned. Perhaps she should get up and make a cuppa. It was cold, though. She dragged the duvet up around her shoulders and tried to think of something positive. What had she learned yesterday? How could she help? Her mind automatically turned to Harley's sister, Scout. She'd been there in the park on the morning that Harley was murdered. She'd visited his shrine when she thought no one else was around. What was going on there? Was this just the normal behaviour of a grieving sister, wanting some quiet time to remember her brother, or was there more to it? The received wisdom in Kingsleigh was that the Creech family was a close one, drawn closer still by the death of Connor. Perhaps she should find out a bit more about them.

She did a bit of googling, but all the references were either to Harley's death or to Connor's. One family. Two tragic incidents. But what was the reality behind the headlines? Bea felt the tingle of excitement as an idea formed — a plan of action for the day. It was too early to recruit any help, though. Perhaps she'd try and get a bit more sleep. She shut her laptop and put it on the bed next to her, then reached for her book. She read a few pages, then found her eyes going over and over the same few sentences, the words not making sense, and then the book was slipping through her fingers, and she was away.

When she woke up again, it was light outside. She could hear Queenie clattering about in the kitchen. She checked her phone. Half-past ten. She really had needed a lie-in after all. She put her dressing gown on, used the bathroom, then went downstairs.

'Hello, sleeping beauty,' Queenie said. 'Do you fancy a fry up?'

An array of saucepans and frying pans was on the top of the stove, but she hadn't started cooking yet.

'Actually, Mum, I wondered about going out for something to eat.'

'No need, lovely. I've got all the stuff in.'

'Yeah, but we can have it another time. I'd like to treat you. A little thank you for everything you do.'

A flush of pleasure spread to Queenie's face. 'Oh, that's lovely! Where are we going? The Ship?'

'No, I was thinking of lunch at the diner. It's still open and it would be nice to show them a bit of support.'

'That's a good idea. It's a bit of a trek, though. All the way to the Bristol Road.'

'Yeah, I thought I might see if Dot wants to take her Micra for a little run out and give us a lift.'

Queenie smiled. 'You're crafty, you are. Go on, text her and see.'

After a minute or two, Bea's phone pinged and then she gave Queenie the thumbs up.

'Bob's gone off to the allotment, so she suggested asking Ant. She can pick him up on the way here. Come on, Mum, shall we go smart casual?'

It was a while since Bea had been anywhere other than the pub or the café. The diner didn't have a great reputation for food, but at least it was somewhere different, so after a quick scan of her wardrobe, she decided on a nice shirt and smart jeans, along with a suedette jacket. She didn't have time to do her hair properly, so she swept it up into a high ponytail and tied a little scarf round it which was a nice 50s touch, she thought. She used the rest of the time to make sure her make-up was on point. She was just blotting her bright red lipstick when she heard a car draw up outside and a horn beeping. She grabbed her bag and clattered downstairs. Queenie was in the kitchen, all ready to go.

'Oh gawd,' said Queenie as they approached the little purple car waiting outside their front gate. 'I'd forgotten how small it was. We're not going to fit in there, are we?'

'We'll be fine,' said Bea, breezily, but by the time she and Ant had clambered over the tipped forward passenger seat into the back and Queenie was installed in the front, she did wonder if their antics were being filmed, prior to being sent into 'You've Been Framed'. How many knees and elbows did Ant actually possess? However many it was they seemed to be everywhere.

'Budge up, Ant. You're taking up all the space.' She barged her shoulder against his.

He barged back. 'I can't budge any further, mate.'

'Can you move your seat forward, Mum?' Bea could feel an uncomfortable pressure on her legs, squeezed between her seat and the back of the one in front. Queenie faffed about trying to find the lever and then wiggled backwards and forwards in her chair, ramming it repeatedly into Bea's shins.

'I think this is as far as it goes.'

'It can't be.'

'No, that's it, love,' said Dot, taking a quick look. 'Have you all got your seatbelts on?'

'Buckle up, it's going to be a bumpy ride,' muttered Bea, thinking about the various traffic calming measures between their house and the Bristol Road. Beside her, Ant sniggered.

'What's that, Bea?'

'Nothing.'

The journey to the diner was mercifully short and they soon saw the familiar pink neon sign in the front window, crafted to look like sloping handwriting, Patsy's Diner. The car park at the front was busy, but there were still spaces, although they were a bit small, even for a Micra. Dot drew up beside one, close to a rank of motorbikes. A couple of enormous men in full leathers were standing by the bikes, which both had large paniers on either side, drinking coffee in takeaway cups.

'You lot get out and then I'll squeeze in here,' Dot said.

Getting out was easier said than done. Bea had seized up and couldn't seem to get enough momentum to propel herself forward and out.

'Do you need a shove?' Ant asked.

Bea could easily imagine where he would apply the pressure and squawked, 'No, no, I've got this! Keep your hands to yourself!' She took hold of the edge of the doorway with one hand and the folded-over seat in front in the other and heaved. She emerged into the daylight in an ungainly tangle of legs and arms, grateful that she'd chosen the jeans and not a denim miniskirt or cute little dress. Ant scrambled after her. As they stood with Queenie and watched Dot manoeuvre the Micra into the space, Ant said, 'Grateful for the lift and everything, but who buys a purple car the size of a rabbit hutch?'

They heard one of the bikers snort with laughter and looked round. 'Sweet ride,' he said. 'Don't knock it.'

Bea couldn't decide if he was being ironic or not, but there seemed no malice in him.

'Purple, though,' said Ant, shaking his head.

They all trooped towards the entrance.

'It's all right to be coming here, isn't it?' said Queenie in a low voice to Bea. 'It almost feels a bit ghoulish.'

'No, Mum. Like you said, we're here to show our support. It's a nice thing. They've still got to pay the bills, haven't they? They don't want people avoiding them, 'cos it's awkward.'

'True.' She and Bea both knew what it felt like to see people lost for words or crossing the street out of embarrassment after a loved one had died. 'Come on, then. Let's do lunch.'

CHAPTER THIRTY

Despite the presence of a decent number of customers, the diner had a forlorn air. There was hardly any conversation going on and the rockabilly music playing through the ceiling speakers seemed over loud and out of place even though it was completely in keeping with the 1950s prints, the red vinyl seats, and black and white floor tiles. Bea and her party stood by the *Wait to be Seated* sign just inside the doorway, but nobody came to welcome them. She found her eyes drawn to the large, framed photograph of Harley, propped up near the till and garlanded with red plastic roses. He looked so young and Bea was hit again by the magnitude of the tragedy which had happened only a few days ago. How terribly sad it was. Maybe lunch out had been a bad idea. Maybe it was a day to hibernate and reflect and count your blessings.

Out of the corner of her eye, Bea saw a waitress, in a gingham blouse and pink pedal pushers, approaching them.

'Welcome to Patsy's,' she said. 'Table for four? Would you like a booth?'

'Ooh, I love a booth!' said Queenie.

'Yes, please, love,' said Dot.

The girl smiled and she showed them the way to a booth at the far end of the room.

'I'll be back to take your drinks order in a minute.'

The laminated menus were next to a vase of plastic flowers in the middle of the table, tucked into a sort of large paperclip. There was an additional sheet offering *2 for 1 on American breakfasts* with a photograph of a rather temptingly overloaded plate of fried goods. Ant handed the menus out and started to look at his. Dot put hers on the table without reading it.

'I know what I'm having,' she said.

'What's that?' said Bea.

'An American breakfast. Anyone want to be my bogof?'

'I will,' said Bea, 'unless you want it, Ant? Ant?'

Ant was concentrating so hard that he didn't hear her. She caught Dot's eye and put her fingers to her lips, both realising that it was a special moment.

When the waitress came back, they ordered drinks and food. Two American breakfasts, an 'Everything' burger for Ant and pancakes, bacon and maple syrup for Queenie. Ant asked for coffee and watched with disbelief as Bea and Dot opted for Diet Coke while Queenie ordered tea. As the waitress went off to the counter to fix their drinks, Ant put a menu on the table and planted his index finger on one line.

'Guys, what are you doing? It says here that they refill your coffee for free, as many times as you like, all day long. Think of the value!'

Dot smiled. 'Have you tried their coffee? I can't get to the bottom of one cup, let alone ask for a refill.'

'If it's free, Dot, I'm going to enjoy it. Trust me.'

Dot smiled. 'We'll see.'

When the drinks came, Ant took a big slurp of his coffee. 'Nice?' said Dot.

'Yeah, brilliant,' said Ant, picking up the glass container of white sugar and pouring some through the metal spout into his cup. He gave it a stir and tried another taste. 'Just the job.'

He had time for a second and third cup before their food came. No one could think of much to say. The one hot topic of conversation was out of bounds here, of course. They'd been waiting for at least forty minutes and were just having a whispered discussion about whether to complain or at least ask if they had been forgotten when the waitress finally appeared, bottom first, between the swing doors to the kitchen, carrying three plates of food.

'Two breakfasts?' she said, looking to see who would claim them. 'And a burger. I'll be right back with the pancakes.'

'Don't wait for me,' Queenie said. 'You all start while it's hot.'

'You all,' said Ant. 'Don't you mean y'all?'

They all took turns putting on American accents with varying degrees of success, while they applied salt, vinegar, and red or brown sauce to their plates. Queenie's pancakes arrived — a great pile of them with a little jug full of syrup on the side — and it was generally agreed that she had hit the jackpot, although Bea did wonder why on earth she had chosen them, a day after she'd cooked them at home.

Bea's breakfast was nothing like the photo on the menu, making her wonder if they had just cut and pasted an image off the internet, rather than photograph something made on the premises. If she was more malicious it would be quite funny to take a snap of this sorry offering and post it on Insta or wherever as a 'What I Ordered. What I Got' meme. Still, it smelled quite promising, and she was absolutely starving, so she dug in.

'I can't see the King and Queen coming to Costsave, with the town in such a state. I mean, throwing stones at firemen. What an awful thing to do,' said Dot, loading her fork with a generous piece of pancake, dripping with syrup.

'We don't look good at the moment, do we?' said Bea. She was trying to enjoy her breakfast, after the long wait, but the hash browns were swimming with grease. Honestly, she thought, you could wring them out like a sponge. She pushed them to one side of her plate with her fork and tried the 'Collard greens' which looked suspiciously like spinach out of a frozen packet.

'I don't think the King will let that put him off,' said Queenie. 'I mean, the royals are always going to deprived areas and meeting the people who are trying to make things better, aren't they? It's one of their things.'

'Is that what we are now, deprived?' said Bea.

'No, I didn't say that. We're . . . troubled. We could certainly do with a bit of encouragement, something to bring everyone together.'

'Like someone coming in a limousine to shake a few hands at a food bank before going home to a nice organic three course dinner cooked by a private chef?' said Ant, then contorted his face, pulling the sides of his mouth down and continuing in his poshest voice, 'You're doing a marvellous job!'

Bea, having rejected the greens which were, indeed, watery spinach, now had a mouthful of baked beans. As she tried to stifle a laugh, a stray bean threatened to come down her nose. She extracted a paper serviette from wedge in the menu holder and covered her face, just in case.

'Ant! That's not fair. Not fair at all!' Queenie was starting to get upset.

Bea managed to swallow the beans and took a swig of Diet Coke to wash them down.

'Mum, calm down. He's only teasing.'

'Well, it's not funny. Charles has only just lost his mum and he's doing the best he can. I think he's shaping up quite nicely.'

Ant opened his mouth to say something but caught the warning look in Bea's eye and shut it again. He took another fry, dipped it in ketchup and popped it in his mouth.

'Sorry, Mrs J. Didn't mean anything. Each to their own, yeah?'

Queenie sniffed hard, but she was calming down.

'Quite so, Ant. We can agree to disagree, can't we?'

'Nice and civilised,' he said, licking his ketchup-covered fingers. 'Do you want one of my fries?'

'No, ta, love. I don't think it would go with pancakes. I'm full anyway,' she said, sitting back from the table and easing her fingers round the waistband of her trousers. 'They have rather defeated me. American pancakes are quite a different texture to English ones. Can you finish them?'

Ant's expression brightened dramatically, as if he'd just found out he was holding a winning lottery ticket instead of another fry. 'Really?'

Queenie pushed the plate across the table towards him. 'Be my guest.'

While they were talking, Bea had given up on her lacklustre breakfast. It had definitely overpromised and underdelivered. She was quite keen for her plate to be taken away — it was a depressing sight. She spotted someone clearing the tables at the other end of the room and felt a flutter of excitement in her still rather empty stomach. It was Scout.

Bea got up.

'Just going to the loo,' she said.

'They're right round the other side, through the back,' said Dot.

Bea walked the length of the diner. Scout had an armful of half-empty plates and was heading for the same door.

'Let me,' Bea said, darting ahead and then holding the door open.

Scout smiled. 'Thank you,' she said, automatically, then hesitated. In that moment, Bea knew that Scout recognised her from the morning under the bridge. It was a delicate moment, like snagging a fish on the end of a hook and needing the lightest of touches to reel it in.

'Hi,' she said. 'I . . . think I saw you the other morning. We were both paying our respects. I'm so sorry about your brother.'

Scout looked at her warily.

'Thank you,' she said.

'Okay, I'm just, um . . .' Bea tipped her head towards the doorway to the rest room, which was adorned with a decal of a girl with a ponytail wearing a sticky-out skirt.

Another awkward smile and then the girl walked past the toilet doors to one marked 'Staff Only' on the other side of the corridor. She backed into it, pushing it open, and was soon through and gone.

Bea rolled her eyes. That hadn't gone very well. Her fish had slipped off the hook and got away with barely a wriggle. Bea went into the loos for the sake of appearances. She didn't actually need to go, but she went into a cubicle and stood there for a minute or two before flushing. Just going through the motions, she thought, pleased with herself at the pun.

She stood at one of the two washbasins and squirted soap onto her hands. She was rinsing them under the tap when the door opened. Expecting it to be Dot or Queenie, she glanced up in the mirror and saw that it was Scout. The girl didn't head for a cubicle but stood just inside the doorway, hands clutched in front of her.

Bea turned round, dripping water onto the floor. She picked up a puny paper towel from a heap on the counter.

'Hello, again,' she said.

'Hi. Um, you won't tell anyone you saw me, will you? That morning.' The girl spoke very quickly and very softly.

'No, of course not.' Well, she wouldn't tell anyone *else*. 'It was a private moment.'

'Thank you. Did you know Harley?'

'No. Not really. I was in the shop that morning. I work at Costsave. I was just, you know, sorry.'

Scout nodded. She didn't seem in a hurry to leave.

Bea waited, wondering if silence would encourage her to say more. There was an agonising gap, then the sound of plates clattering to the floor drifted in from elsewhere in the building and a woman shouted Scout's name. Scout virtually jumped out of her skin. 'That's me. I've got to go.'

'If you ever want to talk, you can find me at Costsave. I'm on checkout six. I'm there most weekdays, weekends sometimes too.'

Another little smile. 'Checkout six, okay?' Bea repeated, and then Scout was gone.

CHAPTER THIRTY-ONE

None of them could face dessert. Even Ant declined the offer.

'I actually feel full,' he said. 'Those pancakes sort of sit in your stomach, like you've eaten a cushion or something.'

'Yes, I found that,' said Queenie. 'They were an odd texture, weren't they? Not something you'd normally associate with food.'

'Do you want a coffee? Help it go down?' said Dot, with an undernote of mirth in her voice. 'Ant, want another top up?'

He was up to number four by now, but a fifth was beyond even him. Everyone else shook their heads, too.

'I would quite like one,' said Queenie, 'but not here. And not coffee. Shall we just have a cuppa at mine? You're all welcome.'

This seemed like an excellent suggestion. Their waitress brought the bill. Bea added a tip in her head and then divvied it up and they all chipped in without any argument, then filed out and shambled across to the Micra.

'Pile in!' said Dot, opening the door and pushing the driver's seat forward.

Ant looked at the tiny space and puffed out his cheeks.

'I don't think my stomach will take being crammed in the back again. I reckon I might walk back to yours, Mrs J, if that's all right. It won't take me long. It'll give it a chance to all shake down a bit.'

'I'll join you,' said Bea.

'You sure?' said Queenie.

'It's quite a nice day now.'

'All right, love. See you back at ours in a bit.'

They watched as Queenie and Dot got into the car and drove off, Dot giving them a cheerful toot on the horn in salute as they turned out of the car park.

'That car . . .' said Ant, chuckling to himself.

'Be nice to have one, though, wouldn't it? You could go anywhere.'

They walked past the rows of bikes and cars and off the forecourt onto the pavement.

'Do you know how to drive, Bea?'

'No. Perhaps I should have lessons.'

'Do it, Bea! Never too late to learn.' He gave her a knowing smile.

'I dunno. Expensive, aren't they? And then I'd have to save up for a car.'

They were standing by the side of the road, waiting for a safe time to cross. The traffic had built up while they were in the diner and it was busy now. Every time a gap opened up one way, there was a queue of cars in the other direction. Finally, they grabbed their opportunity and half ran across to the other side, then started walking back towards Kingsleigh.

'But, like you said, you could go anywhere,' said Ant. 'Where would you go, if you could?'

'Well, I can get to Bristol and Bath on the bus. And London and Cardiff on the train. So, somewhere else . . .' Bea wracked her brains. 'Cheddar Gorge?'

Ant burst out laughing. 'Cheddar pigging Gorge? Is that it? Think big, Bea. Cornwall, Blackpool, Scotland! France!' He was dancing along the grass verge now, his arms spread out wide.

'I'm not driving to effing France, you silly sod. I can't even drive on the left-hand side of the road yet. I'm not going to go somewhere they drive on the right. Be real. Oh—'

They were at the official town boundary, which was marked with a sign, which normally read, '*Welcome to Kingsleigh.*' Somebody had been busy with a spray can, though, and the 'King' was firmly and clearly crossed out.

'I'm not the only one, then,' said Ant.

'You're not. There's a whole online thing, *No King in Kingsleigh.*'

'Is there? I haven't seen that. I mean, I don't really care one way or another. Well, I care about the waste of money. I mean it's wrong to have kids going without dinners in the school holidays while the royals swan around all over place, isn't it? Yeah, actually, maybe I do care.'

'It wasn't you with the spray paint, was it?' She was joking, but she wouldn't have been totally surprised if it had been Ant.

'No. Not this time. It's pretty funny, though, isn't it?' He took a snap on his phone. 'If you take the King out, what does that make us? Slee. Sleigh. Sleigh-town instead of K-town.'

Bea pulled a face. 'Fine for the Victorian Evening and most of December. Not so great for the rest of the year.'

They pressed on and soon turned off the main drag and into the smaller road that led to the High Street.

'I saw you ever so subtly making a beeline for Scout in there.'

'Oh,' said Bea. She thought she'd been so discreet that no one would have noticed.

'Did you talk to her?'

'Yeah. Kind of. She didn't really say anything, but she did ask me not to tell anyone about seeing her in the park that time. There's something going on there. I got the feeling she wanted to talk, but she couldn't.'

'Well, she was at work and it is her family's place. I saw one of her brothers, Brough, in the kitchen. They live over the shop, too, don't they?'

'Yeah. It can't be easy. I told her where she could find me. We'll see.'

'Good job, mate. That's all you could do. Have you heard from Evan today?'

'No. I reckon he's lying low. He must be terrified.'

'I was thinking about that. Maybe he's at a mate's place, but if he isn't, he's sleeping rough somewhere. I know most of the spots round here.' He said it in such a matter-of-fact way, but Bea knew that there was a world of pain behind the words. 'Do you want me to try and find him?'

'Maybe. We haven't got a case to bring to the police, though, have we? To get him into the clear? And he knows he can text me if he needs anything.'

They were approaching the middle of town now. Next, they would have to cross the High Street and then follow the familiar alleys and paths back to Bea's.

'Ant,' Bea said.

'Yeah?'

'Can we call at the chip shop on the way to mine? I'm starving.'

CHAPTER THIRTY-TWO

The chips were really quite glorious after the disappointing fare at the diner. Piping hot and slightly crispy on the outside, floury and fluffy on the inside, with just the right amount of salt and vinegar. Ant had caved and got a small portion for himself, and they'd taken their cardboard trays, wrapped in plain paper, into the park to enjoy them properly.

'Simple food, done well,' said Bea, in a mock Cockney accent, holding up a chip to the light, then popping it in her mouth.

'Laaarvely,' Ant joined in, then pulled a range of faces, Gregg Wallace-style. They both enjoyed watching *MasterChef* and laughing at some of the fancier creations.

'Didn't think you'd be able to manage any today. I'm impressed,' said Bea.

'Well, it all bogged down on the walk, and I couldn't sit and watch you eat some. That would have been rude, like letting you drink on your own.'

The park was Sunday-afternoon busy. The appearance of the sun seemed to have tempted plenty of families out, even though there was still a cold wind. The play area was rammed and there were kids playing football on the flat areas of grass, and happy shouts and screams drifting over from the skatepark. It was so different from the dark, deserted place Bea had experienced a couple of mornings ago. She looked down the hill towards the river.

'Shall we go and have another look at the bridge when we've finished these?' she said.

'Yeah, okay. What are we looking for?'

'I dunno, but I think the tape has gone now. We might be able to get all the way along the path.'

They finished their chips and threw the rubbish in the nearest bin, then sauntered down the grassy slope. A little boy miskicked a football and it sailed towards Ant. He chested it down, did a couple of impressive keepy-uppies, then booted it back to him.

'You must miss your family. How are they getting on?'

One of Ant's brothers was still in Kingsleigh, but his mum, sister and younger brother had moved to Cardiff.

'Kind of. Mum and Dani are okay. Ken's giving them the runaround, as usual.'

He didn't mention his dad, but Bea knew he went to visit him in prison every few months. When she'd first met Ant, the family had still been together. It was shocking how things could break apart so quickly and now Ant was making his own way in the world and not doing a bad job of it, considering. As they walked along, she gave silent thanks for Queenie and the home she'd grown up in. Things hadn't always been easy for them, especially losing her dad, but they'd always had each other and their little house, and it felt like something solid.

As they approached the river, they were met with the scent of hundreds of bouquets, still on the ground by the bandstand. They stopped to look at some of the tributes then walked on. The bridge was casting a shadow over the path, and Bea shivered. Out of the sun, it was still a cold day. The police tape had, indeed, gone. It didn't matter whether it had been removed officially or unofficially — they could get into the place where Harley had died now. They both paused, contemplating the space in front of them.

'Come on, mate,' Ant said. 'It's all right.'

He took the lead and walked slowly forward. The hum of car tyres on the road above them came and went, echoing round the space. The concrete pillars were so tall, it felt more like a building than a bridge, but it was undeniably bleak. It had always been one of Kingsleigh's least picturesque spots, despite the river flowing alongside. It was so deep in the cutting here that it was almost hidden. As soon as the bypass had been built in the nineteen sixties, people started adding graffiti to the concrete supports. Every time it was cleaned off, more appeared.

Bea couldn't help looking at the ground, wondering exactly where Harley had met his end. It had to be the darker patch she had noticed before. She stood next to it and shivered. Ant had wandered over to the railings and was looking down at the river.

'Let's go, Bea,' he soon said. 'This place is giving me the creeps.'

'I know what you mean. It feels different here, doesn't it? Like the place itself has been changed by what's gone on.'

'It's just 'cos we know what's happened here. It's us that's changed.'

'Unless it's haunted. It feels like there are echoes here, like the pillars could tell us stuff, if we knew how to listen.'

Ant shook his head. 'The only echo is the traffic on the A4, Bea. Places can't remember stuff. They're just places. Come on, let's get out of here, and have a cuppa at yours.' He came close to her and nudged her elbow.

'Just a minute,' she said. She walked toward the concrete ramp at the bottom of the columns. It was covered with layers of bright paint — it was obviously writing but so stylised that, apart from a few words, it just looked abstract to Bea.

'I can't tell what any of it says.'

'Ha! Now you know what it feels like to be me. Weird thing is, I get this stuff. It's easier to read than words in a book.'

'Really? I don't get it.' Bea squinted at one message, trying to decipher it. She could decode some of the letters, but it didn't make sense.

'All right, Grandma, which bit are you trying to read?'
'That one?'
'K-Cru. They're a team of taggers. You see that one all over the place.'
'Oh. What does one that say?'
'Suck my—'
'Okay, okay. Wish I hadn't asked.'
'Some of this stuff has been here for years. I think the council have given up cleaning it off. It's kinda cool.'

Near the bottom of the ramp, Bea noticed some white paint. It was on top of an older message, so it must be fresher, newer — a simple heart with the initials *SC 4 TJ* written inside. She snapped it on her phone.

'SC,' she said, pointing at the heart.

Ant shrugged. 'Could be anyone.'

'Could be Scout Creech.'

Ant's eyebrows shot up. 'Blimey. Do you think so? There must be loads of people with those initials, Bea.'

'Yeah, I know, but what if it is Scout? In which case, who's TJ?'

CHAPTER THIRTY-THREE

'I know that this is a difficult time for a lot of you and for the store itself. It's a situation none of us wanted to be in. All I can say is that we continue to cooperate with the police.'

'Have they found Evan yet?' someone piped up from the back.

George appeared uncomfortable. Beside her, Neville was pale and sweaty, his rather large forehead glistening in the harsh strip light of the staff room. 'Not as far as I know. Obviously, this isn't strictly speaking a Costsave matter now. If anyone has any information about his whereabouts, you should talk direct to the police.'

Bea kept her expression fixed and stared straight ahead.

'If I found him, I'd march him down to the cop shop myself,' said Kirsty. There were murmurs in the room, both agreeing and disagreeing with her.

'Some people are keen to throw him under the bus,' whispered Bea to Ant.

'Some people would drive the bloody bus and run him over.'

The hubbub grew and discussions started to get heated.

'Innocent until proved guilty . . .'

'Have you seen the size of him? That poor boy . . .'

'Didn't stand a chance . . .'

'Said he didn't do it . . .'

George took a step forward, holding up a hand.

'All right, all right. Feelings are running high. I get that, but we are family here and we've got a business to run, so let's park everything else and do what we do best. Provide a safe, friendly environment for Kingsleigh's shoppers.'

She was speaking above the noise, which subsided a little but didn't altogether stop. 'Right,' she shouted. 'That's it! I don't want any more discussion about this. And I don't want to hear it on the shop floor. Our customers do not need it. Neville, if you hear any chat about the current situation from any staff, please report it me.'

The room fell silent now. Neville went even paler and wrote a note on his clipboard.

'Now,' George continued, 'there will be a task force meeting straight after this one, but everyone else should start getting ready for the day. We can't control what's going on in the world, but we can make this little corner into a happy space to work and shop in. Let's do it!'

It was a distinctly unhappy workforce that trooped out of the staff room, though. That was the closest most of them had ever got to a telling off from George, who was universally considered to be the best and fairest manager Costsave had seen. Maybe, under a bit of pressure, she was the same as all the other bosses. Ant raised his eyebrows at Bea and shambled out of the room, muttering under his breath, 'Happy, happy.'

George left the room rather abruptly and the task force members regrouped, huddled together and shuffled forward, like a little flock of sheep, a tactic that, as it turned out, didn't protect them at all from another tongue-lashing. This time it was Neville and he did not hold back.

'I've got to say, I'm extremely disappointed in you. Apart from Dot's rather grand plans for the Ladies' facilities, I haven't seen any progress at all from the task force.'

Tyler put his hand up, but Neville shook his head. 'No,' he said, sharply, 'I don't want to hear your excuses. We will be under the spotlight soon, and we will be found wanting, because you have simply not put the effort in. I don't know why you volunteered in the first place when you clearly weren't committed.'

Tyler put his hand back down by his side, but Bob was made of sterner stuff.

'Wait a minute, Neville. I don't think that's entirely fair . . .'

'Oh, you don't, do you?' said Neville, his voice rising in pitch. 'Well, thank you for that opinion, Bob, but none of you, not one, seems to appreciate the urgency of this. There's still so much to do and—'

'. . . so little time,' muttered Dot.

Neville homed in on her like a heat-seeking missile.

'What was that, Dot? Did you have something to say?'

Dot blinked rapidly and started to blush, taken aback at his reaction to a very mild remark.

'No, Neville. It was nothing.'

'I think it was something. Do you want to repeat it?'

'Honestly, it's not worth it. It was just a throwaway thing. Can we move on?'

'I don't think we can. I'm waiting for you to tell me what you said.' His words were those of a bullying teacher. His tone was close to a piccolo. The effect was quite unnerving, and Bob wasn't having it.

'Now, wait a minute. You can't talk to Dot like that,' he said, his voice, in contrast to Neville's, oozing calm authority. Everyone looked at him, sensing that something spectacular was about to happen. Bea wished that Ant was there to see it.

'Dot is an employee here, Bob. I am her manager.'

'You could be good King Charles himself for all I care, Neville. You can't talk to Dot like that. You need to apologise.'

Neville's pasty face was mottled with pink spots now. 'I most certainly won't,' he said.

There was a pause, during which everyone in the room seemed to be holding their breath. Was there going to be a punch up? There was no doubt in anyone's mind over who would win in a fight between Bob and Neville.

Neville stared at Bob. Bob stared at Neville.

Then Bob said, with an admirable display of dignity, 'In that case, you can stick your task force where the sun don't shine. I'm going back to work. Anyone else with me?'

He looked at the others. As his eyes met Bea's, she felt herself nodding in agreement. Some things were worth taking a stand for.

'Me too,' she said.

'And me,' said Dot, taking hold of Bob's arm.

Tyler looked torn. It was a lot for the most junior member of the staff to have to make a choice like this so early in his Costsave career and no one would have blamed him if he didn't want to step out of line. He chose solidarity. 'I'm with everyone else,' he said, and Bea felt a ripple of pride.

They all filed out of the room.

'No, wait!' They could hear Neville calling after them, but it was too late. Things had gone too far. 'Come back! You can't do that! You can't—!'

CHAPTER THIRTY-FOUR

'You know I can fight my own battles,' said Dot, at the top of the stairs. Bea wondered if she was about to tell Bob off. She really hoped not and she noticed that Dot was still holding Bob's arm, which was a good sign. 'But the way you handled that was . . . magnificent.' Dot stood on tiptoe and planted a big kiss on the side of Bob's face, leaving a beautiful scarlet impression of her lips on his skin.

'Hey, steady,' said Bob, but he was beaming with pride. 'He was out of order, and he knew it.'

'He was, wasn't he? Quite nasty, really. It rather upset me.'

'Are you all right to work?' said Bob.

'Oh yes, I'm fine. I think I might rather enjoy it today. It's nice knowing someone's got your back.' She fluttered her eyelashes at Bob, who was looking extremely pleased with himself.

'I think you need to wash your face, Bob. You've got a little bit of lipstick—' Bea held her finger up to her own cheek to indicate where he needed to clean.

'Spoilsport,' said Dot. 'I was hoping he'd keep that all morning. Give the customers something to smile at.'

Bob peeled off to visit the men's washroom, while the others trooped downstairs.

'What happens now?' said Tyler, nervously.

'We just keep calm and carry on,' said Bea. 'And wait and see what happens. They can't host a visit like this without staff cooperation. It's a non-starter.'

'Does that mean it's off? My mum will be ever so disappointed.'

'They won't call it off, but somebody will have to eat a large slice of humble pie. It'll be interesting to see how long it takes him.'

'Will we get in trouble?'

Bea remembered her first shifts at Costsave. She'd started there as a Saturday girl, eager to please, desperate not to make any mistakes. Dot had soon taken her under her wing.

'Absolutely not,' she said. 'The only person in trouble this morning is Neville. I imagine he's trying to explain the situation to George as we speak. I don't envy him, because she was in a mood, too, today. Let's leave them to it and have a bit of a laugh today. Are you back in stores?'

'Yeah, helping Ant.'

'Nice. See you at break time.'

She and Dot settled down at their tills and prepared to face their public. It was a quieter than usual Monday, and Bea had plenty of time to keep an eye out for Neville on his way to the Customer Service desk, but he didn't appear. Instead, George herself turned up on the shop floor. Bea could see her walking along the back of the store and then pausing at the meat counter.

'Uh-oh,' she said to Dot. 'Bob's got a visitor.'

Dot swivelled her chair and leaned to one side so she could see down the aisle to the far end.

'He hasn't done anything wrong, as far as I can see. If George disciplines him for this, I think we should take action.'

'What? Strike?'

'If it comes to it, yes.'

'I'm up for it,' said Bea, 'and I reckon most people would be, too.'

After a few minutes, George came down the frozen food aisle. She then walked along the row of checkouts, having a word with everyone as she passed, but stopping when she got to Bea and Dot. Bea had a customer with her and, after giving George a brief smile, carried on processing their shopping, but Dot was unoccupied.

'I understand that the task force meeting didn't go well this morning,' said George. 'I've had a word with Bob and told him I'll chair tomorrow's meeting. I think Neville could do with the extra support.'

'What did Bob say?'

Bea glanced across and could see George tidying an already tidy heap of plastic carrier bags. Dot was twirling one way and then the other on her chair.

'He said, um, well he said that he wouldn't be there. He'd resigned from the task force.'

'We all have,' said Dot. 'It's a task force of two, now, as far as I can see. You and Neville.'

George issued a nervous laugh. 'Well, obviously, feelings have been hurt and I understand that this is extra work for everyone. I'm sure things will seem better in the morning, though, and you will all remember what an absolute honour it is to have a visitor like this. I'm sure you will all rally round.'

Dot stopped twirling.

'We will not be rallying round, as you put it, unless there is an apology for the unacceptable behaviour from management today.'

'A few cross words . . .'

'It felt like bullying,' said Dot. 'That's what it felt like.'

Bea stopped beeping shopping and looked round. George's face was a picture, as if she'd just been slapped.

'That's a very serious accusation. Do you want to make an official complaint?'

'No, not at present, but I do want an apology. That's my bottom line. No apology, no task force.'

'I see.'

George replaced the heap of plastic bags onto Dot's packing area with such force that they made a resounding smack. With that, she turned on her heel and marched to the Customer Service desk, which was where she stayed for the next hour.

Bea and Dot felt like they were working under a spotlight. Whenever they glanced in her direction, George was watching them. It was uncomfortable and unnerving.

'I might use the loo, then have my break outside,' said Bea. 'I could do with a bit of fresh air.'

'Agreed,' said Dot. 'Who'd have thought a royal visit could cause so much trouble? Ridiculous.'

It was still over an hour until break time, though. The morning was passing so slowly it felt like the clock was going backwards. Just after ten, a police car drew up outside. Tom and a uniformed officer walked into the store and had a word with George, then all three approached the checkouts.

'Now what?' muttered Dot. 'A little tiff at work isn't a police matter, is it?'

But it wasn't Dot they were heading for. They all stopped at checkout number six and George said, 'Bea, can you log out, please? These officers need a word. You can use my office.'

Everyone was so solemn. Bea's first thought was that something had happened to Queenie.

'What is it?' she said, searching Tom's face. 'Is it my mum? Is she all right?'

'It's nothing to do with your mum, Bea. We need to talk about Evan. We can do it here, or you can come down to the station. Your choice.'

'What are you talking about?'

'Not here, Bea. This is serious. We have reason to believe that you know where he is.'

CHAPTER THIRTY-FIVE

It was all getting a bit much for Ant. He liked covering for Dean in the stores and Tyler was a very willing workmate, but, if anything, he was over-keen, always asking questions and wanting Ant to find him something to do. He hadn't yet got the hang of enjoying the rhythms of the working day, including the art of just chilling out when things weren't busy. Ant decided that if he wasn't going to get snappy with Tyler, he needed some time, just him on his own, with a cigarette and a bit of peace and quiet.

'Listen,' he said. 'I'm just going to make sure the recycling's ready for this afternoon's collection.'

'Shall I come?' Tyler was already on his feet.

'No, I need you to stay here and . . .' he struggled to think of something to occupy his protégé, '. . . tidy up the unpacking area. We don't want to give anyone an excuse to have a go at us, do we?'

'Okay.'

'I won't be long.'

It was a bit like leaving a puppy at home for the first time. Ant could feel Tyler's eyes boring into him as he walked out of the stores and into the yard. He couldn't face seeing his sad little face, so he didn't turn round.

'He'll be fine,' he muttered to himself, half-expecting to hear the patter of feet catching up with him.

The recycling area was one of his favourite hidden spots. It was busier during peak shelf stacking hours, but apart from that, it was only really the stores staff that came here. As he crossed the yard, he noticed that the air was a couple of degrees warmer than over the past few days. No rain, either. He looked up at the grey sky and watched a pigeon fly overhead. Freedom, he thought, as it flapped over the boundary wall and headed for St. Swithin's church tower. It's all relative, though, and just now, a fag break and a quiet five minutes would do just nicely.

Ant's heart sank when he saw a figure sitting on the ground by the big metal cage that contained Costsave's cardboard for recycling. He'd have to find somewhere else now, maybe the trolley park at the far end of the forecourt. Then he looked a little harder. They were leaning forward, head resting on their bent knees and arms wrapped round them. In fact, they were curled up pretty tightly, Ant realised, and gently rocking backwards and forwards. He could hear little keening noises like a grizzling child.

With a shock, he realised it was Neville. Knowing he hadn't been spotted yet, Ant considered turning around swiftly and walking in the opposite direction, but the poor guy was obviously in distress, so instead Ant approached him cautiously.

'Um, Neville? Are you all right?'

Neville didn't respond directly, but tightened his grip around his legs, making himself into the smallest ball possible, as if he wanted to disappear.

Ant crouched down next to him.

'What's wrong, Neville? Are you hurt?'

Gossip about the task force boycott had reached the stores within a few minutes of it happening, but Ant didn't put two and two together. Or, at least, he considered it, but didn't think anyone would get that upset about a silly workplace argument. It must be something else. Maybe bad news about Carol or one of the kids.

He hesitated, then put his hand gently on Neville's back.

'What's happened? Can I fetch someone? George or someone else?'

This finally got a reaction. 'Nooo!' Neville wailed, his voice muffled by his own arms. 'I don't want to see anyone. Leave me alone!'

Ant removed his hand, but said, 'I'm not leaving you like this. If you don't want to talk, I'll just sit with you till you feel a bit better.'

He perched on the bottom edge of the cage opening and stretched his legs out. He badly wanted to have a smoke, but he knew Neville disapproved, so he just sat quietly and waited, turning his lighter over and over in his hands. It took two or three uncomfortable minutes until Neville stopped crying and loosened his grip around his legs slightly.

'That's it,' said Ant. 'Do you want to sit up a bit, take a few deep breaths?'

Still not speaking, Neville unwound a little more. His face was streaked with tears and snot. He made no attempt to wipe either away.

'Here,' said Ant, handing him a crumpled but clean tissue.

Neville took it and dabbed at his face, then blew his nose.

'Do you want tell me about it?' said Ant. 'I mean, you don't have to, if you don't want to.'

Neville's chin wobbled.

'I can't,' he said.

'Can't tell me?'

'Can't go on.'

The wobble was quite violent now and the little muscles either side of his mouth were twitching. Ant's hand went out again and he gently rubbed Neville's back.

'I'm sorry,' he said. 'I'm sorry you feel like that.'

'I mean it.' Neville was staring at the ground. 'I can't do it anymore.'

'Maybe it's not as bad as you think. Maybe I can help. What's happened?'

Neville pressed his thin lips together, suppressing another flood of tears. Ant waited again. He heard a noise and saw George appearing in the door to the stores. Her face brightened as she realised who was sitting there and started to walk towards them. Ant put his finger to his lips and then flapped his hand away from him, indicating that she should leave them to it. He winced inside, realising he'd just dismissed the boss of the whole store, but George obviously understood the delicacy of the situation. She nodded, turned round and retreated back inside.

'Who was that?' said Neville, catching the movement as George disappeared.

'Just Tyler.'

'Young Tyler? I think he might do rather well here, if he applies himself.'

This was more like the Neville Ant knew.

'Yeah, he's doing all right. He's bright, too. Perhaps he'll go into management, like you.'

Ant wondered if it was too soon to turn the conversation back to Neville, but it seemed he'd hit just the right note.

'This is where I started,' Neville said. 'In the stores. Twenty years ago.'

'Did you? I never knew that.'

'It was a chap named Alf in charge then. Bit of a tyrant. Old school. I didn't want to go back after the first day, but I did.'

'That's just like me. I nearly didn't come back, but here I am. Nowhere better to go, I suppose.'

Neville managed a watery smile. 'Don't do yourself down, Ant. You're an important part of the team now.'

Ant snorted. 'Hardly. Anyone can round up trolleys or lug cardboard about.'

'But not everyone is as keen to learn as you. Not everyone can get on with people, get the best out of them. Take young Tyler. He's doing well because you've been showing him the ropes. Don't think I haven't noticed.'

Ant felt a warm glow inside, the same feeling he got now when he managed to read something new.

'Thanks, Neville. I appreciate it. I'm so used to being told I'm useless. At school and that.'

'You are very far from useless, Anthony.'

'Okay, I'm blushing now. We'd better stop before I can't get my head back through the door. Talking of which, do you want to go back in?'

Neville's body immediately tensed up. His shoulders hunched and held onto his knees again.

'I can't. I don't think I can ever go back in, Ant. It's over.'

'But you love it here! You know this place inside and out. To a lot of people you *are* Costsave.'

'To use your word, "hardly".' It sounded bitter coming from Neville's mouth. 'I know what you all think about me, how you laugh about me behind my back.'

It was true. He was often the butt of jokes in the staff room, but, Ant thought, it wasn't malicious. It was the sort of everyday banter that made work bearable, enjoyable even. He'd never really thought of it from Neville's point of view.

'We all rate you, Neville. We might have a bit of a laugh about the rules and regulations, but it's harmless. You're like the glue that holds us together. This place would fall apart without you.'

'Well,' Neville sniffed. 'you're about to find out if that's true or not.'

'Oh, come on. We need you. With the King coming and everything, Costsave needs you. The country needs you.'

'You're doing it again, laughing at me.'

Ant hadn't meant his comments to be mocking at all. He was rather stricken that Neville had taken them like that.

'Neville, I wasn't laughing at you. I was just trying to be funny, but Costsave does need you.'

It was too late, though. Neville had plunged back into despair. His voice was rising as he fought back tears.

'The royal visit is going to be a disaster. And no one will help me because I shouted at Dot, and I didn't mean to, but nobody understands how important it is and everyone treats everything as a joke and I'm the biggest joke of all and everyone hates me . . .'

He buried his face again and his shoulders shook.

CHAPTER THIRTY-SIX

'Tom, what's all this about?' said Bea. She was sitting in George's office and Tom and the other officer, PC Watkins, were on the opposite side of the desk.

'It's Detective Constable Barnes,' said Tom, quickly, as his colleague looked rapidly from him to Bea and back again. 'This is a serious matter, Bea.'

'In that case, it's Miss Jordan, and you'd better give me a clue why you are here, as I haven't the foggiest.'

Tom sighed and produced a couple of pages of A4 paper.

'We have an arrest warrant for—' Bea's heart skipped a beat. For her? For helping Evan? — 'for Evan Edwards and I think you are in contact with him.'

'No,' said Bea, which at that particular moment was true. Right here, right now, she wasn't in contact with him. In fact, she hadn't heard from him for thirty-six hours or so.

'Bea. Come on. These are Evan's phone records and this is your mobile phone number.' Bea glanced up at him. He was very familiar with that number, wasn't he? He met her eyes and didn't flinch. Was he being professional or just cold? Maybe both. 'He rang you here and here and here,' he said, his finger pointing to various points on the page.

Bea didn't need to see the printout. She sat back in her chair, which creaked ominously as she shifted position.

'Yes, okay. I've been in contact with him, but I never knew where he was, and I don't know where he is now.'

'You'd better tell us exactly what you do know, Bea, Miss Jordan.'

Bea told them a potted version of her phone calls with Evan. She didn't include her early morning mission to the Rugby Club car park.

'The thing is,' she said, 'he spoke to me just after he'd come back to work after chasing Harley. He told me all about it. Evan said he rugby-tackled Harley to the ground, but that he was okay after that. He was sitting up and talking. He told Evan that he hadn't nicked — stolen — anything, and Evan believed him, felt sorry for him, actually. He let him go.'

Tom was looking past her as she was talking, not paying full attention.

'We interviewed Evan and he gave us an account.'

'The same as that?'

'That's police business, Bea.'

'Miss Jordan.' He twitched his face with irritation. 'But you still want to arrest him?'

'We do. And we will. With or without your help. And I need to warn you that obstructing the course of justice is an offence.'

'Fair enough,' said Bea. 'Are we done now?'

She headed straight to the Ladies' washroom, passing George in the corridor. She shut herself into a cubicle and sat down. Despite her bravado, she was shaking like a leaf.

CHAPTER THIRTY-SEVEN

When Bea emerged from the Ladies' she bumped into Ant.

'Not break time yet, is it?' she said, checking her watch.

'No, I'm going to see George.'

Bea's eyebrows shot up. 'Caught smoking behind the bike shed again? Need some *Kingsleigh Bugles* to tuck down the back of your trousers?'

There wasn't a glimmer of a smile from Ant, which brought her up short.

'She might have still have the cops with her,' she said. 'I've just had a grilling.'

Now it was Ant's turn to be surprised.

'Yeah? What was that about?'

Bea shrugged. 'I'll tell you later. Catch up at break time?'

Wondering about Ant's trip to the management suite helped to take Bea's mind off Evan and her brush with the law, as she walked back to checkout six. She was aware of Dot watching her approach.

'You okay?' Dot asked, as she sat down and logged onto her till.

'Yeah. They've been monitoring Evan's phone and I texted him.'

Dot's mouth formed a little 'o'.

'Don't tell your mum,' Dot said. 'She'll go postal.'

'Good point.'

Bea resolved to keep Queenie in the dark about the interview. When she got home tonight, though, she'd google 'obstructing the course of justice' and see how much trouble she was really in.

She removed the *Checkout Closed* sign from her conveyor belt and smiled as a customer approached. Her face froze as she realised it was Patsy Creech. Dot had clocked her, too. She swivelled round in her chair and started to give her packing area a quick spray and wipe down.

'Are you open?' Patsy said. Bea nodded and Patsy started putting the few bits and bobs she had in her wire basket onto the belt. Bea didn't want to stare at her but couldn't help sneaking a peek as she started to beep her shopping through. At first glance, she looked exactly as she had the last time she was here — blonde hair held in a messy up-do by a tortoiseshell claw, gold hoops dangling from her earlobes, leather jacket over a black T-shirt. Her face was different, though. She was wearing less make-up for a start, and her skin was dull, the lines around her eyes and mouth more noticeable. Frankly, she looked ten years older. The past few days had taken their toll.

Bea's heart felt like it was breaking for her. How on earth does anyone cope with losing a child? She wanted to say something, show that she cared, but was desperate not to put her foot in it. Maybe the woman had come here for a bit of normality and wouldn't want sympathy from a stranger. It wasn't like her to be tongue-tied with a customer, but the more she tried to think of something to say, the harder it became.

The next item was a family pack of Crunchies. 'Chocolate,' she said. 'I read somewhere that Yoko Ono started eating chocolate after John Lennon . . .' She stopped, unable to say the 'd' word, and realising that she'd probably picked an awful thing to say anyway.

'Crunchies,' said Patsy, staring at the packet. 'I didn't even know I'd put them in my basket. They are — *were* — Harley's favourite.'

'Oh god, I'm so sorry,' Bea said. 'Do you want me to put them back?'

Patsy blinked hard, then looked at Bea. 'No, I'll keep them. The boys will eat them.'

Bea finished ringing the shopping through. Patsy paid with cash as usual. As Bea handed her the change, she said, 'I'm sorry for my clumsiness. I just wanted to say that we're all so, so sorry for your loss. Everyone here.'

Out of the corner of her eye, she noticed Dot turning round, flashing a sympathetic look.

'Thank you,' Patsy said. She picked up her carrier bag and walked towards the exit. Bea faced Dot and rolled her eyes.

'Bloody hell, Dot, talk about awkward. Be honest, did I make a complete tit of myself?'

'No, love. You were fine. It's better to say something rather than nothing, even if it's the wrong thing.'

'Was it the wrong thing?'

'Well, the John Lennon stuff perhaps wasn't the best, but the rest of it was lovely.'

Bea leaned forward and buried her face in her hands for a few seconds, groaning, until Dot nudged her — 'Customer, doll.' — and Bea had no alternative but to sit up, take a deep breath and plaster a smile on her face. The smile soon turned genuine when she saw that it was Charles, with his normal purchases of a meat pie, a sliced white loaf and two tins of dog food. Although he had slowed down a lot since his last spell in hospital and was using a stick, he still managed to have a walk to Costsave most days and trundle his shopping home in his bag on wheels.

'Hello, Charles,' Bea said. 'How was Goldie yesterday? I hope we didn't walk her too far on Saturday.'

'She's fine, Bea, but she did sleep a lot. I let her out to do her business, but she didn't want a walk. She's like me, starting to feel her age, I'm afraid.'

'Age? I thought you told me you were twenty-one! Have you been fibbing to me?'

'Twenty-one times four.' Charles winked at her. 'Something like that, anyway. I'm not sure what Goldie is in dog years — she'll be thirteen in a couple of months.'

'Aw, give her a little fuss from me. I'll keep it shorter next time, spare her legs.'

'She loved it, Bea. She always likes seeing you.' He took hold of the walking stick, which he had leaned against the side of the checkout, and grasped the handle of his little trolley. 'Bye, love. See you tomorrow.'

'Bye, Charles. Take it steady.'

As she watched him make his slow, slightly unsteady way out, she noticed that the Customer Service desk was unattended. On one level, it was a blessed relief not to have Neville breathing down their necks, like usual. On the other hand, it was rather eerie to see the desk empty. It was an unsettling reminder that all was not well either at Costsave or Kingsleigh in general.

This latest development wasn't going down well with customers. Every few minutes someone would stand near the desk, looking around and wondering whether to stay there or not. Whenever she spotted someone, Bea would beckon them over and try to help with their queries, but it wasn't easy fitting this in alongside dealing with her own customers.

When Dot went on her break, Bea was left in splendid isolation, battling a continuous influx of shopping, queries and complaints.

'It's a bit nuts today,' she told Dot when she got back. 'I'll call in at the office on my way to the staff room and ask George to come down, shall I?'

'Why don't you use the tannoy?' said Dot, with a bit of a twinkle in her eye.

'Ooh, do you think I should?'

The tannoy system was very much Neville's domain. In fact, Bea couldn't remember the last time anyone else had been allowed to touch it.

'Go on,' said Dot. 'I dare you.'

'All right.' Bea logged out of her till and approached the Customer Service desk with caution. The tannoy looked very straightforward. It was just a question of pressing a button and leaning into the microphone. She glanced across at Dot, who gave her two thumbs up, then pressed the button.

'Member of staff to Customer Service desk.' Her voice boomed out from loudspeakers around the store. Did she really sound like that? She always fondly imagined that her voice was similar to the fragrant Fiona Bruce, but the person whose dulcet tones were amplified uncomfortably now was more like a Wurzel on speak-like-a-pirate day. 'Member of staff to Customer Service desk. Please. That's it. Thank you.'

She released the button and scuttled back to Dot, who gave her a short round of applause.

'Beautifully done,' Dot said. 'You're a natural.'

'I don't think so. I quite like the feeling of power, though. I'm off for my break now. Hope it's not too bad while I'm away.'

As Bea reached for the 'Staff Only' door at the back of the store, it opened and George appeared.

'Oh, Bea,' she said. 'Is there a problem?'

'It's just got really busy, George, and there have been customers not knowing where to go with their queries. I've been fielding them as best I can, but Dot's more or less on her own down there now.'

'Right, right. Okay. Thank you.' George pulled down the hem of her jacket and marched towards the front of the shop. Bea set off up the stairs, feeling rather pleased that she seemed to have got away with her foray into the word of public broadcasting.

She made two mugs of tea and was just adding sugar to Ant's when he appeared. The staff room wasn't busy and they decided to stay inside, finding a corner where the two of them could talk without being overheard. They both launched in together.

'What a morning—'

'Bloody hell—'

Then they laughed.

'Ladies first,' Ant said, sweeping his hand forward and bowing.

She checked around the room first. Kirsty was eating a doughnut at the far end of the sofa and Sidney, Bob's new apprentice butcher, had just put the kettle on again, providing a nice barrier of sound. She leaned forward and spoke in a low voice anyway.

'The police have got access to Evan's phone records.'

'Oh, shit.'

'Yeah.'

'What did you tell them?'

'That we'd been talking, that I didn't know where he is. The thing is, that phone's hot now, isn't it? If I try to contact him again, I'll put him at risk.'

Ant nodded and took a big slurp of tea. 'But he might still contact you. He won't know he can be traced.'

'Exactly and I can't warn him. I just have to hope that he's already thought of that. I haven't heard from him for ages.'

'He's on his own, then. Unless he hands himself in or someone finds him.' Ant drained his mug of tea. 'Are you in trouble?'

'I don't know. Maybe. Tom was really snotty, going on about obstructing justice, blah, blah, blah.'

'That's probably just Tom being Tom. I wouldn't worry about it. If the worst comes to the worst, I'm used to prison visiting anyway.'

Bea picked up a nearby copy of the *Kingsleigh Bugle* and batted his arm with it and he howled in fake agony, making Kirsty look up from her doughnut.

'Stop it, you monster!' Ant said, taking the newspaper away from Bea.

'Anyway,' Bea said, 'what have you been up to? Why did George call you in?'

'She didn't. I went to see her.' Now it was Ant's turn to lower his voice. 'I found Neville out in the yard, having a sort of breakdown.'

Bea felt a pang of guilt.

'You know we all walked out of the meeting this morning, after he was arsey with Dot?'

'Yeah. That's what did it.'

'Oh dear. I'm sure nobody meant to upset him, but he was awful. He's been uptight since this bloody visit was announced.'

'I know. I think the boycott was the straw that broke the camel's back. There's a lot of stuff going on under that rather crusty surface. He's more sensitive than any of us think.'

Bea's guilt was more than a pang now. He had been out of order earlier, but, if she'd got time before she had to go back to her checkout, she would try and find him and smooth things over.

'Where is he now? The Customer Service desk has been empty all morning.'

'George sent him home.'

'Blimey. I don't think he's ever had a sick day. He's just always here.'

'It's serious, Bea. I don't want to say anything I shouldn't, but he was pretty broken.'

They lapsed into silence.

'Patsy Creech was in today as well. She came to my checkout. What do you say to someone who's lost a child?'

Ant shook his head. 'I dunno. What did you say?'

'I commented on her Crunchie bars and she said they were Harley's favourite.'

'Fuck.'

'I know.'

An air of gloom seemed to hang in the room like a dark cloud. So many bad things had already happened and it wasn't even lunchtime yet. Bea felt at a bit of a loss how to make things better, let alone keep up a cheerful appearance to the end of the day.

'We broke Neville,' she said. 'I guess we'll have to try and fix him, but I'm not sure how.'

'And we need to find Evan, and work out what happened to Harley, before you get locked up for obstruction.'

'Where on earth do we start?' said Bea.

Ant looked across the room. Kirsty was licking the sugar off her fingers. Next to her on the sofa was a multipack containing at least four more doughnuts.

'We're going to need fuel. Brain food,' he said, decisively and leapt to his feet. 'Here, Kirsty,' he called out. 'Are any of those doughnuts going spare?'

CHAPTER THIRTY-EIGHT

The afternoon shift was much less eventful than the morning one. News of Neville's absence spread quickly. Most people were shocked and sympathetic. It was true that Neville was a figure of fun among the workforce, but he was admired, too. Everyone knew it was largely down to him that the shop floor ran like clockwork, and he could be relied upon to treat staff fairly, if a little firmly. You always knew where you stood with Neville.

Dot was quite upset when she heard. 'Poor Neville,' she said. 'I mean, he was being a bully, and Bob was rather magnificent standing up for me, but I never wanted it to come to this.'

'I know,' said Bea. 'I feel pretty awful now. Perhaps the mass walkout was a bit over the top.'

'Has anyone rung him?'

'Too soon, I think. Ant'll see him this evening, anyway. He can let us all know how he is. In the meantime, we can just carry on with Operation Windsor, do everything we can, so that it's all under control.'

'Yes,' said Dot. 'That's the right thing to do. Why don't we have a task force meeting in the pub this evening? Get all our ducks in a row.'

'Good idea. We can be a guerrilla task force until Neville is back. Makes it a bit more fun. Although perhaps we should tell George what we're doing.'

'Agreed.'

'I could rope Ant in, too. He'll do it for Neville now.'

Dot looked round the store. 'There's a bit of a lull, so I'll whizz round and see if everyone can come.'

Bea watched as Dot bustled off to talk to people, her smart heels clacking on the floor as she headed for the meat counter. It amazed her that Dot could wear shoes like that all day. She herself had posh trainers or comfortable flats for work.

When Dot came back, she reported that everyone was on board. Bob had been the most reluctant to join but had given in after a bit of arm-twisting.

The rest of the day passed peacefully enough, but Bea found the last hour dragging terribly, her spirits only lifting when she spotted the evening shift people approaching the store and knew that it was nearly time to go home. She really felt like heading straight back and hibernating on the sofa until bedtime, but Dot was fired up about their 'secret' meeting now. Perhaps it could be all done and dusted in half an hour or so, then she could enjoy tea and telly with Queenie.

The informal task force had agreed to meet in the Ship at six. Ant and Bea set off first. Bob was taking his time 'showing Sidney how to put the butchery to bed' and Dot lingered to make sure that he didn't change his mind about joining them.

As they crossed the car park, Bea saw someone lurking in a corner, away from any of the streetlights. It was Scout Creech.

'Ant, look,' she said. 'I think she's waiting for me. Do you mind going ahead?'

'Sure. I'll wait round the corner, shall I? I'll see if the pie shop's still open. They might have marked down today's unsold goodies.'

He sprinted away, and Bea approached Scout, who was wearing the dark clothes and hoodie she'd first seen her in.

'Hello,' Bea said. 'Nice to see you.'

'Hi,' said Scout, looking nervously around.

'Were you waiting for me?'

'Um, yeah.'

'Do you want to go somewhere and talk?'

The girl shook her head. 'No, I don't want anyone to see us. It's not a good idea. Can we talk here?'

'Of course. What's on your mind?'

'Harley,' she said.

'It must be so hard. He wasn't much older than you, was he? Were you close?'

Scout nodded and swallowed hard. 'Yeah. And the thing is, the whole thing — him being in Costsave, getting chased, ending up . . . you know — that was all my fault.'

CHAPTER THIRTY-NINE

Scout wasn't crying. She was solemn and deadly serious.

'I'm sure that's not true,' said Bea. 'Why do you think it is?'

'It's awkward.'

Bea shrugged and said, 'You don't have to tell me,' while silently praying that Scout would, in fact, spill the beans.

'It would be good to tell someone,' the girl said. 'The thing is, I asked Harley to go and get something for me. I was too embarrassed to get it myself and he was just the nicest, kindest brother. He said he'd do it. Neither of us had any money. Mum doesn't pay us to work at the diner — it's just something we're expected to do. So, he was going to nick it. The thing.'

'The thing being a pregnancy test?' said Bea.

Scout blushed. 'Yes.'

'He dropped it when he ran off. I found it on the floor. If it helps, I don't think anyone else knows. I just put it back.'

Scout looked at her then. 'It was silly. I was panicking. There was no need. My period started a couple of days ago. I wasn't ever pregnant. I don't think me and my boyfriend even did it properly.'

Bea had an overwhelming urge to hug her. She looked so small and young standing there, so full of confusion, embarrassment and remorse.

'It's not silly to get in a panic like that. We've all done it. Most of us, anyway.'

'Really?'

'Really.'

'I wish I'd had someone like you to talk to before. I've only got brothers. And Mum, well, I couldn't talk to her about it. She says I'm too young for boys—' Bea wondered if Patsy had a point — 'and she didn't know I'd been seeing someone. It was a secret. Only Harley knew. He was really nice about it, though.'

Her voice had been monotone, almost numb, but now it wobbled as she fought back tears.

'If I hadn't asked him, he'd never have been there. He'd never have got chased by that Evan . . .'

'Scout, it's not your fault. If it helps, then I'm almost a hundred per cent sure that Evan didn't kill him. He chased him, but he didn't hurt him. Nothing more than a scraped knee, anyway.'

Scout shook her head. 'He did, Bea. Everyone says he did. He killed him, but it was because of me.'

She looked past Bea and frowned. Bea turned round and saw Tyler walking past the thinning ranks of parked cars on his way to the Ship. When Tyler spotted Bea, he waved, but as he realised there was someone with her, his step faltered.

'Shall I tell him to go away? It's only Tyler. He's started recently. He's a nice lad.'

'No, it's all right. I know him from school. I'd better go home, before I'm missed. I said I was going to netball club.'

Tyler came and stood a couple of metres away.

'Hi, Tyler,' said Bea.

'Hi.'

'Hello,' said Scout. 'I'm just going.'

Tyler shuffled his feet a bit and Bea sensed he was someone else who didn't know what to say to the recently bereaved. None of this was easy. The three of them left the car park together, Tyler on one side of Bea, Scout on the other. They parted ways in the High Street, with Scout turning left to head towards the Bristol Road and Bea and Tyler joining Ant, who was sitting at a bus stop, eating a rather greasy looking pasty out of a bag. He got to his feet when he saw them, wolfed down the rest of the pie and lobbed the bag into the nearest bin.

'Everything all right?' he said.

'Yeah, there've been developments,' said Bea. 'I'll tell you later. It's a bit sensitive.'

'Can't you tell me now? Tyler's practically one of the squad now.'

'Don't mind me,' said Tyler. He fished in his pocket and plugged an ear bud into each ear, then fiddled on his phone and gave them the thumbs up.

'Well,' said Bea, 'Scout just told me that Harley had gone into Costsave to nick the thing that I found on the floor.'

Ant pursed his lips and gave a little whistle.

'She's up the duff?'

'Well, no, she isn't, as it happens, but she was worried that she was.'

'So, Eileen was right that she saw him pocketing something, and Evan was right to chase him,' mused Ant.

'Yeah, I guess, except that, from what Eileen said, he'd changed his mind and wasn't going through with it. If she hadn't seen him, then I reckon he would have put it back and none of this would have happened.'

They realised that Tyler was no longer beside them. They looked round and he was a few metres behind them, standing looking at his phone.

'You all right, mate?' said Ant.

'What?' Tyler wrinkled his face, then yanked the buds out of his ears.

'I said, are you all right?'

'Yeah, just got a text from my mum. She doesn't want me to go to the pub. I'd better bail.'

'Okay,' said Bea, 'we'll tell you all about it tomorrow. See you later.'

He raised a hand, turned round and started jogging back the way they'd come.

'When I was little,' said Ant, 'my mum would just open the door and yell when it was time for tea. Now they can reach you anywhere with a text. Funny, innit?'

'That's progress for you,' said Bea. As she was speaking, a low sound in the distance grew to a roar and two motorbikes sped down the High Street.

'Blimey' said Ant, 'I reckon that might be a search party for young Scout. Her brothers out looking for her.'

'Her family seem very . . . protective,' said Bea. 'I hope she's not in trouble.'

'More trouble, you mean?'

'Yeah. It was weird. I'm only five years older than her, but she seemed so young just now. So vulnerable.'

'Mm, I know what you mean. When I was talking with Neville earlier, he called me a mentor to Tyler. Made me feel about a hundred and eight. Do you know what I think?'

'What?'

'When things have settled down, maybe after this royal visit stuff is over and done with, we should go "out out". Like a proper session, get rat-arsed, do something stupid. I don't want to get old before my time, Bea.'

'Just us?'

'You, me, Saggy, even Dean. Anyone who wants to live it large.'

Bea held her hand up and they high fived. 'It's a deal.'

CHAPTER FORTY

'It feels like more fun this way, like we're rebels or something,' said Dot. She and Bob had found the others in the pub, and they were all about to start their unofficial meeting.

'Rebels, secretly planning to make everything shiny for a visit from the King?' said Ant. 'That is the least rebellious thing I've ever heard. And I've gotta say, I'm here for Neville, not the King. Although even that's weird, innit?'

'World's gone mad, Ant,' agreed Bea. 'Can we wait a minute or two, though? There's one more person to come.'

'No,' said Dot, 'we're all here, apart from Tyler.'

'Well, actually, I invited a VIP of my own,' said Bea, feeling rather smug. 'An ace up my sleeve. Someone who will guarantee that the visit will be a success.'

Dot narrowed her eyes. 'What are you up to, Bea?'

'It's a good surprise. I promise.'

Bob looked at his watch. 'Can we just get on with it? I can't stay too long,' he said.

'Why? Where are we going?' said Dot.

'I've got a little job to do, love,' Bob said. 'Mary Widdowson, lives near Charles, was in the shop today. Said she was having trouble with a leaking bathroom tap. She didn't know who to ask for help. Her Colin used to do all that. I said I'd have a look for her.'

'I can come along,' said Dot. 'Have a cuppa with Mary while you work your magic.'

Bob shook his head. 'It might take a while. I think I should actually go and make a start now. Leave you to it here.'

Dot looked at him quizzically as he got to his feet. 'We've literally just got here, Bob.'

'Yes, and I'm still not sure I want to bail Neville out. He crossed a line today.'

'Bob—'

'See you later. Oh, before I go, if we're going to do the VIP thing, then just buy another bloody red carpet. I'm not going to look for it anymore.'

With that final volley, he took a quick swig of his orange juice and then left the empty glass on the bar. Someone was coming in as he was going out and he held the door for them. Bea was delighted to see the new arrival.

'Anna!' she called out. 'Yoohoo! Over here!'

Anna was the office manager at Costsave. She'd been on annual leave for two weeks to help her two new kittens to settle in at home and had missed all the recent drama and excitement.

'Ah,' said Ant, tapping the side of his head. 'Good thinking, Bea.'

'Hello, everyone,' Anna said, coming over to their table. 'Does anyone need a drink?'

'No, we only just got here. Let me get you one, though,' said Bea. 'Sit down. What do you want?'

Bea fetched a vodka and tonic for Anna. 'So, how is kitternity leave going? How are the babies?'

Anna had already got her phone out to show Ant and Dot pictures of the terrible twosome. They were British shorthairs, like her previous cats, and, everyone agreed, completely adorable.

'It's been full on. You have to have eyes in the back of your head. They're lovely, though. Now, you'd better fill me in on what I've been missing . . .'

It took quite a long time to tell her everything that had been going on. They started with Harley and Evan and then moved onto Operation Windsor.

'This is why we really need you,' said Bea. 'We've all been doing our best, but Neville has been antsy about it from the beginning and now he's fallen off the deep end. You're coming back tomorrow, aren't you? Could you take this by the scruff of the neck and sort it out?'

Anna smiled. 'I would love to, as long as George and Neville are happy about it.'

'I think it will take quite a while for Neville to be happy again, but George will bite your hand off if you offer. And we'll all muck in. I can send you the plans so far, if you like.'

'That's okay. Just talk me through it now, then I'll access all the files tomorrow, first thing. I'm sure everything will be fine.'

With Anna on board now, Bea was pretty sure that it would be too. She and Dot outlined where they had got to.

'Well,' Anna said. 'It sounds like you've done really well. It just needs a bit of action now. Depending on budget, we should get the decorators in or buy a job lot of overalls and recruit some volunteers. Whatever happens, we're going to get a nice upgrade to the staff toilets out of this.'

Dot raised her glass. 'I'll drink to that.'

'Seriously, Dot, I love your plans for a restroom spruce-up. I'll get that underway tomorrow. I can order the decorations, bunting, all that stuff, too. Did the red carpet ever turn up?'

'No. Bit of a sore point, but Tyler got a quote for hiring one along with some posts and rope and stuff. It's not that expensive.'

'Tyler Jackson? School leaver? Has he started? I was there when he came in for his interview.'

'Yes, he's doing all right.'

'Thought he would. He seems like the Costsave type.'

Bea nearly spat her mouthful of white wine out. 'What does that mean? The Costsave type?'

'Oh, you know, down to earth, pleasant, not all that ambitious, not too flashy.'

Bea and Dot exchanged looks of faux outrage. 'I take exception to that, young lady!' said Dot.

Anna laughed. 'I'm including myself, Dot! I mean, we're definitely pleasant, aren't we, but I wouldn't say we were flashy. You're more classy, I'd say. Stylish.'

Dot bowed her head in acknowledgement, but Bea was thoughtful. She stared rather gloomily into her glass.

'Jeez,' she said, 'you're right. There *is* a Costsave type. *I'm* a Costsave type. I am, aren't I?'

'It's not a bad thing,' said Anna, worried that she had managed to upset her friend. 'It's great working with people you like. I wouldn't work anywhere else.'

'Yeah, but lacking ambition. That's not good, is it? I'm only twenty. Am I really going to be on checkout six for another forty years?'

'Could be worse, Bea. I'll be outside, rounding up trolleys and wrangling cardboard boxes with my arthritis playing up and my bunions giving me hell,' said Ant.

They all laughed, but Anna's words had lodged in Bea's brain and wouldn't go away. She was happy at Costsave. She loved her colleagues and her customers — well, most of them — but was that all there was?

'Oh dear,' said Anna, seeing Bea lost in thought. 'I'd better get you another drink. White wine again?'

'No, ta,' said Bea, putting her hand over the top of her glass. 'If I have more than one, I'll settle in for the night and I really need a clear head and an early night. I think I'm gonna go now.'

Anna put a hand on her arm. 'Have I upset you? I didn't mean to.'

'No, I'm not upset. You've made me think a bit, that's all.'

'Thinking upsets me,' said Ant. 'I'll have another pint, Anna, if you're buying.'

Bea gathered up her things, happy at least that Operation Windsor was back on track. She said goodnight to everyone and stepped out of the warmth of the pub into the chilly night air. It had felt like a long day, but at least it had ended well. She set off along the road and saw a familiar figure approaching — khaki coat flapping, hood up.

'Oh, hey, Saggy,' Bea said. 'Ant's in the back bar, if you're looking for him.'

Saggy waved at her but didn't stop walking. 'Yeah, he owes me a pint.'

Just for a moment the streetlight caught his face and Bea saw that he had an impressive black eye.

'Woah, mate, that's a bit of shiner. What happened to you?'

'Run into a door, didn't I? Going to get that pint now. See you later.'

Bea didn't believe him for one minute. Saggy wasn't aggressive, but he wasn't one to back down from a fight either. She wondered who the other party was, and whether Saggy had given as good as he got. She trusted that Ant would be able to fill in the details tomorrow. She crossed the road, heading for the alleyway that would take her past the bungalows and towards the rec, but stopped and turned round when she heard Saggy call out to her.

'Hey, Bea,' he shouted. 'You be careful walking home, okay?'

'I'll be all right,' she called back. 'It's only ten minutes.'

'Text me or Ant when you get there, yeah?'

She screwed up her eyes, puzzled at this unexpected concern for her welfare.

'Really?' she said.

'Really. It's a bit scary out there. Keep safe.'

CHAPTER FORTY-ONE

The next morning, the wind and rain of recent days had blown over. It had been a clear, cold night and Bea noticed patches of frost smattering the grass of the rec as she walked across. She wondered if Evan had blankets with him, wherever he was. Was he waking up cold, or had he found someone to take him in, give him sanctuary for the last few days?

She saw a figure lurking on the corner of the High Street, leaning on the wall of the Leisure Centre, smoking a cigarette, and her heart lifted a little. As she approached, Ant tossed his cigarette butt to the ground and trod it into the paving stone.

'Thanks for the text last night,' he said. They started walking down the street together.

'Felt like a bit of a wally sending it, but Saggy made me promise. He was really weird, when I saw him outside the pub, like he was scared or something. I don't believe he ran into a door, do you?'

'No. He wouldn't tell me who'd done it to him, but they put the wind right up him. He doesn't mind a bit of a bundle, but this wasn't the sort of scrap he'd boast about. I reckon someone jumped him.'

'But who would do that?'

Ant laughed. 'Could be any number of people, Bea. I mean, I like him, he's my mate, but he's not everyone's cup of tea, and he does get involved in some dodgy schemes.'

'Why would he warn *me*, though?'

'Did he? Or did he just tell you to take care. He's a nice guy, underneath it all.'

Bea heard the click-clack of some killer heels on the pavement behind them. Suspecting it was Dot, she turned round. Sure enough, Dot was steaming along towards them at an impressive rate of knots, with a face like thunder.

'Morning, Dot. Not getting a lift from Bob today?'

'Morning,' Dot said, grim-faced. 'No, I'm not. And I'll be walking to work from now on.'

Obviously, Bob hadn't stayed the night at Dot's, and their relationship, which had seemed to be on an even keel again, was rocky once more. Ant and Bea exchanged a knowing look.

'Dot, what's happened?' said Bea.

'He's been lying to me and I won't have it.' Her jaw was tense and there was a steely look in her eyes.

'Not Bob, surely . . .'

'Oh, you all think he's "good old Bob", "salt of the earth Bob", "reliable Bob", but when all's said and done, he's just another man, isn't he?' Her voice had a bitter edge to it, not like her usual warm, chatty tone. Bea found it quite upsetting. 'And any of them — *any* — can and will let you down.'

Ant looked offended but bit his tongue. Bea was a little bolder.

'Oh, Dot, come on. Bob thinks the world of you. Why do you think he's lied to you?'

'I don't think. I know. He was going to stay at mine last night, but he didn't come back to the pub and he wasn't home when I got back at half nine. I texted him and he said he was still at Mary's, it had been a long job and he'd go back to his. Fair enough, but he'd normally ring me with something like that, so I rang Mary and she said that he'd done her taps in under an hour. He'd left hers by seven! So where was he?'

'Dot, there could be a perfectly good reason . . .'

'Oh, come on, Bea. Read the room. He was with some other woman. Honestly, I was so upset last night, I couldn't face talking to him. I had another couple of drinks and good cry. Can't believe I'm still crying over men at my age.'

'Dot, I'm so sorry.'

'Yeah. Me too, but this morning I'm not sad about it, I'm effing fuming. Do you mind if I go ahead? I want to get there before he does, make sure my warpaint is up to scratch.'

'Of course. You look amazing, as always, though.'

'Thanks, doll. See you in a min.'

Dot increased her pace and set off towards Costsave so fast she was almost running.

'I wouldn't want to be in Bob's shoes this morning,' said Ant.

'I can't believe it. What is he thinking?' said Bea.

'Dunno. If he is cheating on her, he needs his head examining. I thought he knew a good thing when he had it.' Dot had been the one to end their brief dalliance, just after Ant started at Costsave, and Bea often wondered if he still held a bit of a candle for her.

They had reached the car park now. As they went to cross over to the staff door, a car slowed and then stopped to let them cross and the driver, Bob, waved at them.

'Should we warn him?' said Bea, waving back with a fixed, fake grin on her face.

'No, he knows what he's done.' Ant narrowed his eyes. 'He'll soon find out how Dot feels about it.'

The grin faded on Bea's face. It felt like it was going to be another difficult day.

'Are we seeing Neville today?' she said.

Ant shook his head.

'Carol says he's got "nervous exhaustion" and is staying at home. Apparently, he came home yesterday afternoon and went straight to bed. I didn't even see him this morning and he usually gets up at half-past six every day for a bit of a morning pray and his exercises.'

'Exercises?'

'Callous-something. He does them in his work trousers and a white vest. It's quite something. Anyway, him and his vest stayed in bed this morning.'

'So you didn't get a chance to tell him Operation Windsor was back on and that Anna was in today and was going to help get everything shipshape?'

Ant shook his head. They were nearly at the staff door. 'Tell you who else is back. Look,' said Bea, spotting the distinctive figure of Dean scuttling along the other side of the car park.

'Bet he can't take any more of Eileen. He's come to work for a rest,' said Ant, then pulled a face and emitted a noise like a whale exhaling through its blowhole. 'That means I'll be back on trolleys. I quite like it in stores. It's interesting.'

'Ask George if you can stay on.'

'Nah, it's been good just me and Tyler. Don't think I want to be cooped up in there with Dean. He's all right these days, but only in small doses.'

They trooped inside and joined the staff briefing. George dealt only briefly with Neville's absence, concentrating instead on welcoming Anna and Dean back after their absences. She also, as predicted by Ant, reallocated some of the staff roles, and, yes, Ant was back on trolley duty. She asked the members of the task force to stay behind. When the others had left, the atmosphere became rather more edgy. Dot was sending daggers in Bob's direction. Standing at the opposite end of the group, he seemed oblivious. Anna filled Neville's place next to George and gave Bea a surreptitious thumbs up as George started talking.

'Before we start, I want to let you know that I am aware of some . . . um . . . upset yesterday over the royal visit. All I want to say on the matter is that I am glad to see you here this morning, and I am sure that we will all support Neville as our task force leader when he returns.' There was a loud cough from Bob. 'Did you want to add something, Bob?'

'No,' he said, looking uncomfortable, then visibly changed his mind. 'Actually, yes. I believe the staff rules about speaking to colleagues with respect should apply to all members of staff. No exceptions. That's it.' There were murmurs of agreement from most people and a very audible, 'Ha!' from Dot.

'Of course,' said George. 'That should go without saying.'

'Apparently not,' said Bob, 'but I've said it now.'

'Okay, let's move on. Anna will be stepping in for the time being. She has the project plan and I've authorised her as a signatory on the budget for this. Given the timescale, I've asked her to find a local company to undertake the decoration work in the restrooms. We'll also go ahead with the best quote for bunting, and balloons.'

'Does that include a red carpet?' said Bob. 'I think we should stop faffing around and just buy one or hire one.'

'Tyler? I believe you got a quote?' said George.

There was no response from Tyler and now everyone's focus turned to him. He was staring into mid-air, miles away.

'Tyler?' George repeated.

He suddenly came to and looked at George like a baby rabbit in the headlights of a ten-tonne truck.

'Did you get a quote for hiring a red carpet?' she prompted.

'Oh, um, yes.' He quickly checked some notes on his phone. 'It's a hundred and thirty pounds to hire a carpet and some pillars and rope.'

'Let's do that, then,' said George, turning to Anna to make sure she had recorded the decision. 'I'm also happy to announce that the budget will stretch to a small buffet in the staff room to be consumed after the visit, as a thank you to staff.'

The mood lightened instantly. Bea smiled to herself at how easily their favours were bought, but she wasn't immune to such things herself, and felt rather cheered by the idea of everyone relaxing together after what might be a stressful day. It was a nice touch from George.

As soon as the news about the buffet spread through the grapevine, the mood in Costsave brightened. Ant was torn between muttering that a decent pay rise would show a bit more appreciation than a plate of pork pies and plant-based savoury bites and anticipating the sheer volume of nibbles he would be able to hoover up. It might be worth going without lunch that day, he thought.

The general good vibes in the store lasted through the morning. The day unfolded with a steady stream of shoppers, mostly leisurely pensioners taking their time and enjoying a chat at the checkouts, but Bea was aware of gathering storm clouds above Dot's head. She tried to disperse them with a bit of banter but Dot remained tight-lipped and increasingly tense.

At lunchtime, Bea offered to treat her to a cup of tea and a bacon sandwich at the café.

'No, thank you,' said Dot. 'I couldn't face eating meat. It would turn my stomach. Might turn vegan after all this.'

'A cuppa and some toast, then. A little break would do you good.'

Dot pressed her lips together.

'There's only one thing that will do me good, and that's having it out with that one.' She tipped her head towards the meat counter.

'Oh, Dot, not at work. Can you keep a lid on things until this evening?'

'I don't know. I really don't.'

And, it turned out, she couldn't. At lunchtime, the storm clouds well and truly burst.

CHAPTER FORTY-TWO

Dot went for her break a few minutes before Bea, who got bogged down with someone obviously doing 'a big shop', which in their case included two trolleys full to the brim with multipacks of basics, enormous sacks of rice and pasta, and enough toilet roll to meet the personal needs of a small army. Bea didn't notice Bob leaving the meat counter but when she had just taken the payment for the mega-shop and handed over a receipt a bit like a dressmaker's tape measure, she saw Tyler running down the row of checkouts, strictly against Costsave policy.

'Slow down, mate,' she said to him as he screeched to a halt, breathing heavily. 'You'll do yourself a mischief.'

'Bea,' he gasped. 'It's all kicking off in the staff room. You'd better come!'

'Okay, I'm just logging out, anyway,' she replied.

'Can you do it quicker?' He looked so agonised that she signed out and quit her station without the usual tidy up and wipe down. She could do that when she came back.

She followed Tyler as he jogged towards the back of the store. 'What's going on?' she said, struggling to keep up.

'It's Bob and Dot. They're having an awful row.'

As they clattered up the stairs, two at a time, Bea could hear raised voices.

'I did not lie to you,' came Bob's unmistakeable tones. 'I went to Mary's and sorted out her tap, like I told you.'

'Yes, but *then* where did you go?' shouted Dot. 'Come on, Bob. You can tell me. I'm a big girl. Who were you with? What's her name?'

'I'm not seeing another woman, you daft doughnut. I swear on my mother's grave.'

'I don't believe you!'

'Dot! I told you I swore on Mum's grave! Isn't that good enough?'

'No. Tell me where you were.'

Bea reached the door to the staff room. Bob and Dot were standing in the middle a metre or so apart, facing each other like two gunslingers.

'I can't,' said Bob.

'Can't? Won't, more like.' There was no mistaking the disgust in Dot's voice.

'Dot, please. Let's not do this here. Come outside and talk. We could go to the café.'

'I'm not going anywhere with you right now. In fact, I'm not going anywhere with you ever again. It's over, Bob. I'm too old to be messed about.'

Dot turned round and started to walk towards the door. Bob's face bore a look of such devastation that it hurt Bea to see it. Surely, this couldn't be the end.

'Dot!' he called out, his voice breaking. 'Dot, please don't go.'

She faced him again.

'I've got no reason to stay, Bob. Not if you're lying to me.'

'I wasn't lying.' He was obviously wrestling with something. Eventually, he said, 'I did go somewhere else after Mary's. I just can't tell you where.'

Without words, Dot turned and stalked past Bea and out of the room, back ramrod straight, shoulders down, head held high. She headed towards the Ladies' rest room.

Bob stood rooted to the rather stained carpet, and Bea was dismayed to see tears trickling down his face.

'Bob,' she said, 'go after her. Just tell her where you were. I'm sure she doesn't want this to be over any more than you do.'

He wiped his sleeve across his face, which had become red and blotchy in the heat of the argument.

'Shall I?'

'Yes,' she urged.

He, too, walked past her and called down the corridor. Dot, halfway into the Ladies, paused.

'Please,' he said, 'please let me explain. Come outside. Do you want me to beg? Because I will.'

Bea sensed a softening in Dot's expression, only a slight one, but it was there.

'No, I don't want you to beg. I will go outside, and I will listen, but you'd better tell me the truth, Bob, or we're finished. End of.'

Dot was only gone for five minutes. The kettle had boiled but Bea was still dangling her tea bag in a mug when she reappeared, on her own.

'Two sugars?' Bea said, seeing the expression on her face.

Dot nodded grimly.

Bea made a second cup and they took them over to the sofa.

'I guess you two haven't made up, then,' said Bea.

'No, love. We haven't.'

'Did he tell you where he'd been?'

The little muscles in the side of Dot's jaw tensed.

'He told me, but I still don't believe him. He swore me to secrecy, but he said he was up the allotments. I mean, who on earth goes to the allotments in the pitch dark in February? I don't think so. I'm done with him.'

'Dot, please don't be hasty. Did you ask him why he was there?'

'No, I just laughed at him and asked if he expected me to believe that. And that's where we left it. Well, not quite. I told him to collect his things from mine later.'

'Oh, Dot. I'm so sorry.'

'Yeah, me too. I thought . . . no, it's silly.'

'What?'

'I thought he was the One. You know, after all the ups and downs with my Darren, I thought that I could live happily ever after with Bob. I know he's not the most exciting man on the planet, but he's solid and kind and reliable and he treats me — *treated me* — like a princess.' She was blinking back tears now.

'Dot, he *is* all those things and he adores you.'

'But he lied, Bea. And that's a red line with me. That's a dealbreaker. Oh bother, I didn't want to do this again . . .' The tears were flowing now. Bea shuffled up the sofa and put her arm round Dot's shoulders.

'It's okay. Everything's going to be all right,' she said, although she wasn't at all convinced that it would be.

They sat together for a few minutes, Dot gently weeping, dabbing at her face from time to time to try and save her foundation. At one point, Bob appeared in the doorway, took in the situation and fled with a stricken look on his face. Luckily, Dot didn't spot him.

What a mess, Bea thought. She found it hard to believe that it was terminal between them, but it was also difficult to accept that Bob had lied to Dot. It was so out of character. What if he wasn't lying? A while back, Ant had told her that he had spent a few nights in an allotment shed when he was sleeping rough. Could Bob have been up there, looking for Evan, maybe even checking in with him, taking him food?

Dot sat up and took a few deep breaths, then announced that she was going to fix her make-up, ready for the afternoon and headed for the rest room. Bea checked her watch. She still had ten minutes left of her break. She went out into the car park in search of Ant and found him at the side of the store, picking up some rubbish which had gathered at the bottom of the hedge.

'There you are,' she said. 'It's been World War Three upstairs.'

'Dot and Bob?' said Ant.

'Yeah. I think they might actually be splitting up.'

'Damn. That's a real shame.' He straightened up, with a handful of receipts, shopping lists and crisp packets, and started sauntering over to a bin. Bea followed him.

'Ant, when you were sleeping rough, where did you go?'

'I had one night round the back of the changing rooms at school. That was rubbish. I tried the park but, man, that was creepy at night. There were random people and foxes and all sorts. Then I had a few days up the allotments. That wasn't too bad, actually. I found a nice dry shed and got some old potato sacks and made myself comfy.'

Rubbish dealt with, they leant against the wall and Ant lit a cigarette.

'The allotments,' said Bea. 'I think that's where Evan is. I also think Bob knows where he is and has been looking after him.'

'Is that where he was last night?'

'That's what he just told Dot. He didn't mention Evan, though, and I'm not meant to know that she knows, so I can't really ask him without dropping her in it.'

Ant leaned forward, resting his elbows on a trolley.

'I reckon we could go and have a look anyway. Be better if we knew where to start, though. There's about thirty sheds up there.'

'Tonight, straight after work?'

'I've got my reading session in the library. I can't miss it. I don't want to mess them about. We could go after that, though. There's no rush, is there?'

'No, I could go home and get changed and bung some food in a bag in case we find him. You could call for me after your class.'

'Sounds like a plan. It'll be about seven when I get to yours.'

'Okay, I might go to Saggy's on the way home, look at that footage again.'

'Bea, we've looked at it twice.'

'Yeah, I know, but the answer's got to be there, hasn't it? I feel like we must have missed something.'

There was a sound behind them and they both looked sharply at each other. Bea held a finger to her lips, eased herself up and crept round the corner. Tyler was bending down, trying to tidy up a pile of crates that had obviously just fallen over.

'Tyler!' said Bea. 'What are you doing?'

'Dean sent me to find Ant. There are two big deliveries due in at the same time. He says we need another pair of hands.'

'Ah, okay. Ant's right here.'

Ant, having heard them, appeared.

'I knew they needed me in stores,' he said, looking pleased with himself. 'My talents are wasted out here.'

'Well, Dean did say "We need another pair of hands, *even Ant's*", but I think he's panicking a bit. His mum keeps ringing him and asking him when he's coming home.'

The staff were meant to leave their mobile phones in their lockers. It was one of Costsave's strictest rules and one which had caused Bea a lot of heartache when Queenie had been suffering from agoraphobia and was unable to leave the house. She had often switched on her phone at break time to find scores of messages. So, she didn't begrudge Dean's rule-breaking one little bit. It wasn't easy juggling work and being a carer. More difficult still, she thought, if the one you were caring for was Eileen.

'What's coming in?' said Ant, rubbing his hands.

'Frozen food and plants. George has said to get the plants out on display round the front as soon as possible, and the frozen stuff won't wait.'

'All hands on deck,' said Ant. 'Muck or frostbite, which do you fancy?'

Tyler grinned at him. 'Muck, I think. It's a bit cold in there anyway and I like flowers and nature and that.'

'Muck it is,' said Ant. 'See you later, Bea.'

Bea watched them walk away together. Neville had been right, she thought. It was kind of lovely how well Ant had taken to supervising Tyler. Who would have thought it?

CHAPTER FORTY-THREE

The afternoon passed without further drama. Dot was subdued but put on a brave face for her customers. Bea kept her topped up with extra strong mints and words of encouragement. When five o'clock finally came round, they both headed for the rest room with a sense of relief.

Bea wished that she could walk Dot home, give her a chance to have another vent, but Saggy's was in the other direction. She had better check he'd be there, though, rather than flog over to his estate and find him out.

She retrieved her bag and phone from her locker and rang Saggy's number. As she waited for him to answer, Dot waved goodbye and went out. The phone rang for quite a while before it was picked up.

'Bea?' said Saggy. 'You all right?'

'Hey, Saggy. Yeah, I'm fine. Can I come and look at the drone footage again? I want to check something.'

'Sorry, Bea. I'm out then,' he said, quickly.

'When?' she said, sharply.

'What?'

'When are you out? I didn't say when I wanted to come over.'

'Well, today, all evening. I'm, um, going to Bristol.'

'No, you're not,' she said.

'Yeah, I am.' Bea wondered how long this particular exchange might go on for. He was clearly being evasive.

'Saggy, you're not. You're a terrible liar. Why can't I see the footage?'

There was a long pause.

'I haven't got it.'

'You gave it to the police and you didn't keep a copy?'

'No, I didn't give it to the police and it got wiped by mistake.'

'It got wiped.' She wasn't buying it. 'You mean, you deleted it.'

'No, I, um, dropped my laptop, and the hard drive's knackered.'

Bea clamped her phone to her ear with her shoulder and started putting her puffer jacket on.

'Saggy, what's going on?'

'You can't see the video, Bea. That's all there is to it. Can you just drop it now?'

'Like your laptop.'

'What?'

'The one you dropped.'

'Oh yeah.' He really was a terrible liar.

'Saggy—'

'Gotta go, Bea. Good chat.'

'Wait! Please! Is this something to do with your black eye? Is that when it got dropped?'

There was a silence so long that Bea was starting to wonder if he was still there. Finally he spoke in very low, quiet tone. 'That was when I was told I had to drop it.'

The rest room was hot and stuffy, but Bea felt a chill run through her.

'Oh, mate,' she said. 'Who was it?'

She pressed her phone closer to her ear, waiting for his reply.

'I don't know.'

'Saggy—'

'I'm not having you on. I really don't know. It was dark. It was all very quick. There was one thing, though. They were wearing motorbike gears, you know, leathers, helmet, the lot. And they went off on a bike.'

A bike. Like the two she saw roaring after Scout yesterday. It was all starting to fit into place, and the more she understood, the more alarmed she became.

'Thanks, Saggy,' she said. 'I hope you're all right.'

'I'm okay. Bea, don't do anything silly, will you? These people aren't messing around.'

'I won't. See you soon.'

She rang off. Her mind was whirring. She could almost hear the synapses crackling as her brain processed the new facts. She had two new pieces of information; someone else thought that the drone footage was important, and the person with something to hide was a biker or had friends who were.

With Saggy's place off the menu for tonight, she realised that she could catch up with Dot after all. She trotted down the stairs and out of the side door. When she rounded the building, she could see Dot halfway across the car park and was just about to shout out to her when she also spotted Tyler. He was hanging around by the nearest trolley park, obviously waiting for someone. Bea had a sudden inkling that she might be the subject of a little crush.

'Hello,' she said.

'Hi.'

She smiled at him, and tilted her head, 'You waiting for me?'

Tyler bit his lip and looked at his shoes. Bless him, she thought. She'd have to let him down gently.

'Hey, Bea!'

The voice behind her could only be Ant. She heard the staff door slamming and looked round to see him jogging over to them.

'Going to pick up some chips before my coaching session,' he said. 'Brain food. Want some?'

'No, ta. I was going to catch up with Dot.' She looked across the car park, but Dot had disappeared now.

'Coaching session?' said Tyler. 'Football, is it?'

Bea looked at Ant, expecting him to go along with Tyler's assumption.

'No,' he said, keeping his voice casual, 'a different sort of coaching. I'm learning to read. I never got on with school. This is different, one to one. I'm doing all right now.'

'Oh,' said Tyler, hardly batting an eyelid. 'That's great. Fair play, Ant.'

Ant smiled. 'Thanks, mate. Okay,' he said to Bea, 'let's leg it! Don't want to cramp Ty's style.'

'Huh?'

As Ant caught hold of Bea's elbow and started whisking her away, Bea was sure he winked at Tyler. What was all that about? They jogged towards the High Street.

'Can we slow down?' said Bea. 'It's been a long day and it's not over yet.'

They cut their pace to a fast walk. 'What did you mean cramp his style?' said Bea.

Ant grinned. 'He's got a girlfriend. He told me and Dean this afternoon. That's who he's waiting for.'

'Oh,' said Bea. 'Oh, I thought . . . never mind. Who is it?'

'He wouldn't say. Someone he knew from school. Sweet, isn't it?'

'Yeah. Did you have a girlfriend when you were sixteen?'

''Course. Tons of them. Look, there's Dot. She's outside the newsagents. I'm going to stop at the chippy, but I reckon you could catch her up. I'll come round to yours about seven, yeah?'

'Okay, see you then.'

Bea started running again, a stately trot along the pavement. It didn't take her long to reach Dot, who was dawdling and doing a bit of window shopping. She was pleased to see Bea and they linked arms and walked along together.

'Do you want a drink?' Bea offered.

'No, love. I'm going to go home, and start bagging up lover boy's belongings, ready for him to pick up. The sooner his stuff is gone, the better.'

'Oh, Dot. Do you think you're being a bit hasty? I've got a theory about what Bob was doing yesterday. I should be able to tell you if I'm right later this evening.'

'Really? You going to follow him to his side-piece's place and take pictures through the window?'

'No, you daft cow. If I tell you where I'm going, can you keep it a secret?'

'Of course.'

So, Bea told Dot her theory about Bob, Evan and the allotments, and her and Ant's plan to investigate. Dot digested it for a little while and then nodded. 'It's not out of the question, is it? And that would mean that he hadn't actually lied to me. He'd just left some bits out.'

'Exactly. And he is kind-hearted. He's always helping people out.'

'Soft, you mean.'

'Yeah, that too. I'll let you know how I get on. Don't write him off yet, Dot.'

They parted company at the far end of the High Street. Bea walked past the bungalows and across the rec. She had about an hour before the expedition to the allotments, plenty of time to change out of her work clothes and have a bite to eat and change her shoes. Neville only just tolerated trainers on the shop floor — he certainly wouldn't appreciate wet, muddy ones. She wondered if he'd be back tomorrow. Costsave had felt different without him today. She resented his ever-present vigilance when he was there, but it was kind of nice to have a foil to play off. Everything certainly ran more smoothly when he was there.

She had crossed the rec and was nearly opposite her house when her phone started ringing. She didn't recognise the number and when she answered it took her a while to realise who it was.

'Bea, I can't get Ant on the phone. I need to tell him something.' It was Tyler, sounding rather breathless.

'He switches it off during his coaching so he can concentrate.'

'Can I tell you? I don't know what to do . . .'

'Of course. What is it?' She was by her gate now, but stopped walking so she could listen properly.

'I think . . . I think I've done something bad. I didn't mean to, but I've put someone in danger. Real danger.'

CHAPTER FORTY-FOUR

Tyler sounded so distressed. Bea couldn't imagine what would cause him so much upset.

'I'm sure you haven't, Tyler. Tell me what's happened and I'll see if I can help.'

She sat down on her garden wall, phone pressed against her ear.

'The thing is, I heard you and Ant talking about Evan and the allotments this afternoon.' Bea narrowed her eyes, remembering hearing a noise and finding Tyler round the corner of the store.

'Go on,' she said.

'And I told someone.'

Bea felt her skin tingling, like electricity was dancing over the surface.

'Okay,' she said. 'Who did you tell?' But as she was talking, she realised that she knew the answer. The graffiti heart under the bridge. 'SC 4 TJ'. Scout Creech for Tyler Jackson.

'Scout,' he said. 'Harley's sister. She's my friend. My girlfriend.'

His girlfriend. The girlfriend who thought she might be pregnant. It seemed so unlikely. They were both so young. Then she remembered that he'd suddenly run off when she and Ant were discussing Scout yesterday. Of course! Why on earth had she taken so long to make the connection? They were young, and foolish, maybe, but that wasn't a crime. But perhaps through a tortuous set of circumstances, it had led to a crime. The very worst sort.

'Is she the one in danger, Tyler? Is it Scout you're worried about?'

'No. It's Evan. On the telly, Scout's mum talked about the family wanting justice, but from what Scout has said her brothers are out for revenge. If they find Evan, they're going to kill him. And I think Scout may tell them where to look.'

And now Bea couldn't help thinking about Saggy and his assailant. Motorbike leathers and a helmet. *They weren't messing around.*

She swallowed hard.

'Okay,' she said. 'Don't panic. I'll go there now. It's not far from here, and the Creech's place is the other side of town. I reckon I can get there first.'

'What about Ant?'

'He'll be out of the library soon. He can meet me there. I don't think I can wait for him, though.'

She was already on her feet. No time to change her clothes or footwear. Every minute counted. Her handbag would slow her down. She dumped it behind the wheelie bin in her garden.

'Bea—'

'I'll get there, find Evan and get him somewhere safe. It'll be okay, Tyler. Don't worry.'

She killed the call and started running, adrenaline injecting added energy into her tired leg muscles. The allotments were a ten-minute walk from her house. Maybe she could cut it down to five. It was another clear, calm evening. The streets and alleys were dark but studded with reassuring pools of amber light. Everything was very familiar, but Bea knew that bad things could happen in the places she knew best. The park, the houses, the alleyways, even Costsave itself — nowhere was truly safe and no one was ever immune to the actions of desperate people. And anyone could become desperate, if pushed into a corner.

Her breath was becoming strained, her chest uncomfortably tight, but she couldn't stop now. She was within sight of the allotment gates. As she got closer, she could see that they were closed, held secure by a padlock and chain. She groaned as she realised that she was going to have to climb over.

She took off her jacket and draped it over the top of the metal spikes, then started clambering up. It wasn't pretty, but she managed, landing on the other side heavily. She left the jacket. Ant would recognise it when he got there and know she was inside. There was no lighting here. As she walked further from the gates and moved out of the reach of the streetlights, she switched on the torch on her phone.

The ground was uneven, but there was logic to the layout, with a series of grassy paths between plots laid out in a grid pattern. Sheds and tool stores were dotted around. Not every plot had one, but there were enough to be daunting. Moisture from the long grass was already soaking through her trainers, making her feet cold and wet. Bea cursed herself for not confronting Bob. She hadn't wanted to betray Dot's confidence, but some things were more important than a lovers' tiff.

She shone the beam of the torch at each shed that she passed, looking for signs of forced entry. *Think Bea, think*, she urged herself. If she was Evan, she wouldn't be near the entrance. She'd be in one of the quieter corners where any activity or break-in was less likely to be noticed. Shining the torch at the ground in front of her, she picked her way across the site towards the far edge.

There were half a dozen sheds on the last row of plots. It was as good a place to start as any. She walked along the path, examining each one in turn. The door on the third shed was closed, but there was no padlock securing the hasp. She approached with her heart in her mouth.

She put her hand to the catch and pulled, gently. The inside was completely dark. She stood on the threshold, listening. She could hear her own blood pulsing in her ears. Was there something else too? Someone else's breath? The slightest movement? She tried to put thoughts of rats and bats and spiders to the back of her mind, and moved her torch around, letting the light play over piles of plant pots, and sacks of compost. There was a bundle of something in the corner, some sort of material half-unrolled. Underneath it, squinting and trying to shield his eyes from the light, was Evan.

CHAPTER FORTY-FIVE

'Leave me alone,' he shouted. 'Just leave me alone.'

'Evan,' Bea said, lowering the torch's beam. 'It's me. Bea!'

'Bea? Oh, thank god. Come in and switch that torch off. Anyone could see it.'

Bea stepped further into the shed and pulled the door to behind her. She didn't switch the torch off but kept it low to the ground.

'How did you find me? Did Bob tell you I was here?'

'No. I just kind of worked it out. Did he tell you to come here?'

'No. I found it myself. Bob came looking for this carpet. That's how he found me. Beats me why he'd want this horrible old thing. It stinks, but at least it's kept me warm. He's been brilliant. I couldn't phone you, Bea. I had to dump my phone. Realised it could be traced.'

'I only twigged that after the police interviewed me,' said Bea. 'They'd been monitoring your calls.'

'Shit.'

'I know.'

'I'm so sorry I've made things difficult for everyone. Do you want to sit down?'

'No. In fact, you'd better stand up. I came to tell you it's time to move or to hand yourself in. I think Harley's brothers are out looking for you tonight and I think there's a good chance they'll come up here.'

'I'm not handing myself in.'

'It might be for the best, Evan. They're out for your blood.'

'Perhaps I deserve it.'

His words brought Bea's racing mind to a standstill. What was he saying? Had she been wrong about him all along?

'Why would you deserve it?' she said, carefully.

'I've had a lot of time to think, Bea. I should never have chased Harley. I made assumptions, got carried away. Yeah, I was right to try and stop him leaving the shop, but I should have left it there. I frightened that kid, put the fear of god into him. That was one of the last things he felt. Fear. Created by me. That's a hell of a thing to live with.'

'But you didn't kill him.'

'No.'

'So you don't deserve the sort of rough justice that's coming your way, Evan. You really don't. Let's get you away from here. You can come to ours tonight, while we figure out what to do.'

'Okay,' he said, reluctantly. 'Hang on. What's that?'

They both fell silent. While they had been talking, Bea had been aware of a background noise. Now, what had sounded like a far-off whine was louder, deeper, nearer.

'Cut that light, Bea,' Evan said.

As they sat in the dark, the throaty roar of an engine drifted across to them. It reached a crescendo, then stopped.

'We've got to get out,' Bea whispered.

'I think it's too late. Get under here with me. Come on.'

Unable to see more than vague, dark shapes, Bea felt her way forward. Evan's large hand found hers and he guided her onto the hard cement floor next to him. Despite him claiming to have been kept warm by the carpet, his hand was freezing. He lifted the carpet over their heads, so that they were in a sort of cave that smelt of must and mould and old leaves. Evan's body was warmer than his hands. Bea was hard up against him, her head level with his armpit and chest. His smell, even after days in a shed, was actually rather nice, and there was comfort in his sheer bulk, as they waited together in the dark.

Bea couldn't hear footsteps. There was no shouting. No noise at all, apart from the screech of an owl from across the nearby fields.

She started to wonder whether the bike rider lived at one of the nearby houses, after all. Maybe they'd put their bike in a garage and had headed inside for the evening, glad to be home after another day at work.

That fantasy died when a beam of light flashed across the grubby window.

Someone was here. Close.

Bea held her breath and shrank down, leaning closer into Evan.

Around the edge of the carpet, Bea could see that there was light illuminating the crack in the doorway where she hadn't pulled it completely shut. Why had she been so careless? Padlock undone. Door slightly ajar. She might as well have attached a neon sign with a big red arrow on it, 'Look Here!'

And, sure enough, they'd been rumbled.

The pale strip became larger as someone slowly opened the door.

CHAPTER FORTY-SIX

The torch beam shone directly at them. Bea and Evan kept their faces hidden under the carpet but the light was playing on the wall behind them, bouncing off galvanised buckets and shiny fertiliser sacks, sending a twilight glow into their carpet cave.

'You can come out now, Evan. I know you're in there. It's over.'

It was a woman's voice. It wasn't one of the Creech boys. Bea felt herself relax, just a fraction. She and Evan looked at each other, their faces almost touching. Evan nodded and slowly moved the carpet away from their heads. Now the torch was directly in their faces. Bea screwed up her eyes, trying to see the figure behind the glare, although she was sure she recognised the voice.

She held her hand up to shield her eyes.

'Patsy?' she said. 'Is that you? Can you move the torch please?'

'You! The supermarket girl,' said the woman, keeping the light full on them. 'What are you doing here?'

'I just got here. I was trying to find Evan before someone hurt him. To persuade him to turn himself in. I'm glad you're here, Patsy. I'm glad it's you.' The woman didn't respond. 'Can you please move your torch?'

The beam moved down a little, landing on the carpet covering their legs, dusty and red, and now Bea could see a little more of the shed interior and Patsy. Her face was familiar and yet there was something different, something harsh about it, which made Bea feel queasy. Perhaps it was just the odd lighting, with her cheekbones and nose casting upwards shadows.

'Mrs Creech,' Evan said, sitting more upright and putting his hand on his heart. 'I need to tell you — I need you to believe — that I didn't hurt Harley. I swear on my life that he was okay when I left the park. I'm so, so sorry for your loss.'

'No one believes that, Evan,' Patsy said, her tone cold and hard.

'But it's true.' He started to get to his feet.

'Stay where you are!' she shouted, her voice suddenly filling the small, dank space.

Shocked, Evan sat down again. He held both hands up.

'I'm sorry,' he said. 'I didn't mean to frighten you.'

'I'm not frightened. I need time to think.'

'Sure, sure. Take all the time you need. You can call the police, if you want to. It's okay. I won't make a fuss.'

Patsy coughed or was it a laugh? 'The police? Not yet.'

'Actually,' said Bea, 'I think perhaps we should. Are your boys heading here? It would be better to get Evan out of way before they get here.'

'You don't need to worry about my boys,' said Patsy. 'They'll do what I tell them.'

'Even so . . .' Bea brought out her phone and woke it up.

Before she realised what was happening, Patsy lunged forward and kicked the phone out of Bea's grasp.

'Hey! What the hell—?' The pain, where the heavy boot had crunched into the back of her hand, was hot and sharp.

Beside her, she could feel Evan reacting, tensing his body, but he didn't move yet. Instead, he turned to her and asked, 'Are you okay?'

'I guess.'

Patsy took a step back. 'No phone calls.' She was the one blocking the doorway and yet, Bea thought, she had the air of a cornered animal, unpredictable, lashing out. That was what grief would do to you, she supposed. And Patsy Creech was clearly a woman in the throes of grief.

'Listen,' said Evan, slowly, 'I can't imagine how you feel. It's a terrible loss. The worst. But I didn't do it. It wasn't me. So, you need to let me and Bea leave here now. I promise I will hand myself in. I will do everything I can to help the police find out who did this. Who killed your Harley.'

'Don't you dare say his name,' she spat. 'Don't you ever — *ever* — say his name. Do you understand?'

'Okay, okay. I understand.'

Bea, sitting on the floor and nursing her hand, which she was pretty sure was broken, appreciated the way Evan was speaking to Patsy. Perhaps talking calmly and kindly would take the heat out of the situation. It was certainly worth a try. She was acutely aware that, despite what Patsy had said about her boys, the chances were that things would turn much nastier if they did turn up. She kept listening out for the sound of more bikes.

'Patsy,' she said, 'You want to know why your son died. You want justice. Closure. And you deserve that — it's only right. You and me, we've done the police's job finding Evan, but now it's time to hand him over.'

'Oh, do shut up,' Patsy snapped. 'If you weren't here, it would all be over by now.'

Over? What did she mean? thought Bea.

'Everyone knows he did it. No one will miss him, not like my Harley.'

Miss him? Had she come here to kill Evan herself? She was tough and not frightened of violence — Bea's hand could vouch for that — but he was twice her size. What on earth had she been intending to do?

'Did you see the flowers in the park, all those people at the vigil?' Patsy's voice was thick with emotion now.

'Yes, I was there,' said Bea. 'It was very moving. He was loved, by his mates at school and his family, you, his brothers, Scout.'

'Scout? What do you know about her? Keep her out of it.'

'She and Harley were close, weren't they? I . . .' Bea wondered how much to say, but the important thing seemed to be to keep the dialogue going. '. . . I saw her at the memorial, early one morning.'

'She's got nothing to do with this.'

Bea didn't want to drop her in it. 'Maybe not,' she said, 'but she needs you, Patsy. Your boys need you. You mustn't do anything silly that would take you away from them. Let's all get out of here. We can go and talk at my place, if you like. It's not far.'

Bea turned to Evan. 'Can you help me up? My hand's hurting like hell.'

'Sure.'

Evan tucked his feet under him and crouched, then put an arm around Bea to help her.

'No!' Patsy screamed. 'Don't move! Stay there!'

Bea looked across at her and now she saw that Patsy had, indeed, come prepared. She was still holding the torch in one hand but had something else in the other. Bea was staring down the barrel of a gun.

CHAPTER FORTY-SEVEN

'Oh, Patsy, no,' Bea said.

'Holy shit,' Evan murmured.

It seemed as if all Patsy's jitteriness had gone now. She was quiet, determined and steady. The gun was aimed directly at Evan's chest.

'Patsy, you can't do this,' said Bea. 'You've got the wrong person. Evan did not kill your son. This is blind revenge, Patsy. It's not justice.'

'You really don't get it, do you? I don't need revenge. I need him to be guilty. Everyone thinks he did it, and once he's dead, then it will be case closed.'

'But why . . . ?' Bea's stomach, already tying itself in knots, gave a lurch. The truth was staring her in the face.

'You were there in the park, weren't you? Were you following Scout? What happened with Harley?'

'Shut up! I'm thinking. Two of you. Two . . .'

As she was talking, Bea was shuffling forwards trying to position herself in front of Evan.

'What are you doing?' Evan hissed.

'It's you she's after. Get behind me.'

Evan grabbed her shoulders firmly and held her where she was, next to him. She had no chance of moving now. 'No, Bea. I won't let you do it.'

'Ah, isn't that nice. Fighting over who gets a bullet, as if it makes any difference. You idiots, I'm going to have to kill you both.'

In the distance, Bea thought she could hear an engine, or was it two?

'Murder-suicide, that's the best way,' said Patsy, talking to herself, with a hint of triumph in her voice. She moved the gun so that it was pointing at Bea. 'Right. I need you over here. Slowly, okay? And you,' she said, waving the gun back towards Evan, 'don't even think about moving. Stay right where you are.'

Bea wondered if Evan was thinking what she was — Patsy splitting them up like this could work to their advantage. There was more chance of one of them tackling her and, maybe, one of them surviving. It was difficult to see how this could end without someone being shot, though. The thought of the gun actually going off was making her legs turn to jelly as she tried to get to her feet.

'Where do you want me?' she said, her voice wobbly.

'Near me. We're going to swap places.'

She was going to fake Evan murdering her first and then his suicide, thought Bea. Risky, because that would bring her nearer to Evan who, surely, would go for her. Bea inched her way around towards the front of the shed, as Patsy moved the other way, keeping the gun trained on Evan. He was obviously seen as the main threat.

'Just inside the door,' said Patsy. 'That's it.'

The door was open. Bea wondered if she should just make a run for it, try and get help. Patsy could read her mind, apparently.

'If you run out, he's getting a bullet to the brain. And then I'll hunt you down.'

Bea tried to think but it was too hard. Whatever she did, the consequences were awful. If she did nothing, she and Evan would both end up dead, anyway. She'd have to try something, though. She wouldn't go down without a fight.

There were all sorts of garden tools leaning up near the door — a spade, a rake, a fork. If she picked one up, it would surely distract Patsy, put her off balance and then Evan could disarm her. She glanced across at him. He seemed to have got his feet under him, so that he was crouching, ready to spring. Yes! This could work.

She edged a little closer to the tools, backing up to the side of the shed. Patsy was constantly switching her attention between her and Evan. If Bea moved slowly, she might get away with it. She felt behind her and her fingers found the handle of something. It didn't matter if it was a fork or a spade — the movement alone and the surprise of an object swinging through the space between them would be enough. She'd have to just trust that Evan would react quickly. Okay, she thought, trying to calm her nerves, she'd do it on a count of three.

One . . . her fingers tightened on the handle . . . two . . . she braced her shoulder, ready to heave the implement round as quickly as possible . . .

'Mum, what are you doing?'

Bea looked behind her. Scout Creech was in the doorway. There was someone else further back, but Bea couldn't see who.

'Go home, Scout,' Patsy said. She had swung round and now the gun was trained on the doorway, pointing towards her own daughter. 'You shouldn't be out. Just go home and forget you ever saw this.'

'Are you arresting them? Have you called the police?'

'Yes. Yes, that's what I'm doing. Citizen's arrest.'

'We'll stay, then, until they get here.'

'We? Is Norton there, or Brough? I heard the bike,' Patsy half-closed her eyes, trying to identify the person behind Scout.

'It was me on the bike, Mum. The boys are looking after the diner.'

'Scout,' said Bea. 'She hasn't called the police. Do it now. Call them. Please!'

Scout peered at Bea, frowning and confused. 'What do you mean?'

'Just call them. We need help!'

Patsy pointed the gun towards Bea, who felt her heart hammering in her chest. It was as if the last few minutes had been taking place in slow motion and now everything was speeding up, getting out of control.

'Don't listen to her!' snarled Patsy. 'Just do what I say. Go home!'

'No, Mum. We're not going.'

Bea could hear another voice now, 'Police, please. It's urgent. The Fouracre Road allotments. The guy you're looking for, Evan Edwards, he's here.' Behind Scout, Tyler was calling it in.

'Hey, you!' Patsy shouted. 'Stop that! Put the phone down! Scout, take it off him! Do it!'

With the gun pointing at her, Scout had no option. She took the phone out of Tyler's hands and threw it on the ground.

'Who the hell is that, anyway?' Patsy growled.

Tyler stepped forward, to stand next to Scout in the doorway.

'This is Tyler, Mum,' said Scout. 'He's my boyfriend.'

'You! The one who got my daughter sneaking around. Who got her up the duff. Who got my son, my darling son, stealing, lying and covering up.' Patsy's composure had crumbled. She was practically steaming with rage.

'Mum, I'm not—'

'Shut up, Scout. It's your fault Harley's dead. If you hadn't disobeyed me, none of this would have happened.'

'Mum!' Scout wailed.

'What did happen, Patsy?' said Bea. 'What happened to Harley?'

Patsy was staring around, wild-eyed now. The gun was pointing this way and that, up at the ceiling, then back at Scout or Tyler or Bea. Scout was crying. Tyler had his arm round her.

'It was an accident,' she said. 'He said he'd been trying to steal from the shop, told me what he was trying to steal and why. I told him he'd betrayed me. Covering up for his sister, instead of coming to me. He wouldn't apologise. I clouted him. Not hard, but he fell backwards. Hit his head. I knew he'd gone. I just knew it.'

The gun was wobbling now, her grip on it loosening. Maybe, thought Bea, someone could gently take it from her hand.

'That must have been terrible,' she said, quietly.

'It was.' Patsy's eyes seemed to glaze over, like she was looking far away.

'Here,' said Bea, 'let me take that.'

She took one step towards Patsy, her arm outstretched.

'Bea, be careful,' Tyler said.

At the sound of his voice, Patsy seemed to wake up. She put both hands on the gun, tightened her grip, raised her arms and pointed it straight at Tyler.

'Not Scout's fault,' she said, her voice low and steady. 'Yours.'

Her finger started to squeeze the trigger.

'No!'

Bea lunged forward at the same time as Evan launched himself at Patsy's legs. The gun going off in that small place sounded like an explosion. It filled Bea's ears, along with Scout's screams, as she saw Patsy topple towards her, the gun still in her hands. She was knocked to the floor, Patsy on top of her and Evan crowning the heap. The gun was squashed between her body and Patsy's. She could feel the hard metal pressing against her ribs. None of it seemed real. It was like a film where someone had pressed the mute button. It was dark and confusing and silent. There was something wet on her face, but her hands were pinned to her sides so she couldn't wipe it away.

She lay there, struggling to breathe under the weight on top of her. Patsy's head was on her shoulder, her body across Bea's. She wasn't moving.

It seemed like a long time until the weight was lifted away and Bea could breathe freely again. The air was cold and full of dust and mould, but it seemed as sweet as anything to Bea. She didn't try to get up, just lay there for a while as faces appeared above her. Their mouths were moving but she couldn't hear what they were saying? Why didn't they speak up? Someone shone a torch at her, making her squint. A hand reached out and wiped her face with a tissue. When they moved it away she could see it glowing red in the torchlight. Blood. Was she hurt? She couldn't feel anything, but she was so tired. All she wanted was to lie here for a few minutes longer and get her breath back.

CHAPTER FORTY-EIGHT

She was still living in a silent movie when the paramedics helped her out of the shed. Confusing images filled her vision — lights, faces, uniforms — as she picked her way along grassy paths, supported on either side by the firm grip of strangers. Ahead of her, the entrance was lit by the bright glare of headlights. Half a dozen vehicles were parked in the lane at crazy angles. There were two ambulances, their back doors open and waiting.

She watched as a stretcher was loaded into one of them, its contents shielded by a posse of people hovering around. She picked out Scout among a sea of uniforms and realised that it must be Patsy. She hadn't moved when she'd been lying on top of Bea, but that didn't mean she was dead, did it?

A figure emerged through the light, barging past the police, heading straight towards her. He was calling her name, although she could only hear a muffled suggestion of the sound. As Ant careered up to her, one of the paramedics put their hand up to stop him, like they were directing traffic. He halted and stood awkwardly next to them, searching her face, his mouth making the words, 'Are you okay?' over and over.

'I'm all right,' Bea said, her own voice sounding as if it came from somewhere far away.

Ant blinked rapidly, watching from the sidelines, as Bea was loaded into the ambulance and helped to sit down.

From her perch inside the vehicle, Bea could see a succession of people trailing in and out of the allotments. Scenes of crime officers in white paper boiler suits were going into the gates, while Evan was led out by two uniformed officers. Tyler followed on his own but was then taken to one side by Tom. Two guys on enormous motorbikes drew up and started running towards the gates, when one of them spotted Scout by the second ambulance and called the other one over. Bea watched as Scout had a tearful conversation with them, and they both wrapped their arms around her.

Watching, Bea felt like she was swimming underwater. A paramedic fixed a blood pressure monitor to her arm and gently encouraged her to lie down. As the doors to the ambulance closed, she caught a glimpse of Dot and Bob standing on the edge of things. She didn't have time to wave to them. The doors closed, the engine started, and she closed her eyes.

CHAPTER FORTY-NINE

Two Weeks Later

It was a big day for Kingsleigh.

'Are you coming down later?' Bea asked Queenie, as she put on her coat and gathered up her shoulder bag.

'Yes, love. I'll be there. Wouldn't miss it.'

The morning had dawned bright and clear and as Bea walked across the rec she was filled with a sense of optimism and well-being. After all the drama of recent weeks, it was going to be the sort of day which showed the town at its best, with the community coming together to celebrate each other as much as the people visiting. Whether it was the King and Queen or Bobby Ball, everyone liked the frisson that celebrity brought; the sense of occasion.

The High Street was looking spick and span already, but even so Bea was pleased to see Ivan, the council street cleaner, out with his brushes and little bin on wheels. There were strings of bunting along most of the shop fronts and displays of flags and photographs in the windows, with one or two notable exceptions. The second-hand bookshop had a rather pointed display of titles on politics, economics and environmentalism. There was a framed photograph in one corner, but when Bea inspected it, it turned out to be a black and white image of the bookshop owner posing with Tony Benn. Bea smiled at the quiet, polite note of dissent. This, rather than the defacing of town signs and vitriolic TikTok rants, was the Kingsleigh she knew and loved.

A piercing whistle assaulted her ears and she turned round. Ant was fifty metres behind her. She stopped and waited for him to catch up.

'Today's the day, then,' she said as he joined her.

'Yup.'

'Is Neville all right?'

'He's done his exercises. He's had some sawdust and blueberries. He set off for work ages ago.'

A truck drove past them and pulled up at the Costsave end of the street where a police officer in uniform was waiting. Two men in high viz jackets jumped out and started unloading grey metal barriers.

'Blimey,' said Ant. 'How many people are they expecting?'

'It'll be a fair few, Ant. Whatever you think about our royal overlords, it's going to be a spectacle.'

'Two posh pensioners in a shiny car,' he said, glumly.

'Stop being so miserable.' She plucked a union flag on a stick from of a nearby planter and waved it near his face.

'Give over,' he said, 'and stop ruining the lovely display. You'll get us into trouble.'

He snatched the flag and planted it back where it came from and Bea realised that they were being watched by a man in a grey suit, standing on the other side of the road. He had an earpiece and microphone in place and was looking rather conspicuous in the otherwise empty street.

Bea nudged Ant. 'Secret service?' she said, indicating their observer.

'Probably.' He gave him a thumbs up. 'What a load of old cobblers this is.'

'But think of the buffet . . .'

That seemed to cheer him up and they set off at a brisk pace.

'Stevo once ate fourteen full-size sausage rolls,' he said, referring to one of his older brothers, 'but I think that could be beaten. I'm willing to give it a try.'

As they turned the corner and crossed the road to the Costsave car park, it was clear that Operation Windsor was very much in full swing. The site was immaculate; shop signs washed and polished, trolleys gleaming, bunting around the front entrance fluttering gently in the breeze.

'Nice,' said Bea, stopping to take a photo on her phone. You didn't get the full effect yet, as the red carpet wasn't in place, but that was all part of the plan. Tyler and Ant would lay it out at ten past two, exactly half an hour before the visitors were expected. Plenty of time to brush it, hoover it and give the posts a polish. It was important not to peak too soon.

A car drew into the staff car park and Bob and Dot emerged. Bob was carrying a cardboard box containing various jugs and vases, while Dot had an armful of fresh flowers, wrapped up in paper.

'Ooh, they're nice,' said Bea, as they met at the staff door.

'They're destined for the bogs,' said Dot. 'Fresh flowers to complete my vision, darling. I'd better get a move on.'

'After you,' said Bob, holding the door open. He and Dot were very much an item again since she'd discovered the reason for his previous evasiveness. In fact, Dot now considered him something of a hero. On the night of Bea's adventures, she had asked him about Evan and he had confessed all, then had taken the decision that things had gone far enough and rung the police. That phone call meant that both Patsy and Bea got the swift medical treatment they needed. The fact that he'd gone to the allotments looking for the Costsave red carpet, which he himself had taken up there to use as a weed suppressant on Charles's plot twelve years before, was quietly overlooked by George and everyone else at Costsave. No need to muddy the waters.

Dot was a little late getting to the staff briefing, but entered the room with a large arrangement of flowers. The gathering parted like the Red Sea as she carried the vase through, wafting the scent of freesias as she went, and placed it on the coffee table to murmurs of approval.

'I had a few left over,' she said.

'That's lovely,' said George. 'We're just waiting for Neville. He was in the office ten minutes ago. Has anyone seen him?'

'I think he was heading for the bogs,' said Ant.

'Nervous tum, I expect,' Dot whispered to Bea, who nodded. They'd all been there.

'Would you mind just checking on him, Ant?' said George, checking her watch again. 'Time's marching on.'

Ant threaded his way out of the room and set off down the corridor. Dot's grand plans for the staff facilities had included the men's toilets. They weren't quite as chi-chi as the Ladies', and there were no vases of fresh flowers here, but they were newly painted, neat and tidy. One of the cubicle doors was firmly shut and there was a gentle keening sound coming under the door.

'Um, Neville,' Ant called out. 'Are you in here?'

The keening stopped. Ant waited, not knowing what to do.

'Neville?' he said at last.

Silence.

'You can't stay in there all day. Open the door, mate. Let's have a chat.'

'I'm not coming out.'

'Are you kidding me? You'll miss all the fun! This is it, Neville. The glory day.'

'I can't face it.'

'But everything is ready. It's all planned, bought, cleaned, painted, scheduled. You've done it. Open the door, please. It's too weird shouting at you like this.'

He heard the sound of the lock being drawn back and the door opened tentatively. Neville was sitting on the toilet, although Ant was relieved to see that the lid was down and his trousers were up.

'That's better,' said Ant. 'Do you want to come out and wash your face? Everyone's waiting for the briefing. George sent me to get you.'

Neville closed his eyes, like he was trying to make the world go away.

'I'm not coming out. You can't make me.'

Ant had a very strong urge to laugh, but he knew that this would be the worst thing he could do and swallowed it down.

'Come on, Neville,' he said. 'You've done all the prep, now it's time to enjoy the day.'

'Something will happen. Something will go wrong.'

'Why would it?'

'Because it always does.'

Ant was puzzled. Costsave usually ran like clockwork. Under Neville's stewardship hardly anything went wrong, and when it did, it was soon put right again. He had a strong feeling this wasn't about everyday life, though. He had a hunch it went deeper. Something in the past had lodged in Neville's brain and had been eating away at him ever since the visit was announced.

'Neville,' he said. 'What happened when Bobby Ball came to Costsave?'

CHAPTER FIFTY

'I can't talk about it,' said Neville.

'So there was something. Please, just tell me. You've been stewing about it for a long time. Most things are better out than in, Neville.'

'You'll laugh at me.'

Truthfully, thought Ant, he might, but he'd try his best not to. 'I really won't.'

'Promise?'

'Promise.'

Neville took a deep breath and told him. Once he'd started, it all spilled out. How twelve years ago he'd been quite junior, like Ant. Everyone at the store had been excited about their VIP visit and he had been the same. He'd been given various jobs to do to in the run-up, and on the day, he'd spotted a stray toffee paper on the carpet just as Bobby arrived. As the VIP clambered out of the limousine and waved to the crowd, Neville had darted across in front of him to go and pick up the paper. His foot had caught on the edge of the carpet. He hadn't fallen but he'd staggered almost the length of the walkway, flailing his arms to recover his balance. Bobby Ball had watched with glee, then pointed to him and said, 'Enjoy your trip, son?' The whole crowd had laughed and then Bobby had walked forward, shaken some hands, and cracked some more jokes before formally declaring the new deli counter open. Everyone agreed it had been a brilliant day and an amazing PR success for the store.

'Was that it?' said Ant.

'I can still hear them, Anthony. Laughing. Hundreds of people.'

'Oh, Neville. I'm so sorry.'

'It was humiliating. Just mortifying.'

'He didn't mean any harm, by the sound of it.'

'I know. It was just a throwaway thing, a funny remark. He was a lovely guy, everyone said so.'

'It was awful for you, though. Being so young and everything. Maybe . . .' Ant tried to find the right words. '. . . maybe it's time to let that one go, though. To move on.'

Neville sniffed. 'Perhaps you're right,' he said. 'Saying it out loud, it kind of doesn't seem so bad. I don't suppose anyone else even remembers it.'

'That's the spirit,' said Ant. 'And twelve years later, you're deputy manager, not the trainee. You're practically running the show. Come on, let's go back to the staff room. You've got a job to do.'

After a little face wash and lot of nose-blowing, Neville was ready to face the world again. Ant walked with him back to the staff room and then went and stood with Bea, as Neville took his place at the front of the room.

Neville ran through the schedule in minute detail. He was flanked by George, who kept nodding approvingly, and Anna, who held the back-up folder, brimming with project plans, emergency numbers and role allocations. She didn't need to step in, though, because it was clear that Neville had it all under control.

'And so,' he concluded, 'I will be doing a uniform check as you enter the shop floor today, although, just looking round the room, I can tell that you've all made a tremendous effort.' His gaze lingered for a moment on Ant, lolling against the wall, chewing. 'We need to lose the gum, Anthony,' he said. 'Come on, it's not work appropriate.'

Ant looked at him with disbelief. Was Neville really picking on him after everything they'd just been through? He made a show of pretending to look at a non-existent watch on his wrist. 'Really, Neville? There's still six hours to go. Even I can't make gum last that long.'

'Spit it out. We don't have chewing gum in Costsave.'

Bea could see Ant wrestling with the urge to direct Neville to the many varieties of gum in the displays next to every till. Happily, he overcame it, and made do with a theatrical sigh before he spat the gum into a tissue.

'Right,' said George. 'Thank you for that, Neville, and thank you to everyone who has worked so hard to make this day special. I'm extremely proud of you all. We've still got a shop to run, though, so let's get started and do what we do best. Good luck, everyone!'

CHAPTER FIFTY-ONE

With half an hour to go, the store was officially closed and a crowd was gathering in the Costsave car park. Further barriers had been put in place to the right and left of the entrance. George walked along the barriers, greeting people. The atmosphere was chatty and friendly. People were speculating about what the Queen would be wearing and whether the royal couple would actually buy anything in Costsave. Would they be tempted by this week's special offers, which included a stew pack of vegetables for a pound, four lamb burgers for one pound forty-nine pence, and a wooden bird box for a fiver? The consensus was that the King would favour the bird box. The local primary schools had been let out early and there were plenty of children adding to the noise and excitement. Everyone made room, so that they could stand at the front without feeling squashed. Bea went along the line handing out little flags for them to wave.

Keisha, a former colleague on the checkouts, had arrived with her daughter Kayleigh. The little girl had been in and out of hospital as a baby and toddler and had become Costsave's unofficial mascot. Customers and staff had raised money to send her and her family on a trip of a lifetime to Disneyland after her final round of chemotherapy. It was natural that she had been everyone's first choice for someone to present the King and Queen with a bouquet.

'How's she doing?' Bea asked Keisha.

'Brilliant. She's at pre-school playgroup now. She's a little bit behind some of the others, but she's catching up fast. She's so excited about today.'

Bea crouched down next to Kayleigh's pushchair.

'Are you all ready to give the Queen some pretty flowers?' she asked.

Kayleigh looked serious for a moment. 'Is it the real Queen?'

'Yes.'

'But the real one?'

This wasn't the time or place to debate consorts, second marriages and the constitution, so Bea kept it simple. 'Yes, darling. You'll see. I'll hand you the flowers when they get here. Not long now.'

Kayleigh clapped her little hands together and kicked her feet against the webbing of the footrest.

An audible 'Oooh!' rose up from the crowd as the front doors swooshed open and Ant and Tyler emerged carrying the red carpet. When they unrolled it, there was a ripple of applause and Ant turned to face them and gave a bow, which resulted in much laughter and a couple of whistles. Evan carried out and set up the metal posts and gold rope. The powers that be had determined that a two-week suspension was sufficient punishment for overstepping the mark when it had come to chasing Harley, and he had started back at work again a few days ago. He and his mum, who had quickly recovered from the effects of smoke inhalation, had found a temporary flat the Kingsleigh side of Bristol to stay in while the future of their burnt-out home was decided. Kirsty gave the carpet a once over with a cordless vacuum cleaner. Neville hovered close at hand, pointing out where she'd missed a bit.

Bea spotted Scout at the back of the crowd. It was only a few days since the town had come out for another occasion — Harley's funeral. People had lined the pavements as the cortege passed along the High Street, headed by a black hearse, and followed by a hundred or so motorbikes. Patsy was still in hospital, recovering from the grave injuries caused by her own gun. The police had told Scout (who had told Tyler) that when she was well enough, she would be charged with manslaughter.

Now, Scout was standing next to Ginny's parents, who had taken her and her brothers under their wing somewhat — two families drawn together by loss. She was waving at someone and when Bea looked she saw Tyler waving back and felt a little glow of warmth. They were probably too young to stay together, Bea mused, but you never knew and, for now, their relationship was rather sweet.

By a quarter past three, the mood had changed. The children had gone quiet. One or two were jumping on the spot to keep warm. Bea had fetched a chair for one older woman, who had been visibly struggling to stay standing for so long.

'Where are they, then?' Queenie asked, when Bea strolled down to see her. They both looked towards the far side of the car park, where a couple of police officers were stationed, looking bored.

'I expect they're just running late. I'll try and find out when they're expected.'

Bea could see Tom near the entrance. He was walking away from George and Neville, pressing his hand against an earpiece and frowning. She went over to him and hung around a few metres away. He noticed her and turned his back. Rude, thought Bea, but she didn't let it put her off. She took a step back, though, so he knew she wasn't trying to eavesdrop.

'Okay. Roger that,' said Tom. He finished the call. When he turned round, Bea could see by his expression that it wasn't good news. He looked at her and then pulled his finger across his throat.

'What's happening?'

'Accident on the bypass. Big tailback. They've been stuck in traffic for a while. A certain someone is going ballistic, apparently, and saying that heads are going to roll.'

'Are they still coming?'

He shook his head.

'They've gone down the back way to Bath. They're missing out Kingsleigh altogether.'

Bea glanced across at the welcoming party; George, standing with a fixed grin on her face, Kayleigh in her pushchair, now with a blanket tucked round her legs, and Neville, ashen-faced, eyes scanning the entrance road for a glimpse of a shiny bonnet and a flickering royal standard.

'Oh blimey,' said Bea. 'Who's going to tell them?'

CHAPTER FIFTY-TWO

It turned out that the paperwork on Neville's clipboard did not include a back-up plan for a royal no-show. Anna, however, had contingency plans and as soon as Tom told them what was happening — or rather not happening — she had a word with George and then was seen running into the store. A minute or two later, and before any announcement was made, she was back with two carrier bags.

Rumours were starting to spread through the crowd. Someone had seen a photograph on Twitter apparently showing the royal limo on one of the country lanes to the south of the town. The mood wasn't exactly ugly, but people were starting to get rather cheesed off.

George stepped onto the red carpet and a hush fell over the crowd.

'Ladies and gentlemen,' she boomed, 'I'm very sorry to announce that due to circumstances beyond our control, the King and Queen have had to change their plans. They are not coming to Costsave today, but—' Howls of disappointment drowned her out. She waited patiently for the noise to subside — 'but, I'm very pleased to say that we *do* have some VIPs gathered here today . . .' Everyone looked around, hoping to spot someone selfie-worthy, but without success. '.

. . you! At Costsave, we love our customers. You are why we are here every day, and we never take you for granted. So, the store will reopen in five minutes, and we invite you to walk our red carpet, take as many selfies as you like, and choose a complimentary pen or a balloon, as long as stocks last.'

She looked around the crowd. Bea half-expected boos and catcalls, but, while a few people were peeling away and starting to plod across the car park, most were obviously minded to stay and make the best of things.

Queenie bustled up to Bea. 'Can I help?' she said.

'You any good with a balloon pump?' said Bea, and they had soon joined a little production line with Tyler and Ant, blowing up blue balloons printed with 'I heart Costsave' in bold red, knotting the ends and tying on red string.

'I can write the *Bugle*'s headline for them this week,' said Ant.

'Yeah?'

'If they've got any balls, it'll be *No King in Kingsleigh*.' Everyone laughed.

At twenty-five past three, George invited Keisha and Kayleigh to be the first people to walk along the carpet. At the far end, Keisha whispered in Kayleigh's ear, and she turned to face everyone and said, rather shyly, 'I do declare . . .' She faltered and stopped and her mum prompted her again, '. . . that the shop is open. Can I have a balloon?'

Everyone laughed and Bea presented Kayleigh with a balloon. She got back into her pushchair, the doors opened and they went in. Customers formed an orderly queue and started to take their turn in the spotlight. Poses were struck. Selfies were taken. The carnival atmosphere was restored.

Later, word went round that the buffet in the staff room was still going ahead and it would be a free for all for those coming in for the evening shift as well as those clocking off from the day shift. Ant stopped by checkout six to have a moan.

'I don't see why the evening people should have any. They weren't even here for the unroyal visit. They'll get in before us and clean up.'

'Don't be daft. Did you see how much stuff was in the staff fridge earlier? There'll be loads for everyone. Can you imagine if the evening shift were excluded? I think K-town has had enough riots for one year. By the way, what was up with Neville this morning? You were in the bogs for ages.'

'He was reliving an old trauma. That's what had been getting to him the whole time. Apparently, when Bobby Ball was here young Neville tripped up on the red carpet in front of everyone. I told him that it was time to let it go. No one else would even remember it.'

'Oh my god, I do!' squawked Dot from the next check-out. 'I'll never, ever forget that. It was one of the funniest things I've ever seen.'

Bea was right about the food. When she and the others went to the staff room at the end of the shift, the trestle table was still groaning. Ant made a noise which sounded very close to a purr as he surveyed the spread, before loading up his paper plate to full advantage. George, Neville and Anna emerged from the management suite. Bea had expected Neville to be devastated by the day's turn of events, but he was surprisingly chipper.

'You okay, Neville?' she said, as she watched him select a cheese straw and nibble the end.

'I am, Beatrice. Maybe it was all for the best,' he said. 'We can hold our heads up high. We did our bit. We adapted. Now, thank goodness, we can get back to normal.'

Everyone turned their heads as George coughed and held her hands up for silence.

'You'll be pleased to hear that I'm not going to make a speech, but I just want to say a big thank you to everyone for your extra efforts over the past few weeks and for rallying round today. I know it hasn't been easy, but in the end, we pulled together and we showed the town what we're made of, and I'm very proud of each and every one of you.'

'Sounds like a speech to me,' Ant muttered to Bea, through a mouthful of quiche and crisps.

'Shh, Ant.'

'One person was driving our efforts and I'd like to recognise them. So,' George continued, reaching behind the table to bring out the bouquet which had been destined for the Queen, 'I'd like to present these to Neville.'

Neville, still holding half a cheese straw, turned bright pink.

'Oh, I couldn't,' he said. 'I mean, if anyone deserves these, it's our backroom wizard, Anna.'

Anna shook her head. 'No, no, Neville. You were the mastermind behind the plan.'

'Really, Anna, I think you should take them . . .'

Suddenly, Bob was at the front of the room. Ant and Bea looked at each other, quizzically.

'Now what's the silly sod doing?' said Dot, who was standing beside Bea.

'Actually,' Bob said, 'if you don't mind, there is someone I'd like to give these flowers to. To me, she's the heart and soul of Costsave. Because of her, we now have the best staff toilets in Kingsleigh, and probably the southwest. But she doesn't just transform toilets, she's changed my life and I can't imagine ever being without her. Dot,' he said, gently but firmly taking the flowers from George, 'will you marry me?'

Everyone in the room now turned to face Dot. Bea thought she heard her say, 'Bloody hell' under her breath, but she wasn't sure.

Dot's face was solemn as she started walking towards Bob. The crowd parted to clear her path. Bob looked like he was in physical agony. Little beads of sweat were breaking out on his forehead.

When Dot reached the front of the room, she shook her head and sighed.

Oh no, thought Bea. Please, no.

Then Dot started to speak.

'Bob, this is probably the single most embarrassing thing you've ever done, and I'm never going to let you forget it.' Bob swallowed loudly, not yet sure of his fate. Then Dot smiled and it was like the sun coming out. 'But I can't imagine life without you, either. And so, yes, I will.'

THE END

ACKNOWLEDGEMENTS

Since Joffe Books relaunched my cosy crime series as *The Supermarket Mysteries*, I have been blown away by how many new readers have been enjoying the books. I would like to say a big thank you to all at Joffe, especially my wonderful editor Steph Carey, and to my lovely agent Sarah Hornsley at PFD.

I'd also like to thank the many supporters and encouragers who have kept me going through a difficult year, my dear writer pals in real life and online — too many to mention but a special shout out to Emma Pass and Sheena Wilkinson, Paddy Magane at Lyme Crime (the best little crime festival in the UK), Derek Farrell, Sophia Bennett and Colin Scott — the hosts and fellow writers at London Writers' Salon's Writers' Hour, and, of course, my family.

Perhaps most of all, I'd like to thank the readers and reviewers who have sent me feedback or recommended my books to others, or just quietly enjoyed spending time in Kingsleigh — it feels like we are building up a community of Ant and Bea fans. As George would say, you are all valuable members of the Costsave crew!

Rachel Ward
September 2023

THE JOFFE BOOKS STORY

We began in 2014 when Jasper agreed to publish his mum's much-rejected romance novel and it became a bestseller.

Since then we've grown into the largest independent publisher in the UK. We're extremely proud to publish some of the very best writers in the world, including Joy Ellis, Faith Martin, Caro Ramsay, Helen Forrester, Simon Brett and Robert Goddard. Everyone at Joffe Books loves reading and we never forget that it all begins with the magic of an author telling a story.

We are proud to publish talented first-time authors, as well as established writers whose books we love introducing to a new generation of readers.

We have been shortlisted for Independent Publisher of the Year at the British Book Awards three times, in 2020, 2021 and 2022, and for the Diversity and Inclusivity Award at the Independent Publishing Awards in 2022.

We built this company with your help, and we love to hear from you, so please email us about absolutely anything bookish at feedback@joffebooks.com

If you want to receive free books every Friday and hear about all our new releases, join our mailing list: www.joffebooks.com/contact

And when you tell your friends about us, just remember: it's pronounced Joffe as in coffee or toffee!

ALSO BY RACHEL WARD

THE SUPERMARKET MYSTERIES
Book 1: THE MISSING CHECKOUT GIRL MYSTERY
Book 2: THE MISSING PETS MYSTERY
Book 3: THE MISSING BABYSITTER MYSTERY
Book 4: THE MISSING RED CARPET MYSTERY

Milton Keynes UK
Ingram Content Group UK Ltd.
UKHW030942061024
449279UK00004B/76